He went down the curving, plush-carpeted staircase and crossed the lobby. He became aware that someone had stepped in behind him. Carver began to turn—and a fist slammed into his neck. Another punch to his kidneys. He felt himself fall, and then he was suspended in air. He felt as if he were cargo floating in a gantry net.

Carver was dragged into the darkened auditorium. He opened his eyes, dimly aware of the carpet passing beneath him. He felt as though his head had connected with a brick. Or a brick had connected with it. Or something. Anyway, it hurt.

They held him by the armpits, one on each side; Carver figured that out. Good. Swell. Fine. He wasn't unconscious. His powers of reason were not dimmed, nor were they scrambled eggs. Carver shook his head as the two men hauled him onto the stage. They dropped him onto the wooden floor. He heard them step away from him.

The oak floor felt smooth and cold. He pushed himself to a sitting position.

"Feeling all right, are you?" a voice asked.

Fawcett Gold Medal Books
by Kenn Davis:

MELTING POINT

NIJINSKY IS DEAD

NIJINSKY IS DEAD

Kenn Davis

FAWCETT GOLD MEDAL • NEW YORK

A Fawcett Gold Medal Book
Published by Ballantine Books
Copyright © 1987 by Kenn Davis

Library of Congress Catalog Card Number: 86-91819

ISBN 0-449-13096-7

Manufactured in the United States of America

First Edition: May 1987

This is dedicated to
my wife, Elizabeth Calkins Davis, with
lots of love. Lots.

"O body swayed to music, O brightening Glance
How can we know the dancer from the Dance?"
William Butler Yeats

"If you want to dance you must pay the piper."
English proverb

ONE

Blindness can be for a lifetime. Or for a second.

Momentarily Joel Burck was blinded. He cursed the driver behind him. He squinted, trying desperately to see through the silver-dazzle of headlights that bounced off the rearview mirror. The dark road was bad, a series of treacherous curves around the summit of Twin Peaks. Thank God traffic was scarce at four o'clock in the morning.

Was the car following him? Burck chewed on his lower lip. Was he getting paranoid? His anxieties getting the better of him? All the obsidian fears he had suppressed the past few days hammered at him. Go away! he screamed silently at the blinding lights in the mirror.

The headlights swerved away. As though the other driver had read Burck's mind. For one brief moment Burck was both surprised and amused.

Fears. Doubts. He had desperately needed a diversion to get his mind off his fears. That was why he had accepted Eric Hudson's invitation. The party he had left only ten minutes before would continue till the first orange flecks of dawn. That's all right for some of the dancers—Don Terman, Joyce Kittering, Gloria Loo, a few of the others, they were younger, didn't need as much sleep for rehearsals.

Then—then Burck's terror began again. The other driver pulled his big sedan alongside. On the curving road there was little room for two cars. The sedan slammed into the side of Burck's car.

There are few sounds worse to the human ear than the scream of automobiles scraping together. Joel Burck shuddered at the sound of metal ripping. Fright filled his mouth with the taste of tinfoil. His car, his expensive BMW, goddamn it, was sliced open like a tin can.

The car shuddered spastically. The BMW's headlight jittered over the tortuous road, illuminating the grass and gravel on the shoulder. The BMW was battered again and again, forced closer to the edge.

Spasms of terror swept through Burck's body. He gritted his teeth and held on to the steering wheel. His armpits were clammy with sweat; he smelled the raw odor of fear from himself. He glanced quickly at the black sedan deliberately grinding into his car.

Drunk driver? No, damn it. No! The driver had deliberately smashed into the BMW. Somebody wanted him dead. And twenty-eight was too young to die. Thoughts ran helter-skelter through Burck's mind: too many "accidents" in the past few weeks. One could have crippled him—and for a ballet dancer that was certainly the kiss of death. Worse than death.

He felt the gravel skidding under his wheels. He was close to the edge. Beyond the cliff was a dark void, the bottom sprinkled with the streetlights of the Noe Valley district.

He was going to be killed.

The two cars split apart. In Burck's mind the metal-rending din lingered. The other car had gone on ahead, around the curve, out of sight. The danger had lasted only a few seconds—but was long enough for Burck to remember the other accidents.

He edged the car back into the center of Twin Peaks Boulevard. With a trembling hand, he wiped sweat from his forehead and let up on the accelerator. Burck drove on, carefully maneuvering the switchbacks.

Obviously he needed help, but what kind?

Burck stopped at an intersection, waited for the light to

change, then turned left onto Portola Drive. His breath still came in gasps, and tremors trickled through his arms and legs. Thank God he would be in his Russian Hill apartment in less than fifteen minutes.

Perhaps he should go to the police? But what could he offer? He had never reported the accidents. Burck had been reluctant to bring in the authorities because the Golden Gate Ballet Company might not like the publicity. They'd had enough in the past month.

The memory of the first accident sent shudders through Burck. He didn't even want to think about that one. The second accident . . . Several weeks ago, early morning, he had left his apartment. His BMW was parked on the street rather than in the building garage. He seldom parked on the street.

There had been early morning fog, which blurred and fuzzed the nearby buildings. Foghorns had sounded in the gray water of the bay. The searchlight on Alcatraz Island had been a mere wash of light.

When he went to his car, Burck had discovered a flat tire. No problem. He would change it. Plenty of time to get to rehearsals.

He had jacked the BMW off the ground. And behind him, as he worked, a car—on an inclined driveway—began to roll. In the fog all the sounds of creaking metal were muffled. If a neighbor hadn't seen the car moving downhill and shouted a warning, Burck's legs would have been crushed against his own car.

An accident? At the time Burck thought so. But then there had been others: the faulty elevator in his apartment building that suddenly dropped several stories, until he had hit the safety brake button. That was the third.

Burck shivered.

Maybe one, possibly two incidents might be considered accidents. But three? And now this. Almost forced over a cliff. Number four.

A large sedan pulled out from an intersection. Headlights off. Burck's mouth hung open. God! The same car! Without lights.

3

The nightmare continued. The big sedan slammed into the rear of the BMW. Terrified, Burck twisted wildly at the steering wheel. *Slam!* The sedan hit him again. A madman! Unreasoning fear screamed in Burck's brain.

Again the car pulled alongside and again metal shrieked against metal. And again! Burck had to steer away from this crazy man. Or was it a woman? He didn't dare take his eyes off the road for a fast look.

He stomped on the brake, but the heavy sedan plowed into him, forcing the BMW toward the parked cars. Burck clamped his teeth. A piece of tooth enamel chipped off from one of his canines. Through terror-wide eyes he saw a side street—he might make the turn.

Tires screamed as Burck forced his car into the side street. He fishtailed, struck a parked car a glancing blow, then skidded out of control and crashed head-on into a small tree.

The BMW stopped. Headlight glass tinkled on the sidewalk. Burck was slumped behind the wheel. Then he raised his head. He blinked his eyes dazedly and felt a thick film flowing into them. Blood. He wiped his face with his hand, smearing the blood. He looked out the side window. The other driver had gone on.

Joel Burck shut off the ignition and climbed unsteadily out of the BMW. Hadn't anyone heard the commotion? Apparently not; the street was silent. He stood in the faint glow of a street lamp; he used a handkerchief to wipe the blood from his forehead.

A light went on in a nearby window. Somebody had heard the crash.

Then he heard a car engine roaring. And a car with unlit headlights swung into the street. Burck stiffened and gasped. The car!

The sedan stopped about fifty feet away. The driver got out. Burck stared. A man? A woman? Not enough light to tell. Just a figure in a dark knee-length coat. And something in his hand—which he raised, bracing his arm over the opened car door.

Burck turned and ran, his athletic legs carrying him

across the sidewalk. He thought he heard a soft popping sound. With a perfect *grand jeté*, he leaped over a five-foot fence into a flower garden. More strides, graceful and flowing carried him through the backyard. One-handed, he vaulted over another backyard fence. Then another.

Thorned bushes snagged at his jacket, brambles scraped at his slacks. His patent leather shoes were wet and slippery with morning dew. Burck felt perspiration on his face; the fusty smell of his own sweat mingled with the perfume of sweet-scented camellias.

More lights went on, and Burck heard a window raised.

He changed direction smoothly, his well-trained dancer's muscles in complete control. Down a garden path, across a dark street, into another garden. Joel Burck was a master of motion, flowing like an elegant river over rock and wood.

This was crazy! He could stumble and break a tibia! Or smash a patella against a stone garden gnome. Just slicing open the cruciate ligament in the darkness would mean not dancing for weeks. Slow down, he ordered himself.

He stopped. He walked along an alley to the next lighted street. He stepped into the deep shadow of a doorway. Burck waited many minutes. Several autos went by, but none was the big sedan that had terrorized him. He looked at his hands, his fingers, and realized that he had been biting his nails, leaving ragged crescents. He forced his hands to his sides. Get hold of yourself, he said to himself.

His angular face was grimy, sweaty. Pale, summer-grass brown hair stuck to his wide forehead. Burck's light-colored eyes stared ahead, reading thoughts inside his mind. Someone was trying to kill him. Unbelievable! He bit at his fingernails again.

In the distance he heard a siren, and growing louder. Had to be police. Probably a neighbor had heard the crash, probably had called them. Joel Burck walked cautiously back to his car.

A single police car was parked near the BMW, its red light striking the nearby houses, the tree, the glass glittering on the sidewalk. Two police officers were standing near Burck's car. Several people in pajamas and robes stood on doorsteps, watching.

"Thank God, officers," Burck said. "I'm glad to—"

"This your car?" one officer asked. He stood with a clipboard in his hand, a ball-point pen in the other.

"Yes, it is," Burck said. "You see, I was coming from . . ." No, he had better not mention the party. "Another car tried to run me off the road. You can see where the side of my car is all battered."

"Looks like you went out of control, fella," the second cop said, joining his younger partner. His manner was slow, his words rumbling out. His uniform was tight, pinching his heavy neck, stretching at the belt. A thin film of perspiration coated his face.

"Let's see your driver's license," the young cop asked. His voice was stern, almost theatrical, as though he was trying hard to sound older.

Again Burck tried to explain as he took out his wallet and showed the officers his license.

"What do you do, Mr. Burck?" the young cop asked, barely moving his lips. Really tough.

"I'm a dancer in the ballet," Burck said.

"Oh, did you hear that, Dan?" the cop said to his older partner. "Our friend dances. My, isn't that sweet?"

"You a faggot?" the second cop asked. The words rolled out slowly.

"I don't see what right—"

"He's very, very gay, Dan," the first cop said.

Dan, the older cop, held out an object, with what appeared to be a balloon hanging from it.

"Mind taking this? You just blow into it, right there in that little tube. Right up your alley."

"Officers, I assure you that I am not drunk," Burck said. "The other car hit me . . what is that word? . . . sidehit . . . sideswiped, yes, that's it. The other car hit me, up there near the top of Twin Peaks. Then he tried to hit me again, when I came down here."

"Okay, fella," the older cop said, "just blow into this gadget. Won't hurt a bit."

"What happened to your clothes?" the first cop asked. "Looks like you been rolling around in a fight or somethin'."

"I ran away, through those gardens. The bushes ripped my clothes."

"Yeah?" The cop said dubiously. "That's a pretty high fence."

"I'm a dancer," Burck said, "and it was an easy jump."

"Blow."

"What?" Burck said.

"Right there," the second cop said. "The little tube. Like I just told you."

"Look, officer, I am not drunk. I could jump that fence again, this very moment, and—"

"That's probably better than walking a white line," Dan said.

"I'm trying to tell you that someone has been trying to kill me. Right after I crashed into the tree—"

"Who's been trying to kill you?" the first cop asked.

"I don't know," Burck said, his voice rising, exasperation tainting his words. "Now listen, let me start my story over."

"Fine, sure, we love stories," the second cop said. "After you blow into this gadget. I've asked twice, and you don't want me to ask too many times. Why, I'm liable to think you've had a few too many drinkies."

"Now listen, I've had about enough," Burck said, holding his anger in tightly. "I'm Joel Burck, a principal dancer with the Golden Gate Ballet Company. I was—"

"And you don't want to have your breath analyzed, either," Dan, the second cop said.

"The other driver had a gun," Burck yelled.

"Sure he did," the young cop said patronizingly.

"He tried to shoot at me . . . I mean he did shoot at me."

"Sure he did. Don't get hysterical, sweetums. We got ears, we can hear you."

"But that's just it, you aren't listening."

7

"Just blow into this thing, and we'll take all the time you need to tell your story. Isn't that what you called it, a story?"

Burck looked hopelessly from one policeman to the other. Obviously a lost cause. He'd have to go through the routine these ignorant prejudiced officers demanded. Burck blew into the Breathalyzer and waited while they checked the gauge. The first officer got a camera from their patrol car and took photos of the crashed BMW. The officer then went to the patrol car and called for a tow truck. The older officer filled out a form and had Burck sign the bottom line.

"What's this for," Burck asked.

"Citation. Reckless driving, and driving under the influence."

"I tried to tell you—" Burck began, then stopped.

The situation was hopeless. They didn't want to hear. He signed the citation. The officer, Dan, tore off the top sheet and handed it to Joel Burck.

"All the info you need is on the back of the citation. A tow truck will be along in a few minutes and take your car to the police impound garage." He went to the patrol car and opened the rear door. "Get in, sweetie."

"This is crazy!" Burck cried. "I've been forced off the road—not the first time. There have been other times that I was almost killed, almost crippled."

"Yeah? Don't get hysterical, faggot," the first cop said.

"I'm under arrest?" Burck asked.

"Yeah, fella," Dan said. "Get in. You can tell all about it tomorrow morning in court. Unless you can make bail tonight. But first, we gotta take you in."

"I am not drunk!"

"Nah. Get in."

"I've been humiliated before, Myron," Joel Burck said, pacing back and forth in front of the penthouse window. He mashed his hands together, forcing himself not to bite his nails.

"Haven't we all," Myron Moseby said.

Gray light filtered through tall windows, filling the main room with a pervasive coolness. The penthouse was atop a Nob Hill apartment building that had been built in 1934. Moseby had lived in it for more than a dozen years. He had decorated it in authentic Art Deco, and hung selected paintings and sculptures from the art gallery he owned on Sutter Street.

Moseby stood near a built-in bar, mixing a drink. Inches under six feet, Myron Moseby seemed taller. He held himself erect, and moved with a dancer's grace. As a young man, Moseby had seen himself as another Fred Astaire, but his wealthy father had discouraged such frivolous pursuits. Trim and athletic, he appeared to be in his mid-thirties; actually he was edging closer to fifty. Distinguished feathered and layered gray wings swept over his ears, evidence of a vain man. As he mixed a cocktail, diamond rings sparkled on the little fingers of his manicured hands.

"Yes, dear boy, haven't we all," Moseby repeated. He carried a vodka martini to Burck, who still looked out the window.

Joel Burck sipped from the glass, grateful for the chilled liquor. The cold vodka contrasted with the first warming rays of the morning sun touching his face.

At that moment Burck felt like a man turning the corner into old age. He took immense pride in his own physical fitness, in his prowess and grace as a dancer. There was nothing, absolutely, positively nothing he would rather do than dance. But now . . . he felt as though he had been mentally bludgeoned by fear. He told Moseby all that happened, including the other accidents.

He sipped more of the liquor and faced Moseby.

"Thank you for coming to the police station and bailing me out."

"I was glad to do it," Moseby said. He shrugged with a smile. "After all, we can't afford to have one of the finest dancers in the city languishing in jail. Particularly since I have a financial investment in the ballet company."

"You're the only one I've told," Burck said.

"Surely you've told Bart," Moseby said.

"Yes, of course I've told him. But outside of you and Bart I just couldn't tell anyone else. And now . . . God, I'm scared." He gulped down the last of the vodka. He walked to the bar and rapidly mixed another martini. He gulped down half the liquor, then stared at Moseby. "I need help, Myron."

"Yes, dear boy, that is quite obvious. And I am glad, quite glad, to offer a suggestion."

"Like what? The police didn't seem interested in anything I tried to tell them. After I was booked—and fingerprinted—" He paused and shuddered. "There seemed little sense to continue to protest that I was the victim, not the perpetrator. I hate them. They hate us. I don't want anything to do with them."

"Don't let those two minions of the law twist your thinking. Most of our city police are more adept at dealing with gays. Perhaps they had a tough night. But of course I cannot excuse their ignorance. They are merely part of the homophobia we deal with day to day."

"This help you spoke of . . ."

"I have a friend," Moseby said slowly, "a private detective. He also has a law degree."

"Is he gay?" Burck asked.

"No, Joel, this man is not one of us." Moseby shook his head and sipped his tequila sunrise. "But he's a very good private detective. His name is Carver Bascombe. He understands our problems, since he is a minority himself. He's black. If the police can't or won't help you, then this man will. I think . . . no, my friend, I *urge* you to see him."

"In which capacity, Myron?" Burck asked. "As a private detective or as a lawyer?"

A good question, Moseby thought to himself. A very good question. One that even Carver Bascombe might not have an answer to. Certainly there was more status and prestige in being a lawyer. More lucrative, too. Yet . . . and yet, Carver had not hung up a shingle. He wasn't actively looking for legal clients. He had merely placed his framed bar certificate in his office. Under his framed state investigator's license. Moseby noticed things like that.

Of course, hanging out a shingle didn't guarantee clients, and Bascombe already had clients for the detective agency.

Moseby knew what ate at Bascombe. A need. Call it a craving. Bascombe was a hunter. And as he got older, this need to know the why, the who of certain cases was an obsession. That ravening need was strong, driving Bascombe on and on.

"Probably both, Joel," Moseby finally said. "He has much more experience as a detective, and he's easy to talk to. Bascombe is good at what he does."

"So . . . You've known him a long time? Old friends?"

"More than friends, Joel," Moseby said, fingering his silk shirt at his waist.

He felt the scar where a bullet had struck him years before. Carver Bascombe had saved his life. He remembered vividly the murky, smoke-filled stairwell at the art museum. He could never forget the forlorn look in the eyes of the lady art dealer as she pulled the trigger, putting a bullet into him. She was going to kill him, there had been no doubt. Unless Carver killed her first. Moseby shook his head slightly at the memory. What was her name? Willard. Frances Willard. Yes . . . Carver Bascombe had saved his life.

"He's a person who can be trusted?" Burck asked.

"I wouldn't send you to him if there was even the slightest doubt of that."

"I'll see him, then," Burck said, "as soon as I've had a few hours of sleep."

"If he agrees to help," Moseby said, his manner brightening, "bring him by tomorrow night."

"Why tomorrow?" Burck asked.

"The party, dear boy," Moseby said gleefully, and consulted his wristwatch. "Thirty-eight hours from now, here in my penthouse manse. A paean to the GGBC. Food and drink as only I can supply, equalled only by the talent of my guests. A great party. A dazzler. A party catered by the gods."

"I had almost forgotten," Burck said, shuddering at the thought of yet another party, so soon after this nightmare.

"Every one will be here. You and your friend Bart, and Carver, if you hire him. And Bob Swaine, Joyce Kittering, Polivitch, Hudson, all the ballet dancer and choreographers. Yes, I daresay, you and all the great terpsichorean spirits."

And probably, Burck thought to himself with a shiver, the one who was trying to murder him.

TWO

"More coffee, Mr. Burck?" Rose Weinbaum asked.

"Thank you. I guess I didn't get much sleep."

"I figured that," Rose said, refilling Burck's cup. "It's not often we get early-bird clients waiting in the corridor outside the office."

"I was anxious," Burch said, settling himself on the office sofa. "What time did you say Mr. Bascombe would come in?"

"You *are* tired, Mr. Burck. I didn't say." Rose poured coffee for herself, then sat behind her desk. As she efficiently twirled paper into her typewriter she looked at Burck. "Usually he's here before me."

There was no reason to inform a client that Carver Bascombe had a small apartment connected to the main office.

After opening the office and letting in Joel Burck, Rose had plugged in the coffee machine and checked the answering machine. There was only one message—from Myron Moseby, that he was sending a client to see Carver. She had gone into Carver's office and knocked on the apartment door. No answer. She looked in. The bed was nearly made. Not slept in. Rose had then come out and offered a cup of coffee to Burck and told him she had no idea when Carver Bascombe would return to his office.

"I'm sure Mr. Bascombe will be here shortly," Rose said. And Carver would probably be damned tired, too, she thought to herself. Might need a few hours sleep.

Joel Burck nodded his understanding and sipped his coffee. He went to the bay windows overlooking Fillmore Street.

The telephone rang, and Rose fended off an office building realtor who offered new office space in a new building.

Joel Burck continued to gaze out the window. "It's an interesting neighborhood," he said. "I'm not too familiar with this part of the city. It seems nicely integrated. Racially."

"Yes," Rose said noncommittally, still typing reports.

Never explain, Bernie Weinbaum had often said. Rose shook her head as she remembered her late husband. Almost a golden rule. A private detective had to think for himself, he had said. Better keep hunches to oneself until they prove out.

She heard the inner door open, and then Carver Bascombe poked his head around the connecting door. Rose thought he looked tired. At his quizzical look, Rose pointed to Joel Burck. Carver nodded, almost without understanding, like a habit without meaning.

He went into his office and slumped behind his desk, his chin on his chest. He sighed, more of a moan actually. Rose stepped in, and he looked at her and waved a feeble hand in greeting. He pulled his feet out of his handmade loafers and rubbed his toes over themselves.

"Tough night, boss?" Rose asked sardonically, coffee cup in one hand. "She must be a tiger."

"Don't be cruel, Rose," he said, almost in a whisper. "Be tender. Treat me gently. Who's the man outside?"

"A friend of Moseby's," she said. "There's a message on the answering machine."

Carver grumped and slumped further into his chair. He

loved listening to Rose; her voice was throaty, sexually inviting. Almost a lewd contrast with her plain, dignified looks. Framed with loose, desert-rock-colored curls, her bony face had a terrific smile. What whims the gods have, Carver thought, putting a sensual voice in a plain woman like Rose. Ah well, he sighed.

At six feet two, Carver's toes stuck out from under the desk. His lean, sinewy hands trailed over the ends of the armrests. His unshaven beard darkened his cocoa-brown skin. He rubbed a hand over the stubble.

"I need a shave," he said.

"You need a client," Rose said. "And there's one right out there—ready, willing, and able. Name's Joel Burck."

"Yeah? Really? Burck? Joel Burck? The ballet dancer?"

"He says he's a dancer."

"Give me ten minutes to wash up and shave," Carver said, "then send Mr. Burck right in."

He yawned, and went to the tape recorder placed next to a filing cabinet. Above the recorder hung a private investigator's license and a law degree. The law degree was positioned below the investigating license. Maybe that placement meant something. Maybe not.

Carver turned on the tape player. The music from Bernstein's *Fancy Free* filled the air. He went into his apartment and in ten minutes was back at his desk, freshly shaved and washed.

He had changed into slacks and a casual Brioni jacket. A cup of coffee was on the desk, and Carver drank it, savoring it. The pungent coffee smell floated in the room. Ah, didn't that aroma mix well with the toe-tapping music? Yeah. Good old Lenny.

Rose ushered in the potential new client.

Carver stood and shook his hand, then indicated a chair.

"Since you're a friend of Myron Moseby's," Carver said in a businesslike tone, "and I know your excellent rep as a dancer, we can dispense with the preliminaries. What's the problem."

"You've heard of me?" Burck asked, unconsciously glancing around the office. He was not impressed.

"Yes, I know your work. I'vve seen you dance," Carver replied. "Some ballet lovers say you're even better than you appear. I'm not enough of an expert to tell. I've heard them say you could be as good as Nijinsky if you wanted to."

Joel Burck jerked, then sighed.

"Nijinsky is dead," Burck said, "and I want to stay alive."

"That sounds like you have a serious problem."

"I *think* so," Burck began, hesitantly, the word drawn out. "I hardly know where to start. But first, could you turn off that music, Mr. Bascombe? It makes me nervous. No . . . not nervous. Actually I like it. I've danced to it many times. It stops my thought processes, though. The music sets up habit patterns in my mind and my muscles. Very distracting at the moment. I can't concentrate."

Carver turned off the tape machine and nodded to Joel Burck to continue. As Carver returned to his desk, Burck noticed that the detective had no shoes on.

"I think," Burck said hesitantly, "I need a bodyguard, Mr. Bascombe."

"Call me Carver."

"Yes. I've had a series of what you could call . . . accidents." He bit down on the word. "Until just recently I believed them to be just that. Accidents. But now, especially since last night . . ." Burck paused and rubbed a hand over his brow. "Actually this morning . . . Well, I think someone is really trying to kill me."

"Why did Myron send you to me? Couldn't the Police Department help?"

"I tried to tell the police last night, Carver." He wondered if he was doing the right thing; the man had no shoes on. Ah, well, Moseby said he was good. "Listen, please. I'll start with the first accident, and I'll bring you to date. Particularly about last night. Actually, early this morning."

"Right. Just a sec."

Carver flipped the intercom and asked Rose if there was any important business.

"Not so's you'd notice. A guy called about showing us some office space downtown."

"Forget that. Cancel anything else."

"There isn't anything else."

Carver flipped off and then placed a micro-cassette recorder on the desk. He thumbed it on.

"The beginning," Carver said.

"The first incident was several weeks ago. You know about ballet slippers?"

"Yeah, the satin ones with squared-off toes, lots of ribbons."

"Those are the ballerina's. The men wear plain slippers. Mine are custom-made. I use about ten pairs a week. Only I can wear them. Several weeks ago I was about to rehearse, at a place . . . well, never mind that. I put on a pair of my slippers and began to excercise. *Pliés, tendus,* the usual. I felt a sharp pain in my toes and took off the slippers. The inner linings and heels had been packed with ground glass and small glass shards. My feet were bloody."

Carver said nothing, just gazed at Burck. Unseen, he rubbed his own stockinged feet over each other.

"Well," the dancer said, wiping at the sheen that had gathered over his eyebrows, "that was the first 'accident.' But it was obvious that someone had deliberately tried to cripple me."

"Go on."

"The next incident—I left my apartment one morning to get to rehearsal. I decided to take my car, which was parked at the bottom of an inclined driveway of the next-door building. One of my rear tires was flat. I began to jack up the rear end—"

"I get the picture."

"An automobile that had been parked on an inclined driveway broke loose. Its brakes had failed. It almost hit me. My kneecaps might have been crushed." Burck stopped and squeezed his hands together, as if trying to mangle the memory. "I could never have danced again."

"Do you usually park on the street?" Carver asked bluntly.

"Sometimes. There's a garage in the apartment building."

"Why did you?"

"Park on the street?"

"Yeah."

"The night before had been balmy, and the rehearsals had cramped my legs. I wanted to walk. It's pleasant on the crest of Russian Hill. I didn't feel like putting the car in the garage and then having to walk out of the garage. It seemed like a lot of trouble."

"Mmm," Carver said neutrally.

"It was horrifying," Burck continued. "All I could think of for days was myself without legs, without the ability to dance, unable to perform or to make a living."

Carver grunted and said nothing else.

Burck continued with the third incident, the elevator that went out of control—and then slowly his words trailed off. he breathed deeply but raggedly.

"And last night?" Carver prompted.

"That was much worse." He related in full detail everything that had happened and his reactions and anger. "There's no doubt in my mind—someone has made deliberate attempts to cripple me . . . and is now trying to kill me."

"But there haven't been any threatening notes or telephone calls?"

"Nothing. Just the incidents. You see the problem I would have in going to the police? Besides, after last night I don't care for the attitude of the police. They won't help me, and I don't want their help."

Carver made another *mmmm* sound and narrowed his eyes. He said nothing else.

Burck bit at his index fingernail, then forced his hands down onto his lap. He felt somehow cheated coming to this detective agency. Was Moseby wrong? Bascombe didn't seem to want to be involved. he's too calm, Burck thought to himself. Too disinterested. Burck felt like getting up and walking out. He felt hopeless and helpless.

"You don't want to get raked over by the cops because you're gay?"

"That's putting it mildly."

"Yeah, you were pissed with those cops, so now you don't want to have anything to do with them."

"Yes, that's right. Myron Moseby understood. That's why he suggested I see you."

"I'll tell you straight, Mr. Burck, I don't do bodyguard work anymore. However," Carver continued, warding off Burck's potential objections, "I think you need help. What we need to do is find out who is trying to kill you. And why."

"How would you do that?" Burck asked.

"I don't know. At the moment. But we're going to be together until we find out who's been terrorizing you. I'll have to call in help from time to time. Even *I* need sleep."

"What will the cost be? Don't misunderstand, I don't measure my life in dollars and cents, but I do like to know what the cost might be. Particularly if there are going to be other detectives to pay."

For the next few minutes they discussed payment, and finally agreed upon a twenty-four-hour-a-day rate. As Burck wrote out a retainer check, Carver reached for his telephone and tapped out the number of Mike Tettsui's agency.

"Mike, this is Carver Bascombe," he said when Tettsui answered. "I have a job for you. You doing anything important?"

"Trying to keep me and my family eating," Tettsui said, "and sleeping in real rooms in real beds, with real sheets and covers. Just stuff like that."

"Consider yourself on retainer. I'll need help later." Carver felt his words were brusque—and he knew why. There was always that chance of trouble for anyone he hired—like the terrible way Bernie Weinbaum had died. Carver forced himself to shrug away the tinge of guilt. "If you can't make it, Mike, line me up someone we both know.''

"No problem, Carver," Tettsui said. "I'm on."

"Right. Thanks. Come by the office sometime today and Rose will give you an advance check."

Mike Tettsui thanked him, said he'd do that, and hung up. Carver turned to Burck.

"I want to see about that elevator, Mr. Burck," he said. "Now?"

"Right now, since it's in your apartment building. There's usually an electrician or somebody that maintains the elevators. Then after that I'd like to see your car. Actually I want to see the tire that went flat."

"The police impounded the car."

"Don't worry about that. We'll get it out."

"I have to be at rehearsal before ten this morning."

"Right. We'll see the car later in the day. I'll have to figure out how you're going to explain my continued presence at the ballet theater. You took a cab here?"

"Yes, I did."

"We'll use my car," Carver said.

He shut off the micro-cassette recorder and tucked it into a shirt pocket. While Burck waited, Carver gave Burck's retainer to Rose and out of Burck's earshot told her to start a check on the dancer.

"Don't trust him?" she asked.

"When did I ever trust anybody?"

"A few times past," Rose said. "A long time ago."

"The Pleistocene Age," Carver replied. "The appearance of modern man."

"Yes, you've come a long way," Rose said.

Carver and Burck left the offices. They walked up Fillmore Street to the Hi-Valu service station. Carver's friend Jimmy Bowman owned the station (and sometime crap-game-at-night emporium), and also operated two other profitable service stations. Standing leisurely by the credit-cards-only pumps, Bowman greeted them.

"Hey, Cahva, how's it goin'?"

"Good, Jimmy, good."

Carver introduced Joel Burck to Bowman, and they spent a few minutes in idle talk.

The morning sun made Bowman squint, creasing his starling-brown face. The light brought out freckles sprayed across his nose and under his bituminous-colored eyes. His narrow shoulders supported an oil-stained, once-white coverall.

"Never been to no ballet," Bowman said with a grin. He ran his fingers over his gray-flecked temples. "Now, Cahva, here, he's always tryin' to get me better ed-u-cated, but, man, I just never seem t'have the time."

"You're just damn afraid," Carver suggested.

"Yeah, you right. I'm afraid I might get to liking that stuff, and I tell you, when I see the prices of a symphony, twenty, thirty dollars, usually more, well I jus' gotta remind myself there's a whole lotta stuff I can do better with that kinda bucks."

"Perhaps I can help," Burck said. "I would be very pleased if you would be my guest at the gala premiere of the new ballet season."

Bowman scratched his chin and grinned again.

"Make it two," he said, "so I can take my latest fox, an' you got yourself a deal."

"Then it's my pleasure."

"Okay, Jimmy, you chiseler," Carver said amiably, "is the car ready?"

"Always, Cahva, always gassed an' ready. An' the alarm system is working jus' fine."

In less than a minute, Bowman drove out a blue, twelve-cylinder XKE Jaguar convertible. Carver opened the passenger door for Burck and then climbed in behind the wheel and drove off. Using Burck's directions, they were at the ballet dancer's Russian Hill apartment in about ten minutes.

The eleventh-floor apartment was decorated in a comfortable up-to-date style, with colors in creams and beiges. Accents of dark browns and bright reds and oranges led the eye from sectional sofa to easy chair to reclining chairs. Underfoot, Carver felt as if he had oozed into the carpet. A marble-faced fireplace was flanked by twin high-backed chairs.

Music from Khachaturian's *Gayne* ballet filled the air. The wall opposite the fireplace was given over to high-tech speakers and a Bang & Olufsen linear-tracking turntable. Carver felt a twinge of envy. Next to the speakers were numerous photographs of dancers, a Renoir print of ballerinas, and several photographs of Burck himself.

"My modest collection," Burck said, pointing out several modern paintings and sculptures.

"Very nice," Carver said, admiring a Chagall etching and a cracking and paint-peeling icon of a Madonna and Christ Child.

"And, Carver, I would like you to meet Bart Meaghler," Burck said, as a good-looking man stepped from the kitchen into the living room, a drink held in one hand. "My friend and roommate."

Carver recognized the euphemisms for male lover.

Meaghler shook Carver's hand and asked if he wanted a drink.

"Not this early, thanks."

Carver guessed Bart Meaghler to be in his early thirties, about Carver's own age. Four or five years older than Burck.

Meaghler had to look up to stare into Carver's eyes. His stocky body moved with false economy, as though he had to prove he could hold his liquor. Light didn't seem to reflect in Meaghler's gray eyes; they were hidden deep under dense eyebrows. His sleek black hairstyle had the "after" look in advertisements for very good wigs.

"Call me Bart," Meaghler said, finishing off the content of the glass. "Joel likes a first-name basis. I'm glad he got someone to help. If Moseby says you're good, then I guess you're good. Naturally he told me about the car trying to run him off the road. And about the two cops. What assholes. In this town, of all places."

"Any particular reason why you didn't drive Joel to my office?"

"Sure, the best. Joel didn't want me to. I offered, but he refused."

"I've been very tense," Burck said, "as you can understand, and I don't want my friends to suffer my nervousness, my peevishness."

"Sure you can't use a drink, Carver?" Meaghler asked.

"No. I mean I don't want one."

"Bart, I wish you wouldn't," Burck said pleasantly, patiently, as though he had voiced that hope many times. "But you know your limits."

Meaghler shrugged and tipped the glass to his lips and emptied it.

Lost Cause Number 587.

Joel Burck stepped to the tall windows overlooking the bay and gazed out. Carver followed Meaghler to a bar near an area of library shelves. A rear light source threw a shadow across the bar, distorting Meghler's squared-off fingers. The dark hair on the back of his wrists shined in the light, as though he had rubbed oil on his arm. Or sweat.

Meaghler busied himself behind the bar, opening bottles, rinsing and clinking glasses. His slate-colored eyes measured another amount of vodka and orange juice into a glass.

"You weren't at the party last night?" Carver enquired.

"No, not me," Meghler said. "I was working late last night. And besides"—he gazed at the liquid in the glass—"I wasn't in any great shape to go, anyway. Wish I could've. I like some of the dancers, drink with them sometimes. Jones . . . Hudson . . . Terman. We talk a lot. 'Bout the ballet."

"Any ideas about these accidents?" Carver inquired.

"I've told Joel what I believe. Some jealous rival. In the GGBC. After all, Joel is one of their great dancers. He isn't publicly recognized as such, but what do you rexpect? Keeps a low profile. But it's obvious to any but blind critics that he's a world-class dancer."

"Any particular rival in mind?"

"No, there are too many," Meaghler said, and drank the screwdriver steadily.

23

"I'll be meeting some of the dancers. I could do better if I had a few names to pay special attention to."

"Okay, you want names." Meaghler cocked an eye at Carver and downed a hefty swig of the screwdriver. "I'd keep my eye on Vassily Visikov. That's one."

"Any particular reason?"

"Certainly. Of course. You'll see when you meet him. Damned obvious, so he probably isn't the one. But Visikov is clever, a real genius, so he might be doing a double reverse. You know. If he's so obvious, he can't be the guilty one, so he really is the one."

"I know the ploy," Carver said. "Any other names."

"Sure. Bob Swaine. He's the big Gouda in the company. Made the GGBC into a world-class ballet company. And John Polivitch. He's the crazy composer. Alex Bellini, God's gift to the dance. Eric Hudson—all-around nice guy, another asshole of conceit. He threw the party last night. Billy Jones, who thinks he's Baryshnikov's only competition. And those are only some of the males. We mustn't forget the prima ballerinas. Deborah Canby. Alice Boygen."

Carver nodded, recognizing a few of the better-known names of the GGBC.

"And then we mustn't forget the corps de ballet," Meaghler added. "All those cute young cunts in tutus. And God, surely we must include Brigham Merkhinn and Graham Maltby and the others on the board of directors. No love lost there. And the backstage crew, all those. Christ, I could name the whole staff. Too many—too many."

"Are you with the ballet company, Bart?"

"No, Carver," Burck said as he joined the two men. "Bart owns a travel agency."

"Plural. Agencies. We have offices in Manhattan, Washington, D.C., Chicago, and Los Angeles. We specialize in international travel, tours, charters, like that."

"You're not working today?" Carver asked.

"Not when Joel needs me. Most of my offices pretty well run themselves. I just poke in once a day or so."

Carver nodded and turned to Burck. "Let's talk to the maintenance man in charge of the elevators. Or is it a woman?"

"A man. I don't know his name."

Burck asked Meaghler if he wanted to come along, but Bart merely hoisted his screwdriver and shook his head. Burck and Carver left the apartment and took the elevator.

As they rode, Carver thought about the elevator incident. When elevators fail they don't fall all the way to the bottom. They drop a few feet before the safety brakes come on automatically. Carver nodded to himself; it had to be someone who had mechanical and electrical knowledge.

But how would someone know Burck's car would be parked on the street? Someone from the ballet company? And the glass in the slippers? That strongly pointed to someone from the ballet company. Meaghler's suggestion of a jealous rival? Possibly.

But he mustn't overlook the obvious, such as the hard-drinking Bart Meaghler. Why would Meaghler want his lover killed? Another lover on the scene? It wouldn't be the first time. And something definitely crackled between the two men—something besides sex and friendship.

No, it wasn't going to be easy.

They stepped out of the elevator at the underground-parking-garage level. The parking area was large and lit unevenly by hanging fluorescent fixtures. Squat, square concrete pillars supported the low ceiling and divided the garage into parking spaces. At least half the parking stalls were empty. The sound of the two men's footsteps bounced off the gray concrete walls. A cold smell, like frozen silk, tickled their nostrils.

The two men arrived at the door to the building maintenance offices. Carver knocked, and they waited. No one answered. Carver knocked again, waited, and then opened the door.

Burck choked and clutched at the doorframe. His eyes were wide, his mouth slack.

A man was slumped across a paper-littered desk. A thin trickle of blood ran from his matted hair onto the papers.

25

Carver reached across the desk, careful not to touch anything, and pressed two fingers against the man's neck. No pulse in the carotid artery.

Joel Burck was iron-rod stiff at the door, his hands clenched into fists at his chest.

"Is . . . is he . . . dead?" he managed to stammer.

"He's dead," Carver said. "Murdered."

THREE

"Was he shot?" Burck stammered. His eyes were wide. He stood shivering, his back jammed against the doorframe. "Was he?"

"No," Carver said, and pointed to a paper spike on the desk. The tip of the spike had dark crusted spots on it. No way a person could commit suicide pushing that spike into his brain—and then place it back on the desk. "The killer probably used that. Jabbed it right into the man's ear."

"It's horrible!"

Burck's voice was high and erratic. He wouldn't look at the body. Carver looked at him. Burck resembled a frightened child, far younger than his twenty-eight years.

"I have to call the police, Joel," Carver said, his words blunt and commanding. "I have to wait for them, but I don't want you here. Go back to your apartment."

"I can't," Burck said, the two words weak and quavering.

Carver saw the fear in the younger man's eyes. "All right," he said, softening his voice.

Carefully using his handkerchief he picked up the desk telephone. He didn't want to smudge any fingerprints. He asked Burck for his apartment phone number and tapped out the numerals. Bart Meaghler answered, and Carver asked him to come down.

Carver gently propelled Burck out the door, and they

27

waited outside the partially closed door. Meaghler showed up with curiosity written all over his face.

"Don't ask questions, Bart," Carver said, "just take Joel upstairs. He'll tell you what's happened."

As soon as the two men left Carver returned to the office and telephoned the Homicide Division. He answered the red-tape questions by the dispatch officer patiently. Et cetera, et cetera, et cetera. Carver hung up the phone and looked around the room.

Behind the desk, a jacket hung on a clothes peg, and Carver went through the pockets. A wallet contained a driver's license, complete with identification photo, several credit cards, and $23.00 in bills.

The photo on the license matched the dead man. His name was, or had been, Ben Rosada. Carver wrote the name and home address into his own notebook. He replaced the wallet. The other pockets of the jacket were empty. So much for that.

Carver waited for the police, thinking about Burck and his lover, Bart Meaghler. The conversation in the upstairs apartment had some strange undercurrents. Carver guessed there was something bothering the two men. But what?

"These things'll kill me," Dr. Wolfram said, grinding a cigarette butt into an ashtray on the blood-spattered desk.

"Nothing's been touched?" Detective Sergeant Arnold Applegate asked Carver Bascombe.

"No, AA," Carver said, using Applegate's initials. "Just as I found it."

"Not AA, Bascombe," the homicide detective said, his lips thin slits, a cold smile. "Sergeant, or Applegate."

Detective Sergeant Arnold Applegate was head of the investigating team. He had already asked Carver several basic questions, and scribbled the answers onto a pad on a metal clipboard.

For the past half hour the forensic specialists had covered the scene. The fingerprint expert had finished moments before, and the crime photographer had put away his cameras and lights. The medical examiner, Dr. Wolfram, stood nearby lighting another cigarette.

The homicide detective pushed aside papers on the desk, and then sat on the corner. He swung one lanky leg back and forth. Occasionally the heel hit the desk. The sound boomed and echoed in the concrete-walled office.

Both Carver and Applegate were tall and lean and thin. Together they were like stick men in a tableau. Applegate was one man who could look Carver straight in the corneas. Years before, he had met Carver on an opera murder case. Then he had looked quite young, and the years since had not given Applegate a look of maturity. He resented his still-youthful appearance. To some he still seemed like a kid playing at cops-and-robbers.

In fact, Arnold Applegate had become an efficient homicide investigator, a dog-at-the-throat on a case. All by the book, of course. Of course.

"Now then, Dr. Wolfram," Applegate said to the ME, "give me your most educated opinion."

"The man has been dead for about two hours," Wolfram replied. He dragged on his cigarette. "The autopsy will narrow the time of death, but not much closer. Death was apparently from a sharp needlelike instrument being pressed through the ear into the brain. Now, me, I'm not the detective, but I'd guess the most likely weapon used was that paper spike. I'd bet those spots on the spike are blood. Anyway, death was most likely instantaneous."

He folded his few instruments into his leather case and left the office. A trail of gray smoke followed him out the door.

Following Applegate's orders, Walfram's assistants bagged and tagged the dark-spotted spike.

"You know, Bascombe," Applegate said, sounding jaundiced, "I learned a long time ago not to trust you." He looked at Carver and compressed his lips. "Have things changed? Can I trust you?"

"Probably not, Sergeant," Carver replied. He leaned casually against a wooden filing cabinet.

"I see," Applegate said slowly.

He reached into his suit coat and pulled out a pipe and a tobacco pouch. He spent long moments filling the bowl, and then more moments lighting the tobacco with a pipe lighter. He sucked noisily as the tobacco glowed. A pleasant odor of warm hickory and sweet honey drifted into the air.

One of the other detectives stepped up and gave Applegate two plastic bags.

"One with stuff from the guy's pants, work coat, shirt pockets," the detective said, "and the wallet from the jacket."

"Okay, Jack," Applegate said.

A couple of coroner's men zipped the body into a bag and put it onto a gurney. They trundled the corpse out of the office. Applegate took the dead man's wallet from the plastic bag and went through it.

"The guy's name was Ben Rosada," Applegate said, scanning the driver's license and credit cards from the wallet. He looked at Carver. "Mean anything to you?"

Carver shook his head without speaking.

"Cash in the wallet," Applegate said, then looked at Carver again. "You found the body?" he asked for the second time.

"Yes," Carver replied, also for the second time.

"What were you doing here?"

"I was visiting a friend. Upstairs."

"You didn't know Rosada? You weren't visiting him?"

"No. To both."

"Why did you come to see Rosada?"

"My friend said he'd had a problem with the elevator. I said I'd see the maintenance man, and I came down to the garage and found him dead. I called you. That's all there is."

"I see," Applegate said, as noncommittally as before. He puffed gently on the pipe. "What's your friend's name?"

"Joel Burck."

"How long had you been visiting Burck?"

"I guess about a half hour. Maybe less."

"What about?"

30

"He was going to get me some tickets to a show."

"Yes?" Applegate said. "And what show might that be?"

"The gala premiere night of the Golden Gate Ballet."

"Oh, really?" Applegate said. "Your friend Burck is some kind of promoter I take it."

Carver shrugged.

"Yes, I know about that premiere," Applegate said. "The department was involved in the permit negotiations. You did know the performance was going to take place on Alcatraz?"

"Yeah. It's been advertised on the classical music radio stations and on TV."

"I've seen the TV ads, and I wouldn't mind seeing that myself."

"I might be able to get you a ticket."

Applegate told Carver that would be a nice gesture. Carver said he'd see what he could do. The homicide detective thanked him, and the two men left the office. Politeness hung like a deadly nerve gas in the air. A policewoman taped a yellow crime-scene banner across the door.

Several police cars drove out of the garage, the sounds of tires and shifting gears rolling hollowly among the pillars and walls. Carver Bascombe and Detective Sergeant Arnold Applegate walked toward the garage exit ramp.

"You know, Carver," Applegate said, "I'm not a fool."

"I never thought so."

"When you say 'a friend,' I don't believe you. Do you know why?"

"Can't imagine."

"Because you don't have many friends. I know about you. I keep up. I read the police reports."

"I believe you," Carver said, doing his best not to patronize.

They stood on the sidewalk, and Applegate looked at the apartments above. He knocked his pipe against his heel, and the tobacco fell into the gutter.

"I think your friend upstairs—Burck?—is not a friend. I'd bet he's a client. Is he?"

"There's no fooling you, Sergeant."

"That doesn't answer the question. Is Burck your client?"

"Yes."

"Then for god's sake," Applegate said, his words dripping with tortured exasperation, "why didn't you say so in the first place?"

"I want my client's confidence. I don't want a reputation of being a blabbermouth."

"I'm a reasonably educated guy, Carver. Does that mean you're a blabbermouth but you're keeping it under control? Or does it mean you're just naturally closemouthed."

Carver shrugged.

"Okay, can I talk to your client?" Applegate asked.

"What about?"

"This killing, of course. He knows you reported it, doesn't he?"

"No," Carver said.

Not really, Carver thought. Of Burck's own knowledge, he didn't know what Carver did after he left. Only what Carver told him he was going to do. Splitting a legal hair.

"Now you've really got me curious," Applegate said. "When did Burck hire you?"

"Looking for an alibi?"

"Just answer the question, Carver."

"This morning. Over an hour ago. In my office."

"What did Burck hire you for?"

"To look into some accidents. One was a car accident."

"Accidents? Why?"

"To find out what might have caused them. There's always the possibility of a lawsuit."

"Say, that's right," Applegate said, a Tom Sawyer grin crossing his boyish face, "I'd heard you got your legal shingle. So—you're out of the private detective business?"

"Not completely."

"Well, well, this is different. Bascombe the lawyer. With a client. Let me congratulate you."

As the two men shook hands, Carver wondered at the

deference once Applegate thought Carver was doing legal work. Applegate chattered away two winds to the east, saying he and Carver had to get together for a drink. He promised to call and they'd do lunch.

Applegate smiled, said goodbye, and walked to his car. Carver watched him drive off and then reentered the apartment building.

"What happened?" Burck asked as he let Carver into the apartment.

"Are they going to question Joel?" Meaghler asked worriedly.

"They don't know he was there," Carver said.

"You didn't tell them?" Bart Meaghler asked.

"No, I didn't. Joel doesn't want anything to do with the police. That was made quite clear when he hired me."

"I see," Meaghler said, his tone dubious.

Meaghler went to the bar and mixed another screwdriver. His actions were brusque, almost defiant. He looked at Carver, practially daring him to start a lecture.

"Do you realize how terrified Joel is now?" he asked. "Do you have any idea how this might affect his performance onstage?

"I think so," Carver answered.

"I wonder if you do. You've got to realize it requires incredible concentration and superb physical condition. Ballet is the impossible art. The human body is not built to do it. Gravity is repealed, torque is turned inside out, inertia is kicked out the window. Nobody can dance on their toes for minutes, for an entire evening. It's unnatural, it's awesome. But they do it."

"I know," Carver said.

"It's all the goddamn arts," Meaghler said. "Nobody can use their voice to push an aria five hundred feet to the topmost balcony of an opera house. But they do! Nobody is supposed to look at a huge block of marble, see what's inside, and then cut all the crap off, and, hey presto, you've got a Michelangelo, a Henry Moore. But they, goddamn it, they do it."

"Easy, Bart," Burck said, his voice low and hushed, with still a trace of quavering.

"Oh, yes? How about you. You start dancing when you're a kid. I mean a *child*. If you start at fourteen, fifteen, forget it, you're too late. Gotta start young. Learn all the steps. Make your body like spring steel. Feel no pain. Eight, nine, ten years of training. And that's just the goddamn steps. Then, then you gotta learn how to refine your technique, clarify all you know, make it perfect. That's called learning to dance."

Meaghler stopped talking long enough to put more vodka and orange juice into a glass.

"Take it easy," Burck said again.

"An' then, maybe, you get to get on a ballet stage and do your stuff," Meaghler replied, and tossed back several ounces of the screwdriver. "And someone wants Joel dead? Just thinking about that is a terror, Carver. It'll fuck up his concentration, his precision. He'll be destroyed."

"I'm here to help," Carver said.

He and Burck left the apartment, and in a few minutes they were driving toward the ballet theater.

Thoughts ran through Carver's mind as he drove. A week or so ago Burck gets into an elevator that fails. Someone with special knowledge had to have gimmicked that elevator. Most likely Rosada, the maintenance man. But before Carver, or even the police, can question Rosada, someone kills him. Carver felt a familiar stirring deep inside himself, as thought a phantom had awakened, stretching and yawning, grinning as from a deep sleep. The huntsman had arisen.

Burck sat quite still and said very little as they drove. The shock of finding Ben Rosada's corpse still hung around him like a pus-colored fog.

Carver figured to get the dancer talking might loosen him up. With a forced amount of animation and interest, he questioned Burck on the problems of the Golden Gate Ballet Company, which had been written about in the local papers.

"I try to stay out of company politics," Burck responded slowly. "I'm an artist, and I make every effort not to take sides."

"But there's animosity between the artistic director, Bob Swaine, and the choreographers and the board of directors."

"Yes," Burck admitted, almost curtly.

"Tell me about it," Carver requested, and reached into his shirt pocket and turned on the cassette recorder.

"Much of that happened before I joined the company. That's one reason why I don't want to involve myself."

"Don't pussyfoot," Carver said. "Involve yourself. There's been one murder, and you don't want to be involved? We're both in it."

"Yes, you're quite right," Burck said and sighed. "Not too many years ago the Golden Gate Ballet Company was in deep financial trouble. Every night there were many empty seats. Several of the dance directors urged the board of directors to get a first-rate artistic director."

"Yeah, I remember reading about that in the papers," Carver said. "A world-class choreographer and director was hired to put the company back on its feet."

"Yes, Bob Swaine. He was the one who hired me, and many others. Some of the older dancers were let go, or stayed on in nonperforming functions. Swaine accomplished a major triumph, hiring Vassily Visikov, who created some of the most daring and beautiful ballets seen in the last ten years. The critics applauded, the public applauded, and the seats were filled to capacity. The company was profitable."

"So what's the problem now?"

"It's the old story," Burck replied, his voice more assured, his attitude more involved. "Swaine is a difficult man to work with. He does want things his own way. Always. And he takes too much credit, when in reality Visikov and some of the other choreographers deserve much recognition."

"Yeah, I've heard that Swaine wallows in self-aggrandizement."

"Brigham Merkhinn heads those members of the board who think Swaine is too arrogant, and that he is getting too much publicity, to the detriment of the company. They want to get rid of him."

Carver mused. Was there any connection between the GGBC's problems and the attempts to kill Burck?

Van Ness Avenue was wide, with three lanes going north and three going south. It ended at Aquatic Park and began at Market Street, to the south. The Davies Symphony Hall, the Opera House, and the modern art museum were a few blocks from Market Street. On a neighboring street behind the Opera House were the rehearsal hall and theater of the Golden Gate Ballet Company.

As they approached the Opera House and ballet theater complex, the telephone poles were plastered with announcements of the forthcoming premiere. The ads featured a stylized silhouette rendering of the notorious island in the bay.

They drove into a parking lot and paid the attendant. From the trunk Carver removed a steno-type notepad and several pencils. He slipped a pair of plain-glass spectacles into his jacket pocket.

Also in the trunk were a 35mm Nikon, several walkie-talkies, and in a locked, custom-built compartment, one of his .357 Python revolvers. Carver removed the Nikon and looped the strap over his shoulder. He locked the trunk and turned on the car's alarm system.

"I'm a free-lance journalist for a ballet magazine," Carver said, spelling out his idea. "I'll be doing an in-depth interview about you and the ballet company. That should explain my presence, and why I'm asking questions."

Burck agreed the idea had merit. "Are you going to use your own name?" he asked.

"Sure. I'm not well known."

"What if they find out?"

"Then I'm a liar," Carver said indifferently.

FOUR

Carver and Burck headed down Franklin Street toward the Golden Gate Ballet Theater.

Constructed in the last decade, the theater building was a dazzling structure of white marble, waterfalls of glass, and soaring dark steel spires. The building seemed made of crystal nocturnes, star-seeking gestures, and fluid muscle. The interior acoustics were praised as though they had been designed in paradise.

Carver and Burck entered by a side entrance, a metal-faced door. The backstage was a jumble of workmen, young muscular men in casual jeans and sweatshirts, young muscular women in leotards, and musicians carrying instruments and instrument cases.

Securing the plain-glass spectacles onto his nose, Carver followed Burck. He sidestepped loose piles of costumes, maneuvered around ropes that went from floor to gloom high overhead. Dozens of lithe young women moved to and fro, chattering, gesturing, many of them swarming out of elevators from the dressing rooms upstairs.

Carver enjoyed backstage atmospheres, and in particular the bustle of ballet artists, the sound of the pianist onstage playing an unfamiliar melody, the smell of sweat, of tobacco smoke, of oil and leather and fabrics. All of it, the feeling of athletic activity. He followed Burck past immense hanging curtains covering the wings.

He photographed several electricians working at a large panel of switches, gauges, and computer monitor screens. This was the lighting board that electronically controlled all the stage lights and the raising and lowering of scrims, curtains, and backdrops.

"Watch it, Burck," one of the young ballerinas said.

She pushed past Burck, her eyes straight ahead. She carried half a dozen toe shoes in her arms.

"Deborah, I'd like to intro—"

"Move out of the way," she snapped, and continued her journey without pause, still staring ahead.

"Sort of pissed," Carver said, watching as the woman went into a large curtained-off room that contained hundreds and hundreds of ballet shoes.

"Yes, I'm afraid so. Deborah Canby," Burck said, without any further explanation.

Burck and Carver took one of the elevators to Burck's dressing room. Carver remained close as the dancer changed into his rehearsal clothes. He wasn't about to lose sight of Burck; anybody could sidle up to the dancer and shove a knife into him. In a few minutes Burck was dressed for rehearsal, wearing loose pants and a belted blouse, attire that seemed more appropriate for a martial arts practitioner. The two men took the elevator down.

On the stage a set of piping and scaffolding covered the back and sides. Stagehands clambered over the structure carrying more pipes, tightening joints, and calling orders to each other. The set had a familiar look, and Carver finally realized that it was supposed to be an abstracted jail or prison, complete with cell doors, bars, catwalks, and tiers. The set seemed odd for a GGBC ballet, more like something for Martha Graham or the Joffrey's modern dance.

The stage itself was not wood but large gray-blue tilelike squares of some sort of resilient material.

Dancers milled about: several young females, half a dozen males. Most of the attention was centered on a husky, older man. Burck pointed him out as Bob Swaine, the center of the company's controversy.

Carver looked the man over, but only for a few seconds. His eyes kept coming back to one of the female dancers. Gorgeous. Auburn hair with strong red tints, pulled back tautly. A tall young woman with high cheekbones and deep, luminescent, Isle of Capri grotto-blue eyes. Pale, moist skin. Probably sweat. Her eyes were tapered at the edges, as though pulling back her hair had stretched the flesh around the eyes.

How old was she? Probably in her early twenties. He tried the old trick of staring at her while she went through a series of stretching exercises; she didn't respond. No survival mechanism, Carver decided, no feeling of eyes on her.

Yet she was an excellent dancer, Carver decided. Better than the others. Artistic excellence was an attraction for him. Something like a rush punched his bones when he met someone who worked with their mind, and when it was a woman who blended mind and body creatively . . . well, that combination was irresistible. He was caught in a storm. The attraction for the auburn-haired dancer was a hard pull on his emotions; he was familiar with it, and seldom ignored it.

Despite the obvious dangers. Emotional, not physical. Although sometimes . . .

"Do you want me to introduce you to everyone?" Burck asked.

"Just introduce me to the top honchos," Carver said, although he was sorely tempted to meet the auburn-haired ballerina. He thumbed on his micro-recorder in his shirt pocket. "I'll sort out the rest of the crowd by myself."

The job of narrowing any suspects down to a manageable level seemed laughable. Starting at the top was always a good bet. Like a pyramid, one person at the peak, with more and more with each underlying layer. Carver hoped the killer—and he was certain there was one—wasn't milling among the hundreds of people at the base.

"So, Mr. Burck," Swaine said loudly when he saw the dancer, "have you been lost, or did you have to make a grand detour to get your compass out of pawn?"

"Sorry, Mr. Swaine," Burck replied.

"Don't think Swaine means anything, kid," a muscular dancer said, his pleasant voice carrying over the hum of noise. "Because he does. He wants you to show us lesser mortals how to melt the floorboards."

"And who is this?" Swaine asked Burck, pointing at Carver Bascombe.

Burck introduced Carver as a journalist to Bob Swaine and to Eric Hudson, the dancer with the congenial baritone voice.

Swaine wore an anodized-blue jogging suit, with soft-soled meringue-colored shoes. He was smaller than expected, around six or seven inches shorter than Carver. He had the look of a medieval monk, with a gray fringe circling his scalp. His movements matched his eyes, quick and sharp. "Knobby" would describe his face: knobby nose, knobby chin, knobby forehead. The color of his eyes matched his hair: gunmetal gray. Wide athletic shoulders made his knobby head seem small. His body was an inverted narrow triangle.

Carver recalled what he had read about Swaine: in his middle fifties, born and raised in New York City, danced on the Continent, then in New York, and began to choreograph about ten years ago. His dancing had been better than average. But his choreography? Magnificent! Instant recognition as a genius.

"What magazine do you work for?" Swaine asked.

"I'm a free-lance," Carver replied. "Although I have the approval of *Dancer's Life* on the project. And Joel Burck's approval. I hope that I'll have yours also."

"Anything that enhances ballet," Eric Hudson said, gently interrupting, "is most welcome. I—we—all of us do love to see our names in print—since it's about the only fame we're going to get."

Swaine glowered at Hudson.

"And when will this article appear, Mr. Bascombe?" Swaine asked.

"In about four months," Carver said, improvising.

"I presume, Mr. Bascombe," Swaine said sarcastically,

"you know a lot about the ballet? Or do you need a guided tour?"

"I'll do fine on my own, Mr. Swaine."

"My name is spelled like the bay, up in Canada," Eric Hudson said lightly, interrupting Swaine's antagonism. "A good encyclopedia will give you the correct spelling, added knowledge about our neighbor to the north, and a lot of information about the fur trade."

"Yes, I suppose so," Carver replied as soberly as he could.

"Not that the ballet, that's spelled B-A-L-L-E-T, has much to do with furs, not even furs in the hearts of our countrymen."

Hudson chuckled at his own idiosyncratic turn of mind.

Carver studied Hudson's good looks, almost aristocratic, with a narrow face, shadowy dark-green eyes, a long patrician nose, a widow's peak of black tousled hair. With that kind of face Carver could almost hear Hudson say imperiously, "Off with their heads." As with the other dancers, there was the excellent musculature, the intensity. Carver guessed Hudson's age: thirty or so, a trifle old to be dancing.

Burck went into several exercises, limbering his legs, his arms, his wrists. Burck seemed a totally different man, without fears, with total confidence. Hardly the person who had been horrified of the sight of a corpse only an hour or so before.

The dancer introduced Carver to several more dancers: Alex Bellini, and a sharp-eyed young man about twenty, Billy Jones, who seemed unable to stand still, but was forever moving, testing his legs, moving his hands, watching himself. Bellini, on the other hand, was more placid, yet seemed powerful in repose, somewhat like a lion or tiger in the zoo waiting for a caretaker to absently leave a door open.

The warm-up exercises were standards, *battements tendus*, one leg centered, carrying the weight of the erect body; the other leg swinging forward, from the hips, the feet arrow-straight, and then back. The same, with a small bend of the knees, a *demi-pliés*.

More complex combinations of movements: *demi-pliés* becoming full *pliés*. *Battements tendus* working more gracefully, changing into *tours en l'aire*, turns in the air. Well-defined, clean beat, nothing tricky. Dancers need great strength, as much as any champion weight lifter, and they need technique, and skill. And most of all, determination.

When the legs begin to ache, when the toes cramp, the calcium deposits grow, the tendons strain, the muscles scream in agony. Then only determination drives a dancer on and on.

Yeah, Carver thought, most of all, determination.

Burck finished his warm-ups and beckoned to Carver. "This will take a while," the dancer said, "since it's *The Prisoner,* Juan Guiterez's original ballet. It's interesting, very modern. Visikov has created the choreography. Very difficult, Carver. Keep watching me, of course, but I feel much better, more relaxed. I am where I am alive. I don't feel in danger."

Carver recognized the peculiar euphoria when a person has had a great shock and then grabs hold of a great interest, an intense absorption in a creative activity. Yeah, determination. Carver placed himself close to the wings, with an overall view of the stage.

The other dancers still limbered up. The older, gray-haired man played chords on an upright piano. The dancers exercised to the melody line the pianist played.

Carver tried once again to stare the attractive auburn-haired ballerina's neck hairs into raising, but she was still ignorant of his ESP attempts. After unsuccessful minutes, Carver quit. And then the ferret deep down inside reached up a hand and tickled the sensors that tightened further the short gnarled hairs on *his* neck. Was someone watching *him*?

Carver turned slowly and glanced around. None of the stage crew. No one backstage. The dancers? Yes. One of the male dancers was watching him intently. Staring. A slim young black man, probably in his early twenties, loose curly hair like dark wet moss, eyes like sunbaked stones, old eyes in a vernal face, eyes gleaming large.

The black dancer smiled, parting his lips slightly, more of a grin. Carver ignored him, turned his back. Carver moved away from the wings and went down the side stairs. He settled himself into a seat in the third row.

After several minutes there was a muttering backstage, and one of the ballerinas pulled aside several of the heavy stage curtains.

"I can do it myself, goddamn it!" a rumbling baritone voice said.

A man rolled in on a wheelchair, shoving aside the stage curtain. He was pushed by a young man, lithe and blond and somewhat vacant-faced. The man in the wheelchair was dressed impeccably in a black pin-striped suit, with a bold blue silk scarf wrapped around his throat.

Anyone even slightly interested in the ballet would have recognized Vassily Visikov. Carver knew who he was as soon as the wheelchair rolled onto the stage.

The dancers made a path for the rolling chair, which stopped in front of Swaine. The man in the chair looked at the audience, saw Carver, and began to speak in a low, train-engine voice. Burck stood close, along with several other dancers and ballerinas.

The crippled man thrust a leonine head at the dancers, giving orders. Occasionally he ran long, twisted fingers through his shock of dark hair. His hair was almost a trademark, long and dark, shaggy, shot with streaks of gray, as though bolts of lightning had once grazed his head.

Carver watched as Visikov ended his conversation, thumping the side of his chair for finality, for emphasis. Burck nodded, and Bob Swaine shrugged. The black dancer who had been watching Carver left the stage and walked to where Carver sat.

"Mr. Viskikov wants to speak with you," the dancer said. He put a strong brown hand on Carver's shoulder; it stayed for moment longer than necessary. "By the way, I've been watching you. I'm sure you've noticed. I might have some interesting tidbits for an interview. My name's Don Terman. That's T-E-R-M-A-N," he said, spelling out the letters.

"And D-O-N-A-L-D, as in Duck," Carver said.

"Funny, but not really," Terman said. "Nice try, though. Come on, you don't want to keep the great man waiting."

Terman took hold of Carver's elbow, being ever-so-helpful getting him to his feet. He smiled and then walked away, expecting Carver to follow. Which he did.

"Mr. Bascombe," the man in the wheelchair said. "I am Vassily Visikov. You know who I am?"

"Yes, sir, you're one of the choreographers of the company."

"And that's all?"

"No, sir, you're one of the great choreographers in the world of ballet."

"In the world of ballet, Mr. Bascombe?"

"In the world, Mr. Visikov."

"That's much better. I was afraid as a journalist for a ballet magazine you were going to fail first off on your assignment."

"Not likely, sir."

"Do not call me 'sir.' 'Mr. Visikov' will suffice."

"All right, Mr. Visikov."

"Good," Visikov said. "You may stay. Remember, we are the ballet, not *A Chorus Line*." He then turned to the man pushing his wheelchair. "Benjamin, move me to stage left. Everyone! I want to see the first few minutes of the new ballet."

Swaine nodded quickly to a young man at the lectern, the stage manager, who thumbed a switch. His voice was amplified through the bitch boxes backstage.

"Okay! All right! Please. Places everyone. For *The Prisoner*." He picked up a hand microphone. "If you please, lights! Number one!"

The first of many lights punched a bright hole through the now darkened theater. Then, as the stage manager gave more orders, more lights blazed on.

Vassily Visikov turned to the older man at the piano. "I

need not tell the composer where to begin, but John, I want the music loud. Very loud. I want those shuffling feet onstage drowned out. I don't want to hear one damned footfall. After all, the music is the thing. Without the music there would be no ballet. All right. Begin.''

The Prisoner used less than a dozen dancers, with Joel Burck performing the lead, a doomed man beset by authorities, by fate. Other dancers represented two prisoners in death row, the priest or minister, Billy Jones as the Interrogator, two guards, a captain of the guard, and Alex Bellini danced a sinister Death. Joyce Kittering and another ballerina in gray shrouds danced silent roles like a Greek chorus.

Even though the piano was the only instrument, the music was powerful, pulsing like a heartbeat awaiting a death sentence. But the music was also depressing, morbid. The dancers' movements were dirgelike, breaking into swift movement when the Interrogator sidled onto the stage. The dancers climbed the prison set, gliding and sliding down the pipes, among the cells, to the strange, gloomy music.

The remaining dancers who were not performing stood in the wings or watched from the audience. Bob Swaine sat near Don Terman and Eric Hudson. Vassily Visikov remained onstage, close to the action.

Several times Visikov stopped the dance by banging on the sides of his wheelchair.

"No, please. Slowly, but do not drag it out. Like this.''

He turned to Benjamin, the young man who stood beside him, and had a whispered conversation.

"Yes, Mr. V,'' Benjamin said quietly. He took the place of the errant dancer and performed the step as Visikov wished.

"Slowly, deliberately, if you please. Billy, watch Joel. See how he rises, carefully, as though he were made of air, that he is weightless. And landing, he is soft, soft, soft as a feather. And then watch Benjamin, Billy, and see, his thighs, they are there, they are strained, they are being used. Now—you do as well, Billy.''

And Billy Jones did his best to imitate the movements of Benjamin, Visikov's alter ego. Jones strained his legs; his thighs were like cannon barrels. And they trembled with the effort. Visikov was pleased. The rehearsal continued.

Another time, and Visikov stopped the action. The dancers froze as the great choreographer snapped his eyes shut, pressed both hands to his face—and thinks, feels the new movement, the new design coming to life in his mind. Again he told Benjamin how he wanted it performed.

"Yes, Mr. V," Benjamin said, and the quiet, almost vacant-eyed dancer did the steps.

Then the corps tried the new design, and Vassily Visikov was either pleased or displeased. On and on. Carver could see the sweat Burck threw off as the dancer spun, pirouetted, a prisoner caught in a tragedy he did not understand.

"Keep the count," Viskikov demanded. "One, two, three. One, two, three. One, two, three, four."

To Carver's untrained eye, the rehearsal seemed composed of jumping rabbits, leaping lizards, and sweaty rumpled swans. Weren't they supposed to be convicts and prison guards? With the new design, occasionally one of them missed a mark or danced out of alignment.

"Damn you!" one of the ballerinas cried out.

She hopped around on one foot, holding the other like some kind of injured family pet. The other dancers backed away from the injured dancer. The other girl tried to apologize, but the victim wasn't having any.

"Little bitch!" the injured girl yelled.

And in seconds the two girls were in a clutch of windmilling arms and legs. Carver got up and moved into the aisle, pulling out his notebook and pen. Had to perform for his cover story; scribble meaningless squiggles. A dancer bumped into him, bodily contact. Pressing close. Carver ignored the contact.

"Certainly know how to scrap, don't they?"

Carver turned. Don Terman smiled at him. Carver ignored him.

Carver watched as Burck, Hudson, and several others tried to pull apart the fighting females. He felt a hand slide along his slacks and over his buttocks. He couldn't ignore the lecherous touching; he turned and stared pleasantly at Don Terman.

"You have a dressing room or something around here?" Carver asked.

"Why certainly," Terman said. He stepped away from Carver and bobbed his head toward the right-hand wings. "Will wonders never cease?"

The black dancer walked away from the crowd around the combat zone and Carver followed him. Backstage some of the stage crew watched the onstage activity. Most ignored the action, going about their business securing flats, repairing scrims, carrying cartons, like that. Carver followed Terman up a metal staircase and into an ill-lighted dressing room.

With one hand on his hip, Terman turned and faced Carver. His eyes, those eyes that seemed to look at life as if they belonged to a worn-out, aged man, those eyes glittered as they slowly looked Carver up and down.

"Lots of guys must have told you that you were good-looking," Terman said. "You are, you know. In a rough kind of way, of course. But then, that appeals to me. I really like your eyes, kind of slanted, like you have some American Indian blood in you. And you must have a good body. In this business, I know about good bodies, and with your good looks you just have to have a great body."

FIVE

Carver pushed Terman hard against the makeup mirror. He crumpled the dancer's leotard in a bunched fist.

"Don't ever touch me," Carver said, his words flat and hard. "Don't put the make on me, don't even think about me, period. Live and let live."

He could feel the dancer tensing, gathering his hard and muscular body for a move. Carver slapped the man across the face once. Terman's cheek went red.

"Don't think about taking me, either," Carver said, the words still blunt. "I'll say it again. Don't touch me, don't brush against me. Do it—and I'll hurt you. You won't dance for weeks."

Terman glared at Carver. Eyes glittering. Hot stones.

"Understand me?" Carver asked. Still tough.

"You hate me," Terman said in a whispery voice infected with anger and hatred. "You hate gays."

"Don't be an asshole," Carver said.

He let go of Terman's leotard. Carver stared directly into Terman's eyes and then left the dressing room. He breathed heavily and shook his head ruefully. He wasn't about to explain to Terman. Carver didn't hate homosexuals. But he detested being hit on. He made a mental note to tell Moseby about the encounter. Maybe his friend could suggest a better way to have handled the situation.

Damn it! He had handled it badly. Homosexuality was a fact of life in the ballet. He knew it, and should've handled Terman better. He wasn't about to apologize, though. Let Terman think whatever he wanted.

Still, Carver could have, should have reacted better. Yeah, he thought, he should've been cool, more tolerant. If anyone should know about intolerance . . . ah, fuck it.

He took off his glasses, wiped them with his handkerchief, and put them back on as a ballerina passed him. She looked at him, and he thought he recognized her. Yeah, the one called Deborah—what was it? Deborah . . . Canby. Deborah Canby. One of the prima ballerinas.

"Is the fight over?" he asked.

She looked at him, her eyes narrowed down to slits, her nostrils pinched.

"Yes, it's over," she replied, her words clipped and fast.

"Who won?" Carver asked, trying to get past her brittle manner with a pleasant smile.

Without replying, Deborah Canby pushed harshly by him and went down the metal staircase. Carver followed, wondering what her problem was. Maybe Canby didn't take kindly to a possible interview?

The rehearsals had stopped, with Visikov talking about making some step changes with the dancers.

Carver went onstage and spoke with the pianist. "You're the composer?" he asked.

"That's correct. Juan Guiterez," the man said, shaking Carver's hand. "They call me John. Juan makes me sound like I'm tired and old, burnt out."

"I'd like to ask a few questions, sort of get a feel about this ballet company. How you work together. What you do outside."

A gray, neatly trimmed Vandyke beard covered Guiterez's strong chin. A narrow gray mustache completed the oval of hair around his mouth. The composer's fingers were long and narrow, but with corded tendons streaking under the skin. Carver guessed Guiterez's age at mid-fifties. Guiterez had a habit, not necessarily nervous, of running those strong fingers over his thinning hair. He had the look of a Spanish grandee.

"I suppose most of your article will be about the dancers?" Guiterez asked.

"Naturally, but I won't slight your contribution. I haven't been introduced to all of the dancers." Carver turned and indicated a ballerina exercising. Gorgeous hair, lithe figure, skin like a porcelain teacup. "That one, for instance," Carver said. "Who is she?"

"Joyce Kittering," Guiterez said, wryly amused. "Very pretty. I don't blame you. For wanting to interview her, I mean."

"Thanks," Carver said, grinning. "Right. Joyce Kittering. All right—let's talk about you, Mr. Guiterez." He made sure his pocket recorder was on.

"Call me John, Carver. You know the theme of my ballet?" John asked, and continued talking when Carver indicated he didn't. "It's a piece set in a prison, with the dancers performing as guards and prisoners. An allegory on injustice, if you will."

"Man's inhumanity to man?"

"You say that glibly, Carver. Don't you think man is still inhuman to itself?"

"Yeah," Carver said, "but I'm not going to argue the point."

"Why not? What is inhumanity after all? It is indifference, it is greed, it is perversion of authority. It is discrimination. You must know about discrimination, certainly. A man of color."

Carver nodded, and scribbled more notes into his writing pad. Yeah, he knew about discrimination. When you're black you live with it, you eat with it, you sleep with it. Even dreams are choked with it. You either go with it, hate it, fight it, or let it beat you down. One thing, you can never ignore it.

He scribbled more lines.

"It is what we do to each other," Guiterez continued. "Artists know about oppression. Jews know it. Gypsies know it. Almost everyone at one time or another has known it. Catholics. Protestants. We never seem to remember, never seem to learn from it. That is what *The Prisoner* is about.

"Everyone is a prisoner, it's just a matter of time and place, and who and when." Guiterez made a temple of his fingers and blew warm breath into the cathedral. "Often we are prisoners inside ourselves, and other times it is imposed. For our own good, we are told. Sometimes. And if there are prisoners, then there must be guards. And there must be people who condemn. The age-old question: who watches the watchers? Does it seem overly pretentious, Carver?"

Carver shook his head and flipped open his notepad. "I understand there's going to be a gala premiere of the ballet on Alcatraz Island."

"Yes, that is so."

"Whose idea was that?"

"Mine and Vassily's. We both have visited several of the county jails for research. We took a boat ride out to Alcatraz when we first came to this fair city. We found the notorious island prison fascinating and inspiring."

"Inspiring enough to have this new ballet performed there?"

"Exactly. Excellent publicity. Have you been to the island, Carver?"

"Yeah, I've been out there."

"Do you know the word 'Alcatraz' is an old Spanish word for pelican?"

Carver admitted his ignorance, and listened as Guiterez explained how a lieutenant in the Spanish navy first saw the island in 1769, covered with pelicans. So: *Isla de los Alcatraces*.

Both composer and choreographer saw an opportunity for enormous publicity if they were to perform Guiterez's music and Visikov's ballet in the infamous prison. After pleading and arguing with the various state and federal agencies, they finally had permission.

"So first we rehearse," Guiterez said, a trace of pride and arrogance in his voice, "and then a one-time-only gala performance on Alcatraz in four days' time. My music joining with the ghostly echoes of Al Capone, Machine-gun Kelly, Alvin Karpis, oh so many other famous gangsters.''

"Sounds exciting," Carver said. "I hope to be there. But for now, about this article, I'd like to get your feelings about the people in the company. You get along with everyone?''

"On the whole, yes, of course. I admire them enormously. Most are obsessed. To dance is their life; they cannot imagine doing anything else. Yet few of them become famous or rich. It is the one thing for which Swaine is disliked: he does not let anyone become a star. Hardly anyone. Even the principal dancers are not well known. The soloists even less so. And the corps de ballet? Forget that they have names. It is one of the few disagreements we have with Swaine.''

"You're in his camp, then?"

"I suppose so. I've played the piano here for many years. And this is the first time that anyone has taken any of my own compositions seriously. Yes, finally, gray-haired, I will have my music played and performed. I owe that much to Swaine. But some of the directors . . . they think going to Alcatraz is cheap theatrics.''

Guiterez pushed a trembling hand through his hair. His eyes seemed far away.

"Over twenty years," he said softly, absently, as if time stood still in his mind. "Twenty years. Three operas. Five symphonies. Dozens upon dozens of suites and tone poems. Unplayed, unpublished. Like unborn children. Over and over again, I begged and pleaded, but there was no one to listen.''

Carver had to cup a hand to his ear, Guiterez spoke so softly, almost a whisper.

"Until Swaine. He listened to me, and he listened to my music. He created a ballet from one of my short tone poems. *Zapata Waltzes*. Even then the world didn't listen. They looked at the dancers, but they didn't hear the music." Guiterez closed his eyes, passing those long, trembling hands over them. "No one listened."

He sat on his piano bench for a while, then breathed heavily and shook himself, returning himself to the here and now.

"I apologize, Carver. Sometimes . . . We never learn from history, do we?"

"People are like that, John," Carver replied. He poised his pen over his notes. "Do you see many of the dancers outside of business?"

"Occasionally, yes," Guiterez said, his voice almost normal.

"Go to parties, do you, that sort of thing?"

"Yes, and as a matter of fact, there was a party last night. At Eric Hudson's apartment."

"I guess you had a good time?" Carver asked, scribbling obvious lines into his notepad. Didn't matter if anyone saw him writing.

"Oh, yes. Good conversation, good friends, good wine, good food. These things I enjoy greatly."

With Carver's prodding, more questioning, Juan Guiterez described the good times, the guests, the jokes, the gossip, who was making out with which young woman or man.

"You were there all the time?" Carver asked, hoping it didn't sound too obvious.

"No, at one point we were running low on liquor. I volunteered a trip to a nearby all-night store for more. Before it closed at two o'clock."

"So you wouldn't know if anyone else left the party."

"Why are you asking these questions?" Guiterez said slowly. "They seem outside the realm of dance interviews."

"Sorry, just nosy. Curiosity got the better of me."

He walked away, putting his notepad in a pocket; he damned himself for pushing too fast, too far afield. In the wings he saw the lovely ballerina, Joyce Kittering, sitting mending small rips in her ballet shoes. Her legs were covered with bulky leg warmers.

"Do you mind?" Carver asked as he pulled a chair alongside hers.

"It's a free country," she said neutrally.

"You dance very well."

"Thank you," she said flatly, looking at him. Aloof.

Blue is a color that is often described as cool. Her eyes matched her voice: not exactly cold, but definitely without interest. Her eyes upon Carver were distant. No, it was less than that. Carver read the indifference and dismissal in her gaze and in the turn of her body away from him.

"Excuse me," Carver said, "have I said something? I'm simply trying to do a story on the ballet."

"You'll have to do it without me," she said.

"I think it would be easier over a cup of coffee."

"Why?"

"For one thing I'd like to know you better. A cup of coffee would give us some time together. I could write a sidebar about a ballerina."

"I rather think not, Mr. Bascombe."

Joyce Kittering gathered her sewing material and her shoes and walked away. Carver watched her, wondering what that encounter had been all about. She certainly had interesting body language. Negative a no-no.

He returned to his seat in the audience and watched the rest of the rehearsal of *The Prisoner*. He mused over Kittering's apparent disinterest. He didn't like to take that sort of thing lying down; his ego had been slashed.

Yeah, Joyce was pretty, but so were many of the other dancers. But the others hadn't snubbed him. He didn't like looking the fool. So? So he wanted to see what it took to overcome Joyce Kittering's hostility. And he wanted to find out why she was hostile.

The allure of excellence often led him into treacherous tides. Oh sure, he often found himself mucking around in emotional ooze, but it was often worth the game.

And there was something else—others were aware he had been put down by Kittering. Any normal male would try one more time. If only for his cover, he wanted to talk to her. Carver grinned at himself. Yeah, make excuses for being attracted to a good-looking woman.

Could she be the one behind Burck's problem? Keep an open mind, he told himself. Some dirty water was trickling under the floorboards. What kind of problems did some of these women have? So there was Joyce's indifference, and there was that odd hostility from that other dancer, Deborah Canby. A peculiar undercurrent seemed to be running through the ballet company.

SIX

Carver read through his minimal notes. Not much to go on; a lot of effort for very little. He watched the rigorous routine that Vassily Visikov put the dancers through. Tough and difficult. As Bart Meaghler had so aptly put it, "Impossible. Can't be done."

Eric Hudson settled into the seat next to him. "Didn't do too well with Joyce Kittering," he said abruptly.

"No," Carver said, shaking his head. "You were watching us?"

"Hard to miss. The journalist snubbed. Love's Labors Lost."

"I guess she doesn't want to see her name in print."

"Oh ho. That ain't the issue, my man. No, no. Most of us toe-steppers like to see our name in news stories. Especially if it's an article in *Dancer's Life*."

Carver studied the dancer. Hudson wiped the sweat from his face and arms with a towel he carried around his neck. He seemed fit enough to lift weights and probably did. A strong, corded neck framed his princely face. His dark green eyes had a casual look, as though Hudson took life very easy. Aristocrats in literature were often described with that look. The indolent look. The hard, lean body contrasted with that look.

"I think," Carver said, "that Visikov's choreography is about as brutal as any I've ever seen."

"Then I think," Hudson said, a twinkle glittering in his eyes, "that you haven't seen too many rehearsals. This routine is just that—routine."

"You found me out," Carver replied, using a quick grin to offset any further inquiries. "I love the ballet, but I've only seen it performed. Never been to rehearsals before. I find it absolutely fascinating. I've gathered a greater appreciation for the art and skill and training. They must need as much relaxation as they can get. What do most of you do for fun?"

"Various things," Hudson said, and laughed. "We read diet books, shop for bargains, pet our cats and dogs—mostly cats. I don't have a cat; I have this strange obsession that cats don't have bones. Ever seen a cat walk? They slink, like a puddle of oil. Boneless.

"Anyway, we talk with friends, most of whom are not in the ballet. We occasionally get married, and again, seldom to a dancer. It is a rare and noble creature, the dancer who can live with another; we do not like to share our aches and pains. And, of course, we rehearse, and rehearse, and rehearse. We also pay a lot of our paychecks to chiropractors."

"What do you do? Personally?"

"Me? Eric Hudson—that's me—likes to have a good time. Just like any best-in-the-world young dancer. I wait for my spot in the limelight. Wait to be recognized. It has to come. My reputation as a playboy of the Western world is undeserved. Why limit the geographical area?"

"Do you often give parties?" Carver asked.

"Do I give parties? Ho ho. As often as the penurious paycheck of the GGBC allows. Not often. Had one just last night. Pretty good, too."

"Any particular occasion? I'm just curious."

"Nope, couldn't think of any. Maybe that's the best kind. I just got up the other day and said to myself, Eric lad—a nasty habit of talking to oneself makes for easy listening—I said, there hasn't been a party for a long while and my numerous and appreciative friends need relaxation. Too bad you weren't here. I would've invited you. A party scene in an article makes for interesting reading."

"Yes," Carver said. "Readers seem to like that sort of thing."

"Of course I wouldn't call my parties deluxe high living. Just a friendly sort of get-together for friends and compatriots. Not a bash like on one of those television soap operas with all those wealthy and powerful soggy cardboard types."

"Are you going to Moseby's party tomorrow night?"

"Now *that's* going to be a bash. Moseby's parties would shame Nero and Perle Mesta. Whoever she was. Before my time for sure. So was Nero for that matter. Anyway, I wouldn't miss it. Are you going?"

"I am," Carver said, and laughed. "I'm supposed to be asking the questions, doing the interview. Tell me about yourself, about your career."

Hudson obliged. And Carver dutifully took notes.

Born in Stockton, California, thirty years before, Hudson was attracted to dancing from watching old Fred Astaire movies on TV. He had badgered his mother and father into letting him take ballet. His father was appalled, and the boy often had to battle his way home from school.

By nine years old he had been spotted by a talent scout for the GGBC. The scout kept her eye on the boy until he was sixteen. Then he was hired to perform—the youngest dancer ever in the GGBC. For the past fourteen years Hudson had worked his way through the anonymous corps de ballet, into one of the few soloist positions, and now, finally, he was among the even fewer principals.

"So that should bring you up to date," Hudson said as Carver folded his notepad shut.

After shutting off his micro-recorder, Carver took several photos of Eric Hudson and of the dancers working onstage. He returned to his seat, his thoughts a turmoil. The dancers going through their rehearsals brought him a memory. The ballet. The first time he had been to the ballet. A violent introduction . . .

*   *   *

He had stood in a large room of the Army induction center with a crowd of young men. He had put his full signature to dozens of forms—Bascombe, Carver Attucks, eighteen years old—and then had been examined, prodded, and poked by doctors.

"Okay, fella," the doctors said, "put your clothes on."

Finally a sergeant wearing a flat-brimmed campaign hat stood at the front of the room and rapped for attention. A commotion was going on in the rear of the room. Shouts and laughs punctured the quiet. Two black guys and a white guy were pushing and shoving at a fourth, slightly built young man backed against the wall. A cheering crowd formed around the four men, yelling encouragement.

"Hit him!"

"Get him good!"

"Do it!"

Carver pushed his way to the front. He guessed the kid couldn't be more than eighteen. And the three guys were older—twenty, twenty-one.

"We joined 'cause we're men," one black guy said.

"Yeah," his white friend agreed, "and we don't want to live in no barracks with no faggot."

"So just get the fuck outta my face, gayboy," the second black man said.

"I'm not gay," the young man said quietly.

Catcalls and boos drowned out his words. Carver turned and looked at the sergeant. The man leaned against a blackboard with a wry smile. He tilted his campaign hat forward, shielding his eyes.

Yeah, Carver thought, you're just going to let this crowd work out its aggression. Some kind of macho game.

Carver grabbed the arm of the meanest-looking black guy, a face of acne pits and small eyes set into beefy sockets. The arm felt as if the brown skin had been stuffed with coconuts.

"Knock it off," Carver said. He hoped he sounded cool.

The guy backhanded Carver into the crowd.

"Give them room!" the crowd yelled. "Yeah! Room! Hey, it's a fight!"

Carver attacked again, but the black guy cursed and slammed an elbow into Carver's ribs. Carver swiveled fast and did a side kick at the guys groin. The black guy bent over, clutching at himself.

"Stay out of this," the kid said calmly to Carver, and repeated it.

"Stay out of it!" the crowd chanted. "Stay out of it! Stay out of it!"

The white guy, tall, broad-shouldered, threw a solid punch at the kid. Whoosh! Nothing but air. The kid had dodged effortlessly. Suddenly he was all movement, almost a blur, bobbing and weaving.

Carver's own fight was brief and losing. He did his best, but his opponent was strong and fucking mean. An elbow slammed into Carver's gut. Ah, shit! Too much. Carver went down.

But the young skinny kid—damn he was fast! Carver saw him lash out with a leg, and the other black guy went down. The crowd bayed and yelled. The kid was okay, untouched. He had bobbed and weaved out of the clutches of the white guy. The second black guy was still on the floor. The black guy who had hit Carver joined his white buddy. Carver cleared his head, clutched his stomach, and got to his feet. Enough of this shit!

The kid was incredible. He moved, he pivoted, he ducked, all with wonderful grace. His body was liquid, one movement flowing into another. He leaped, a high jump, and—one kick to the black guy's chin—another kick—and the white attacker fell backward. The two men were on the floor. Unconscious.

Carver moved fast when he saw the first black guy get up from the floor, a buck knife in his hand. Carver came in from the man's blind side and hit him with a front snap kick at the chin, pivoted, and slammed a spear hand into the guys solar plexus. He kicked the knife away, hearing it bing and clang against the wall.

The crowd was silent, and the sound of the knife lingered

for a moment. The fight was over. The kid looked quietly at the crowd. He had barely worked up a sweat. He looked at Carver.

"Come on," the kid said.

The crowd moved away from him, and Carver followed him.

The young man's name was Elliot Daino. Carver introduced himself, and they agreed a beer was in order. Carver guided him to a bar nearest the induction center. The bartender didn't demand to see their ID. Maybe the bartender didn't care, Carver guessed, or figured they were two guys getting into the Army and deserved a beer. They sat in a booth, two bottles and two glasses between them.

"Daino, where'd you learn to fight like that?" Carver asked, pouring beer into both glasses.

"I learned the moves in ballet school. And I've taken karate."

"Great stuff," Carver said. "What started all that fuckin' around?"

"One of them heard me answer some questions from the doctor. What I did—dance. What I liked to do—dance the ballet. I guess they think every guy who likes ballet is a homosexual."

"Are you?"

"No, I like girls just fine. I had a lot of girlfriends in high school. And in college. I've had one semester. How about you, Carver, what do you do?"

"I've been going to college, but I didn't have quite enough money."

They talked for a while, ordering two more beers. After exchanging phone numbers, Carver and Elliott left the bar. They didn't see one other until their return to the induction center. Both went to Fort Ord, but were in different basic training companies. They often got together at the soldiers' club and went on weekend passes together.

Carver admitted he had never seen a ballet. A terrible oversight in his education, Daino said. With two girls, Daino and Carver went to the ballet in the City by the Bay 120 miles north. *Giselle* and *Swan Lake*. Over the next few months they went several more times. Daino spent time with Carver, explaining all the moves, the strenuous training, and the music.

When basic training was completed, their companies went overseas. Carver wound up in the Military Police, and he never saw Elliot Daino again. When his tour of duty was almost completed, he used his connections in the MP's and Military Intelligence to find out what had happened to his friend. Daino was officially listed as MIA— Missing in Action.

Carver Bascombe sighed and stretched his long legs. The rehearsals were over. Most of the dancers were exhausted. Joel Burck motioned to Carver to come backstage. Carver followed the dancer to his dressing room, which he shared with two other male dancers.

"I caught a glimpse of you earlier with Don Terman," Burck said. "He seemed quite upset. What happened?"

Carver told him.

"I presume he mistook you for a gay because you were with me."

"I suppose so," Carver said.

"I don't think you had to be quite so rough with him. I don't need any further complications within the company. Don't you agree?"

Carver shrugged his shoulders as a statement. Of what he wasn't quite sure. Did Burck want some kind of apology? The dancer would wait a long time for that.

"Now what do we do?" Burck asked as he finished dressing.

"I want to see your car," Carver said, removing the plain glass spectacles. He tucked them into the breast pocket of his jacket.

Within minutes they had left the theater and headed for the Hall of Justice on Bryant Street. They filled out the necessary papers to get into the police impoundment lot, which was located on Potrero Avenue, near 17th Street, only a few minutes away.

A warm breeze wafted through the remains of the afternoons. The impoundment office was a squat single-story building with lots of glass. Several uniformed police were stationed in a glassed-in front office. They were reading reports when Carver and Burck pulled in.

The man in charge was an overweight civilian who didn't seem to like his job. He checked out Burck's papers, and allowed the two men to inspect the BMW. Carver and Burck spent several minutes looking over the vast parking area before they found the car. Carver had Burck open the trunk. He heaved out the tire that had once been on the car's right rear wheel.

"Deliberately cut," Carver said, indicating a slash in the inside sidewall of the tire.

"It was no accident?" Burck asked, his voice quavering at the memory of how close his knees had come to being crushed.

"No, it wasn't. Someone knew your car was parked on the street." Using the Nikon, which he still carried, Carver took several photos of the tire and close-ups of the knife gash. "He saw that the other car was in a good position to ram into the rear end. He—or she—slashed the tire and waited. When you came out, he watched while you were jacking up the car, pulling off this tire, and then he let the brakes go of the car on the incline."

"Wasn't he taking a chance?"

"Yeah, that was taking a chance."

"What if the owner of the other car came out before me and drove away? The killer's plan would have been ruined."

"He'd just wait for another opportunity."

"Then it's quite possible for him to have tried to kill me at other times?"

"Yeah," Carver said.

"And I would have had no knowledge of them?"

"Right."

"I'm very frightened, Carver," Burck said, and turned away and gazed at the darkening sky.

SEVEN

Carver closed the trunk lid of the BMW. A chill wind came up and whipped debris through the compound. Pieces of paper flattened against fenders and wheels of the automobiles parked in the yard. Carver tapped Burck on the shoulder and motioned for him to come along. His long legs ate up the ground, and Burck lagged behind. Carver held his head down, his eyes narrowed, and he nibbled on his lower lip.

Even if he could reduce the number of suspects, he still did not have a motive. Without that his questions were just so many aimless shotgun blasts. Carver felt helpless; he might not be able to prevent an attempted death trap against Joel Burck.

At the office of the compound he put in a call to Mike Tettsui; he asked the Japanese private investigator to meet him and Burck at Burck's apartment.

"On my way," Tettsui said.

Burck had finished the initial paperwork processing to get his BMW released. The car would be towed to a garage for repairs. Burck wrote a check, and then he and Carver climbed into the Jaguar. They headed for Burck's apartment.

"Carver, you have something on your mind?" Burck asked.

"Yeah, but we'll talk about it later. We'll meet Tettsui, and he'll be with you tonight. First thing tomorrow I want to check out Ben Rosada's place. I want to see if a dead man can tell us anything."

Mike Tettsui was waiting for them. He sat in a station wagon that was parked about a half block from Burck's apartment. Carver parked behind him and then introduced the detective to the dancer.

Michael Tettsui's grip was strong and brief. He was third-generation Japanese-American. Like many people living on the West Coast, including Caucasians, he knew a few words of Japanese: *sayonara*, *dozo*, and *moshi-moshi*. But that was about all the Japanese he knew.

As a young man barely out of his teens he had joined the Coast Guard and would have made a career of it, but he had contacted malaria on a vacation to Bermuda. So there he was, in his early twenties, out of a job, and with a lovely new wife to support. The gods must be crazy, all right.

Tettsui went from job to job—supermarket checker, taxi driver, clerk in a law office. He did a few research jobs for a well-known private detective with a large agency and liked it fine. He talked it over with Nikki, his wife, and went after a license as a private investigator. He was good at his new career, and worked out of a small office in the basement of his home in the Richmond district.

His three-bedroom home was only a few minutes' walk from Golden Gate Park.

After being introduced, the three men went up to Burck's apartment. Tettsui met Bart Meaghler and found they had a common interest in playing gin.

"We'll be okay, Carver," Tettsui said, breaking out a deck of cards. "I'll bed down on the couch in the front room. I'll be just fine. No problem."

Meaghler put out some sandwiches on the card table, while Joel Burck went into the study to watch television. Carver told Tettsui that he'd be back in the morning and left.

In his office Carver played back the micro-cassette

in a double-speed machine and took notes. He left the cassette for Rose to transcribe and went into his apartment.

God, he was tired. He had a lot to think about, most of which seemed useless at this point. He was relaxing on his bed, watching the late-night news, when the phone rang.

"Hello, Carver," a seductive voice said.

"Hello, Susan," he replied.

The caller was Susan Munsell, the woman he had gone out with the night before. As he talked to her, images of Joyce Kittering kept intruding. No, he didn't know when they could get together again. He was working on a difficult case. Flash on Joyce Kittering in her warm-up leggings. Yeah, he'd call as soon as he could, when the case was finished. Flash on Joyce swinging those lovely long legs in *battements tendus*. Sure, sure, Susan, sure, he'd call soon. Yeah, yeah, good-bye.

Carver sighed and thought about Joyce Kittering. She seemed a strange woman, who had a hangup about talking to him. Maybe she didn't like his looks? Maybe she didn't socialize with blacks. Maybe she didn't like publicity.

Not that there was any possibility of that, since he was a phony journalist. He wondered how she'd feel when she found out. *If* she found out. Yeah, Joyce was a lovely woman, and probably smart as hell. Now Carver wanted to get to know her, if only to find out what made her tick.

Wasn't she turning into a challenge? Probably. A good reason not to go on with it. Why bruise his ego any further? Because . . . he didn't give up easily. She was a lovely dancer, artistry oozing out of every step onstage. No, he didn't give up easy.

He reached for his telephone book and looked up her number. He wrote it and her address into his address book. He undressed and turned off the lights and climbed into bed. Carver lay in the darkness and wondered—about her? Get off it, he ordered himself. Think about something else.

Like? Like what he would find in Ben Rosada's apartment. With that address in the Noe Valley area, it had to be an apartment.

She kept bumping into his thoughts.

Should he call Joyce? Or shouldn't he? What would he say to her? Say, lady, I really like you? No, that was stupid. He didn't really know her. Should he call her? What would he say?

Carver's self-interrogation problem was solved as sleep stole over him.

In the morning he was awakened by the smell of fresh coffee. Rose was so damn clever, opening the doors and letting the aroma of coffee fill the air. *Mmmm.* A nice cozy warm-bed smell.

Carver threw on a robe and went into Rose's office.

"Hey, you might at least put on slippers or something," Rose said. "You might catch cold or something."

"I'll catch cold if I put slippers or something on?" Carver asked, a real devil him.

"You know what I meant," Rose replied. "It's eight o'clock. What's happening?"

He brought her up to date on the murder of Ben Rosada.

"Oh, that's such good news," she said sarcastically. "One hour on the job and there's a corpse. I think I liked it better in the old days, hanging around fire escapes in the rain, grabbing photos of adulterous husbands and wives."

"Yeah, and bodyguarding some third-rate entertainer."

"Oh, those were the good old days."

She poured coffee for Carver and then put the microcassette into her recorder.

"Anything on Joel Burck?" Carver asked, drinking the coffee.

"Haven't had much time, just local stuff. But I've got some good leads out. I should know more in a few hours. So far he checks out. Good credit rating, pays his mortgage on his condominium. Paid cash for his BMW. His retainer didn't bounce."

"That's the important stuff," Carver said.

"And I've got a college kid researching all the members of the ballet company. He's working at the library. Should have a bunch of clippings sometime today. There's hundreds of people in the GGBC, but I told him to concentrate on just the top twenty or so. The choreographers, the principal dancers, the soloists, the directors of the company."

"Good, Rose," Carver said. He picked up the morning paper from her desk. Rosada's death was on page 4. Carver's name was not mentioned. Good. No mention of Burck. Good. The news story mentioned Applegate plenty. Good.

He dressed, put several more micro-cassettes in his pocket, and in twenty minutes he was at Burck's apartment. Mike Tettsui was freshly shaved and dressed; he had folded up the borrowed bed sheets and covers and had helped Meaghler tidy up the apartment.

"No problem," Tettsui said when Carver asked him how the night had gone. "Won ten dollars from Mr. Meaghler."

Joel Burck was ready for another day of rehearsing, his bag packed with his gear and slippers. Before heading to the theater, Carver and Burck drove to Rosada's address. As Carver had guessed, it was an apartment on the lower floor of a three-story wood frame building.

Entry seemed to present no legal problems, since there was no "scene of a crime" yellow tape on the door. The manager came to the door after Carver pressed the bell half a dozen times.

"What's up, mister?" the manager asked. He was a man in his middle fifties, going to fat, with opaque glasses distorting his eyes.

"We'd like to see Rosada's apartment," Carver said.

"The cops were here yesterday."

"I'm a private investigator," Carver said, showing his license. He jabbed a thumb at Joel Burck. "This is my client, Mr. Jerome Avery, of the Bayside Mutual Insurance Company. Rosada was insured by his company, but Mr. Rosada never left his beneficiary list with Mr. Avery.

We need to look in the apartment for those names, so that his company can pay off those beneficiaries."

"Well, I dunno," the manager said, unconsciously rubbing a thumb over his fingertips.

"It's very important," Carver said, taking a twenty-dollar bill from his wallet. He folded it carefully, as though it were a ritual—which it was.

Tax-free money has a way of speaking. The manager handed over a key, and then Carver and Burck were in Ben Rosada's apartment.

Burck had said not one word since Carver had rung the manager's bell. He seemed oddly dazed by the transaction, and by Carver's matter-of-fact attitude toward walking into another person's apartment.

Carver looked around the rooms, familiar with the cheap living, the underlying smell of dankness. Ben Rosada's life?

On the side wall hung a badly framed reproduction of a mountain stream meandering through autumn woods. Carver glanced at the picture. Very bad, he thought. Glad he didn't have to look at it every day.

The apartment wasn't much, what little of it Carver could see: a front room that served as a living room, a bedroom beyond that, and presumably a kitchen in the rear. He had seen many similar small apartments, complete with the smell of mildew and decades of cooking imbedded in the wallpaper. The size seemed even more compressed by the presence of Burck and Carver.

They went through the contents of Rosada's desk in the front room. They found nothing. Carver wasn't sure what he was looking for—probably a note or a message from someone in the ballet company. Nothing in the dead man's telephone book. Nothing by the bedside nightstands. Nothing in Rosada's clothing in the closet. No little piece of paper with a telephone number. No name, no address, no nothing.

Checkbook stubs the same thing. Except for a deposit of $1,000 a couple of weeks ago. And $500 ten days later. And $250 just a few days ago. In between the $500 and the $250 were several deposits for $473.66. Both the same amount; probably paychecks, Carver assumed. But the other amounts . . .

He rubbed a finger over the deep cut, almost a dimple, in his chin. Funny how some things just blabber blackmail. A good hunch, anyway.

"Was this first date, for the thousand," Carver asked, "before or after the elevator accident?"

"Before," Burck said.

"So the five hundred and the two-fifty came after," Carver said, more to himself. "Blackmail. Which I would guess got him killed."

The front door opened and closed. Footsteps. Carver and Burck both turned, and Carver dropped the checkbook into the nightstand and closed the drawer.

"Just stand there, Bascombe," Detective Sergeant Applegate said. Then he gestured to a sofa, and Carver and Burck sat. "Okay, Bascombe, just what the hell is this?"

"I wanted to see Rosada's apartment."

"Oh, you did? Did you think I wasn't having this place watched? There's a car down the block with two officers in it."

"There's nothing illegal about the manager giving me the keys to a vacant apartment. Rosada is dead, and you've already searched the apartment."

"I remember your telling me you didn't know Rosada. How'd you know where he lived? And who's this man with you?"

"Joel Burck," Carver said, introducing the two men. "Joel lives in the apartment building where Rosada was killed."

"I also remember you told me Mr. Burck knew nothing about this."

"Not exactly. I'll tell you about that in a moment. I got Rosada's address out of the telephone book."

"His number's unlisted, Bascombe. Try again."

"I lied," Carver said. He stood and put his back to a

window; he felt a chill coming through the glass. "I looked through Rosada's wallet before you got there."

"Go on, crucify yourself," Applegate said, staring at Carver and compressing his lips. He looked like a tall broom-handle figure with a razor for a mouth. "Let's hear it all. I think I'll enjoy you sticking your finger on the trigger, pointing the gun at your brains."

A small smile flickered over Applegate's face; he was certain the next few minutes were going to be amusing.

Briefly Carver related Burck's suspicions about the various accidents. He described several in detail, including the elevator incident. Carver continued to stand in front of the cold window, his gestures deliberately restricted. Carver also explained why Burck didn't want the help of the police.

Applegate continued to display a thin, sardonic grin.

"Do you think we're imbeciles?" he asked.

"I've never said so," Carver said, wondering why Applegate often prefaced his comments with questions about his own performance quality.

"Mr. Burck," Applegate said, turning to the dancer, "with all due respect, I think you're wasting your money hiring this man. When Bascombe told me your name I had it checked as a matter of routine. I read last night's report on your drunk driving. There are statements you made to Officers Godwin and Blaisdell about your car's condition. You claim it was not an accident.

"I don't condone the officer's prejudices, but I can't ignore the Breathalyzer test. Even ignoring that, what makes you think Rosada was trying to kill you?"

"Look, Applegate," Carver interjected, "I've told you about the toe shoes, about the slashed tire, about the elevator. Isn't that enough?"

"There have been no formal complaints made about these so-called accidents. And there is no link between Rosada and Burck, no reason why he would want to kill Burck. Are you suggesting Rosada put the glass in the slippers? And slashed the tire? No, I can see from your expression that you don't."

"But you know something we don't?" Carver said.

"Oh, indeed. There's no reason why I should tell either of you any of this, but I'd like to keep civilian meddlers to a minimum. Preferably nonexistent."

"We won't breathe a word of it," Carver replied.

"I know I can't trust you," Applegate said, "but it doesn't matter whether I do or not." He crossed his arms in front of his chest and waited for a moment before continuing. "Ben Rosada was a small-time criminal. He has a record, and he's spent time in several county jails and a two-year term in prison."

Carver and Burck exchanged looks, and Carver turned back to Sergeant Applegate. "Smug" was the only word that came to Carver's mind as he studied the expression on the homicide detective's face.

"Which means what?" Carver asked.

"Rosada's specialty was blackmail. His modus operandi was simple but effective. He'd get a job in some prestigious, expensive building, keep his eyes open, maybe do a little breaking and entering, find out something about persons in the building, something those particular people didn't want the world at large to know about, and he'd blackmail them. Rosada wasn't a greedy man. Just a little taste from a few different people so that he could make a nice piece of change on the side."

"That doesn't discount him in my book," Carver said.

"I didn't think it would," Applegate said. The meager grin continued on his face. "But that's the motive as far as the department is concerned. I'm looking for the worm that turned, a victim that decided the bite was too deep. Enough was enough. It's happened before."

"And yet, according to you, Rosada never took deep bites."

"Maybe he got tired of small tokes. A criminal seldom changes his MO, but they've been known to try for bigger stakes. And that's the typeface on that business card."

"So you don't want to help Burck?"

"We're not concerned with your client. Yet."

"No, not unless you suspect him as one of Rosada's

blackmail victims. He didn't kill Rosada. He's got me for an alibi.''

"It wouldn't be the first time someone has been a patsy. It could even happen to you, Bascombe. No offense, Mr. Burck, we're just speaking hypothetically. It is within the realm of possibility that you were Rosada's blackmail victim.''

"But I assure you I was not," Burck said, his voice strained with puzzlement.

"You might have hired someone to kill Rosada—and your guilty secret would be safe. And as Bascombe says, you'd have a perfect alibi.''

"I presume you're not holding us," Carver said. "We're free to go?''

"No, there's no reason to hold either of you. My job is to find a reasonable motive. I hope Mr. Burck doesn't have one. For your sake, Bascombe.''

Applegate watched as Carver and Burck climbed into the Jaguar and drove off.

Carver said nothing during the drive to the theater.

EIGHT

The rehearsals went on as the day before. First Swaine and Visikov had the dancers go through an hour of exercises: *pliés*, *demi-pliés*, *tendus*, *battements tendus*, and interspersed with *port de bras*. Then the company got down to some serious material.

According to the program, which Carver read as he stood in the wings, the gala performance would consist of three numbers: Aaron Copland's *Rodeo*, followed by Guiterez and Visikov's *The Prisoner*. To offset the gloom and doom of *The Prisoner*, the gala would end on a fun note, an interpretation of Sousa's lively march *The Thunderer*, a frolicking three-and-a-half-minute ballet choreographed by Bob Swaine.

Joel Burck didn't dance the Sousa number but sat on the steps leading to the stage and watched the rehearsal. Carver kept an eye on Burck and also watched the rehearsal.

At first Carver couldn't figure out why the routine seemed familiar, since he had never seen or even heard of *The Thunderer* ballet.

The dancers seemed to be doing pratfalls and silly Molière-like enterings and exitings. The whole thing was absurd and comedic. Finally it came to him: the ballet was a takeoff on several Monty Python routines. The dancers seemed to be having a good time, as if it didn't matter if they were in sync with the music or not.

Perhaps it just seemed that way. Possibly all that whimsical dancing was just as grueling to master as Stravinsky's *Sacre du Printemps.*

He noticed that Joyce Kittering was not dancing in the *The Thunderer.* Alice Boygen and Don Terman were the lead dancers. Joyce was probably backstage.

"Backstage," a voice said, as though reading Carver's mind.

A young male dancer settled into the seat next to Carver. He shook his hand and introduced himself.

"Billy Jones," he said, flashing a quick smile. "I'm one of the dancers, y'know. That's obvious." He laughed, a chilling, insincere laugh. "I seen you pinning Joyce, and you got that wondering look in your eyes, where she is. I seen her backstage, y'know.

"If you're going to write about the company, you can't ignore me. I'm the youngest principal dancer here. Twenty years old. Been dancing for fifteen years. You better take this down. Don't really want to repeat myself."

The guy wasn't about to disappear, so Carver took out his notepad. He also switched on his recorder in his shirt pocket. He poised his pen over the pad.

"Yeah, okay," Billy Jones said. "I was born in Southern California, in Ventura, y'know. Grew up like any kid, but I liked music. I seemed to be always dancing. I even made up my own routines from old reruns of *Peter Gunn.* My mom and dad thought I was plenty weird. A valley guy, y'know. Anyway, my aunt, a real crazy lady, older than my mom, she said why not send the kid—Billy the kid, she like to call me—why not send the kid to dance classes he likes to dance so much.

"So my mom enrolled me in a ballet class, y'know. That's not what my aunt had in mind, and she laughs about that a lot. Anyway, I was the best pupil in that school. Danced my ass off.

"Are you getting all this down? Not going too fast for you, y'know? Okay, so there I was," Jones said, his

75

words coming fast and furious, "the best ballet dancer for my age in Ventura. Some guy from Hollywood saw me dance and said I was the best ten-year-old he ever saw. Why not, y'know? I'd already been dancing for five years. Baryshnikov had nothin' on me. So this guy, Ralph Rocco— honest-to-god, that was his name—sets me up with some auditions, and I'm dancing on all the talk shows. I even got on the Johnny Carson show. Maybe you saw me, huh?

"So I'm taking all this in stride, for a kid, and then I was taken up by a kids' ballet troupe. We danced on weekends, and got paid for it. By this time, my dad, he knew a good thing when money was comin' in. So he gets me a manager, y'know, and the next thing I knew I was a star. A few years later I was taken on as an apprentice by the Golden Gate Ballet Company. Been here ever since, y'know."

"I think I got that," Carver said, "y'know?"

"Great," Jones said, pumping Carver's hand again. "Anything else you want to know about me, I'll be here. I'm dancing *Rodeo* and *The Prisoner,* which is plenty, but I'd sure like to dance *The Thunderer.* Now, that looks like a lot of fun. Y'know? Wish me luck. *Merde.*"

"*Merde?*"

"Yeah, *merde,* French for shit."

"That's good luck?"

"Why not? You want us to say 'break a leg'?"

Jones moved away, his step quick and lively, almost electrical. Carver put away his notepad; if he had tried to actually write all that down, the paper would have scorched. He headed backstage, but stopped to talk with Joel Burck.

The dancer seemed in good spirits. "I'm looking forward to Moseby's party tonight," he said.

"Yeah," Carver said. "We're going straight to your place when rehearsals are over."

"If you're looking for Joyce Kittering, I saw her backstage."

"No, that's all right," Carver said, peeved that everyone seemed to know to whom he was attracted. "I'll just keep an eye on you. That's the job."

And that was a good excuse. Damn, how did these dancers know he liked Joyce Kittering? Maybe it was just a problem in gossip spreading, a brush fire running among dry twigs.

One of the ballerinas passed, a Chinese girl, one of the few Orientals in the company. She stopped and smiled at him—deliberately, it seemed. Carver remembered her name: Gloria Loo. After a long pause, smiling maddeningly, she went on her way.

Damn it, Carver thought, everyone was acting as if they all knew a great secret and needed only the proper moment to blurt it out to anyone. Or to Carver.

Alex Bellini, one of the other principal dancers, stopped and talked quietly with Burck and Eric Hudson. A meeting was scheduled with Bob Swaine, Bellini whispered. Brigham Merkhinn was bringing out Van Doorn from New York. In a week. Things were coming to a head. All the pro-Swaine people had to do something.

Burck shrugged. There was nothing he could do. He hoped Swaine would come out on top of the internal political struggle for control of the ballet company, but . . .

He shrugged again. Burck looked at Carver, who slowly shook his head. "Don't get involved at the moment" was the message. "After the killer is caught, then maybe . . . ." That message passed silently between Carver and Burck.

Alex Bellini clamped his lips tight in anger and frustration. "You're the best dancer in the company," Bellini hissed. "We need your support!"

"Not yet," Burck said worriedly. "Perhaps in a few days. After the gala. Merkhinn isn't going to bring Van Doorn here before that, surely?"

"It might be too late then," Bellini said angrily, trying with difficulty to keep his words low. "I know you don't like Merkhinn's policies. I don't get it, Joel. This is real life-and-death for us. You know what they say, 'If you're not part of the solution you're part of the problem.' "

Burck looked puzzled and said nothing.

Bellini turned to Eric Hudson and began to speak.

"Hey," Hudson said urgently. "Don't ask me."

"What the hell is this? First Joel and now you, Eric? You were one of the first to speak out against Merkhinn and his cronies."

"I'm taking a leaf, a nice fat oak leaf blowing in the wind, taking it from Joel. I'm going to wait and see what happens. Sort of playacting at being a citizen of the Alps—a neutral. Then we'll see what happens. But good luck, anyway."

"Shit," Bellini hissed. "I don't get it."

Carver watched the man stomp away, and he put his memory to work.

Alex Bellini was a latecomer to the dance. He had been a football quarterback star in high school, and had taken up dance to improve his moves. His fame initially rested on his athletic prowess. For a brief while he was a well-known name in Chicago, with all the young girls sighing over his Tarzan V-shaped torso and his bridge-cable thighs. A real powerhouse, Bellini.

Eventually he was brought to the West Coast and joined the GGBC. His ballerina partners at first feared his abrupt, bearlike approach, but soon learned that he had the hands of an angel. When he danced, he seemed to be gazing elsewhere, as if he were interested in something else of more importance. But he wasn't: the ballet was the core of his life.

Bellini was one of the first dancers to go public against Brigham Merkhinn. He was the head of the unofficial organization to protect Bob Swaine, and to keep Swaine the artistic director of the company.

Carver jotted down a few notes concerning Alex Bellini and made a mental promise to check him out in depth.

The rehearsals were over, and most of the going-home conversation was about the party at Moseby's.

The Chinese dancer came by, carrying her clothes in a flight bag. "Hi," she said. "Going to the party tonight?"

Carver shrugged.

"Strong and silent, hey? I like that. I'll see you there. I hope you see me."

She walked away, an enigmatic smile playing over her face.

Joel Burck had finished changing and joined Carver. Without seeing Joyce Kittering—and was that ever disappointing— Carver drove Burck back to the apartment.

Meaghler had bad news as they walked into the apartment.

"A detective named Applegate was here," he said, his face reflecting worry.

"What did he want?" Carver asked.

"About Joel and me. Mostly about Joel." Meaghler twisted a handkerchief in his hands and then went to the bar and poured himself a double-sized vodka. "He wanted to know all about us."

"You told him, of course," Carver said.

"Of course. We have nothing to hide. But he wanted to know if there had ever been any hints of Joel being blackmailed or had done anything to be blackmailed for. I might have talked too much."

"Don't worry about it, Bart," Carver said. "Applegate was on a fishing trip."

"He said he was going to investigate others in the building."

"About blackmail?"

"It sounded like that, yes."

Bart Meaghler emptied his glass and then poured himself another.

"Don't drink so much," Burck pleaded.

Then Burck turned on the stereo. The strains of Glière's *Red Poppy* filled the air. Burck went into the bathroom to get ready for Moseby's party. Carver shook his head; it was going to be quite a job to get these two men to keep their heads.

Meaghler finished his drink—and how many had he had before that?—and went about the apartment, getting Burck's clothes ready. Carver relaxed, mixed a Wild Turkey and soda, and took a book from Burck's library: Hoving's *King of the Confessors*.

Bart Meaghler acted as towel boy, bringing towels and faceclothes into the bathroom while Joel Burck luxuriated in the oversized tub. Carver Bascombe sat in the living room, only one lamp lit to read by, and watched the afterglow of the setting sun. A jumble of questions pattered through his mind. The apartment smelled of warm, wet water, gardenia bathing salts, oak burning in the fireplace.

Carver felt comfortable.

The hunter rested. The ferret-beast rested, with only irregular movements from deep down. Whatever questions were drifting at the periphery of thought were translucently gaseous.

Meaghler came and went from the bath. Ignoring Carver reading, he carried at various times rubbing alcohol, freshly pressed jockey shorts, silk hose, a white dress shirt, and a tailored three-piece suit.

As the room darkened, Meaghler turned on several floor lamps. He sat near Carver and cleared his throat. A prelude? Of course. Carver waited for the man to speak.

In the past half hour not one word had been spoken. Carver sensed the bizarre, almost theatrical quality of the silence. The only sounds had been of the bathing ritual, the opening and closing of closet doors, the splashing of the running water, the slithering sound of footsteps.

"Carver," Meaghler said finally, "I wonder if you think much about the difference between reality and fantasy."

"Sometimes," Carver said, trickling over the syllables.

"I think about them. Not what society means by reality and fantasy. For instance, I see the ballet as a combination of reality and fantasy. It's a matter of perception. To illustrate—once, some years ago, I was in India working with one of my travel agencies. The level of life there was low, the quality of life, as we perceive it, nonexistent. I had occasion to walk by moonlight near the Taj Mahal, and found myself thinking how banal this might seem to a sophisticated gentleman of a certain type.

"Yet I was moved. The reflecting pool, the soft chanting of some kind of religious sect, or perhaps a group escaped from a sanitarium. Nevertheless it moved me. I looked at those gleaming spires, all ivory etched against a deep blue, a sapphire sky. A fairy-tale castle. That was a fantasy, but if I had walked past the reflecting pool I could touch the building, all cold stone. That was reality."

Carver sat quietly, sipping the bourbon.

"Society thinks it wants reality," Meaghler continued, talking at Carver, but just as easily talking to the darkness, "but I don't think it does. Fantasy threatens people and sometimes frightens them. That's why they embrace reality. I've had drinks with Merkhinn, and Guiterez and Hudson, some of the other directors, and we've talked about this. Some agree, some don't, and think I'm a nut. Think I drink too much."

Meaghler brooded and drank most of the glass of vodka.

"Many critics in the arts," he continued, "for instance, praise a play, a book, a movie for it's realism. Yet when an artist gets too close to true reality they want to censor it. On the silver screen, a person is shot, slumps to the floor. Real? Not on your life. A heavy-caliber bullet would knock you on your ass. Blood? Never seen in the old days. Too gruesome. And yet the critics lauded realism as the way to artistic merit.

"Now, I know they really meant slice-of-life dramas. But again, if you were to have a three-act play in real time on the stage, with a real situation, with real people, the audience would fall asleep from boredom. It isn't realism they need but the need for manipulated realism. As for fantasy, perhaps in a singular sense it is the greatest reality. It can touch hidden depths in people's soul as a real family quarrel cannot."

Meaghler paused. He finished his drink, then looked at the empty glass.

"Not too long ago I took a vacation in Nova Scotia. Ever been there? No? It's a bit strange—sort of lonely and foreboding. I had a cottage near the shore, where I could hear the Atlantic beating on the rocks.

"I met some visitors from around the Olympic Peninsula, and they seemed rational. There were six of them, three men and three women. I could never put my finger on exactly what they meant to each other. I mean, you'd think they'd be definite couples, a man and a woman. Or if you see life in one way, perhaps two men. But then, there you are, the social perceptions.

"These six took me in tow, figuring I was a stranger to the area, which I was. Now, Nova Scotia is often thought of as a barren place, full of rocks and mackerel fishermen. But they seemed to have an affinity for the place, even though they had never been there before.

"One night, and I admit I had been drinking, they came to my door. they were all dressed in hoods, like ghosts for Halloween, and they told me they wanted me to come with them, that they were going to show me something wonderful. I thought it a little strange, but we had a few drinks and I went with them.

"At the bluff of the shore they had built a circular wooden platform, sort of like a wagon wheel. It was connected by chains to something like a hangman's gibbet. For some reason I wasn't frightened. Perhaps because the six of them were not threatening, but rather mostly pleasant and quiet. They asked me to take off my clothes and climb onto the wheel.

"I guess I was pretty drunk, 'cause I was persuaded to lay down on the wheel, and they hoisted me up. I gazed at the stars, and listened to the waves close by, booming and pounding on the rocky shore below. The six of them stood at the edge of the cliff and chanted some kind of . . . a mantra, I guess you could call it. I was reminded of the sounds in India.

"I stayed on that wheel, turning slowly in the wind, gazing at the stars, listening to the surf. I don't know how long. Hours and hours, but it might have been much less. time seemed to have no meaning. I think I hallucinated. I thought I was in the sky, floating, and much more. Much more. My parents came to me and talked to me. And I talked with them. I had a visit from a childhood friend who had been killed in an auto accident when he was eleven years old. He was an adult, about my age, when we talked.''

Breathing slowly, Meaghler paused. He put his elbows on his knees and stared at the carpeted floor. Carver sipped his Wild Turkey.

"I won't bore you with the conversations," Meaghler said, speaking softly. "Except to say they were of great importance to me. I've thought about the implications. Anyway, eventually they let me down. I shivered in the night, and they put a rough robe of some kind around me and returned me to my cottage. They said nothing, and we never spoke of the incident again. But I think they knew I had experienced something real and enduring. So was it all a fantasy, or was it real? I have no answers. Perhaps the questions are the realest thing of all.

Meaghler went to the bar and poured himself a screwdriver. He returned to his chair and faced Carver, his face lit by the flickering fireplace.

"So I see the reality of the dance. The ballerinas and dancers are onstage in real time, with real aches and pains, real sweat rolling off their bodies, their feet hurting as if they'd been snapped in a bear trap. But what they are producing is fantasy. Isn't it possible that the dancer might cross over that line? Might feel that there is some reality to the fantasy?''

"What are you leading up to, Bart?" Carver asked.

"As I've told those who would change the company, Merkhinn and Maltby, there is more to the ballet than the reality of the dollar, more than the fantasy of the egos involved.''

The two men looked at each other. Meaghler's discourse was as invisible utterances in the air, bloated, sinister.

"I've got to make a call," Carver said and went into the library.

Rose answered his call.

"I'm at Burck's," Carver said. "Have you come up with anything?"

"Yes, the little man who wasn't there.''

'What do you mean, Rose?''

"I mean," Rose replied carefully, "that you've given me some tough one before, but I don't think even Bernie could do anything with this one."

"Go on," Carver prodded.

"Joel Burck. Dancer. Maybe. Maybe not. He came to the Golden Gate Ballet Company with terrific references. But they don't check out. Not from my connections. I can't find anything about the man from about five years back. No credit rating. A driver's license in New York, but that's all. No previous adresses. Never went to school there. Didn't go to school anywhere. Not in New York, where he got the driver's license. One hotel he was supposed to have lived in never heard of him. I checked with the several New York ballet companies. Likewise nothing. Never heard of him. Like I said, he's the little man who wasn't there."

"What the hell?" Carver said.

"That's the thing of it. Want me to keep checking?"

"Yes," Carver said and hung up.

NINE

A faint odor of Blue Stratos cologne preceded Joel Burck into the room. He was resplendent in a tailored black suit, expensive tie, and matching handkerchief. A pale yellow silk shirt. Monogrammed, of course. Ivory silk scarf. Camel's-hair overcoat draped over one arm. Nice. Tasteful. Costly.

Bart Meaghler admired the ensemble, ooh and aah, very regal indeed, as befitting a prince of the theater. Meaghler wore a standard blue three-piece.

The three men left the building, with Meaghler driving his silver Mercedes-Benz. Burck sat stiffly in the front passenger seat. Conversation was superficial: they were low on paper towels; they needed a new set of cocktail glasses, et cetera. Burck was under a terrific strain; he had said little about Meaghler's encounter with Applegate.

After a monotonous search, they finally found a parking space in an alley two blocks from Moseby's Nob Hill address.

The penthouse elevator opened onto the spacious foyer. Leroy Dolny, Moseby's longtime boyfriend, greeted them enthusiastically. In a crowd Dolny stood out: muscular, well-dressed, an ex-Marine. Mid-thirties, sleek dark hair. He hung their coats in an overflowing foyer closet.

"Not a fit night out for man nor beast," Dolny said, imitating W.C. Fields.

Burck and Meaghler were greeted with big whoops of delight, as if the other dancers hadn't seen them for weeks. Carver watched faces for any sudden signs of hatred toward Burck. Guiterez? No, he seemed glad to see Burck. Likewise Bob Swaine and Billy Jones. Yeah, and Eric Hudson, too. Even Don Terman. And Joyce Kittering. Carver was delighted to see Joyce Kittering.

The dress code was "anything goes." A few were in revolt against *Gentlemen's Quarterly*, wearing flamingo pink and lime-chartreuse pants and orange and lavender overlarge shirts. Trendy ones were in various leather outfits and tropical jackets rolled to the elbow.

The crowd ebbed through the ten-room penthouse. A journalist could be excused resorting to clichés: the guests were shoulder to shoulder. Wandering partygoers opened and closed the French doors to the terrace; a wintry draft chilled legs, and there were cries of "close the doors!"

In the immense living room, three buffet tables were set with a sumptuous display of food and drink. The center table was presided over by a chef in his whites. Servers moved among the crowd, carrying silver trays loaded with hors d'oeuvres. At the tables many of the dancers were ready to fill their plates.

"Kind of like a movie set, isn't it?" Eric Hudson said to Deborah Canby.

"How awful, all that food," Deborah said, her voice somewhat dismayed. "Me on my usual diet. I'm impressed, but what is that stuff?"

"That, mademoiselle," the chef said, "is roast beef Liselotte. And these are cooked apples with Bavarois cream."

"A thousand calories a bite," Deborah said.

"Champagne, then," Hudson said. "At least you can drink."

"Eric, I think I'll have a Perrier."

Carver kept a loose watch on Joel Burck. He strolled through the crowd, looking at the paintings on the walls.

He studied a Diebenkorn, a recent acquisition, all brushstroke slashes of color, the steep hills of the city. Carver found an old favorite, an Irving Norman painting—mankind-as-androids—in a bedroom. Moseby apparently didn't want to annoy the guests.

Carver sought out Myron Moseby and found him near one of the buffet tables, admonishing the head of the catering company.

Moseby was in fine array, his dark hair cut and styled within the past few hours. He wore a custom-tailored midnight-blue suede tuxedo of his own design. The effect was of a flowing, lithe animal, sinews and muscles coiling and uncoiling with natural ease.

Moseby glanced at Carver and then continued his conversation with the obese caterer.

"The pâté is an exquisite product of the European mergansers," Moseby said, enunciating each word with exaggerated clarity, "but it cannot ever be juxtaposed with the salmon Jack Gauer. I distinctly recall stating that the diverse poultry must be centrally located, with the fish dishes arrayed at one side, and the various hams, beef, and venison at the other." He moved his hands theatrically. "I am most vexed, almost distraught, that someone on your staff mixed fish and game."

The overweight man apologized profusely, then hurried to make amends.

Moseby grasped Carver's hand, pleased to see his friend.

"Again you threaten the peasants with dungeons and dragons," Carver said. "You're such a fraud, Myron."

"Ah, dear boy, you know me well. But what would you have me do? Surely you're not one of those plebeian liberals who would spread goose and salmon onto the same morsel of croissant?"

"Heaven forbid," Carver replied.

"Such feeble sarcasm. One of your infrequent attempts at wit. However, you sought me out. What can I do for you?"

"To say thanks. I'm working for Joel Burck. For the time being I'm playing at being a journalist."

"Ah, very devious," Moseby said. "Doing a story on the ballet, able to keep a needle-sharp eye on Burck? Something like that, is it?"

"You got it. But there's something going on between Burck and Bart Meaghler. Other than their relationship. Burck is under a terrific strain."

"Well, someone is apparently trying to kill him."

"No, something else. There's an undercurrent. Anything you might know about?"

"Ah, dear boy, I'm afraid not," Moseby said, running a hand over a gray spray of hair. "Come. You haven't eaten."

Carver glanced around, seeking Joel Burck. The dancer was with John Guiterez. Still alive. Nobody had stabbed him with a serving fork. The composer and the dancer appeared to be discussing something near and dear.

At the buffet table, with Moseby's urging, Carver loaded a plate with beef, celeriac and walnut salad, and a piece of Boursin cheese. He hadn't the faintest idea what most of the foods were.

The table was a gourmet fantasy, decorated with a piled centerpiece of breasts of chicken Belle de Mai in a white chaud-froid sauce. Duck breasts, covered with a rich brown sauce and decorated with swirls of butter, flanked the chicken. The other side was burdened with pike à la Kiev and the cold salmon.

"I've already tried the lamb Innocenti," Alice Boygen said, "and now I feel as if I'm going to have to do *Giselle* at least three times to burn off the fat."

"Then you might as well go all the way, y'know," Billy Jones suggested. "Try that other stuff. Looks great. Deer meat."

"The saddle of venison?" Alice Boygen said with a shudder. "That sour cream sauce will drop me through the floorboards."

"Then I'd suggest," Deborah Canby said, returning for seconds, "you stick with the little stuff. Those petits fours."

"Are you kidding? Those things're are covered with

glazes of kirsch and rum, and lemon sauce with sherry. None for me, thanks."

Carrying glasses of champagne, Moseby lead Carver to a vacant corner alcove.

"You want to know about Joel and Bart," Moseby began. "Well, Meaghler . . . there's not much to tell. "I've used Meaghler's travel services from time to time. So has Leroy. I finally got him off to Europe, you know. But that's neither here nor there. I was introduced to Joel about four years ago. He and Bart were already going together, and in fact had bought the condominium on Russian Hill."

"Yeah. But I sensed something."

"Another man? It happens, you know."

"I don't think so. Something's plaguing Meaghler," Carver said, taking a forkful of beef. He chewed thoughtfully, barely aware of the smoky flavor. "For one, he drinks too much."

"Do you think he's an alcoholic?"

"Close to it. But there's . . . something between the two of them. Anyway, it doesn't feel right."

Carver didn't mention Rose Weinbaum's telephone call. If he had to guess, he would guess there was a connection between Burck's past and the present complications. Including murderous attempts on his life.

"Your hunches are usually rather good, Carver," Moseby said, "and certainly the human triangle is an old story, even among gays. But I'm afraid I can't help you with any juicy gossip. God knows I'd enjoy something along those lines."

"Yeah, well, thanks, Myron."

"Anytime, dear boy."

Carver deposited his unfinished plate of food on the nearest buffet. He moved among the guests, notepad in hand, maintaining his role as a journalist. He dutifully wrote brief histories of several young dancers.

Moving from room to room, he scanned the guests. There in the corner, laughing at something Guiterez had said, was Eric Hudson. And Joyce Kittering. Joel Burck was near the terrace doors, in deep conversation with Don Terman and a narrow-waisted, thin black dancer. Carver didn't know the third man.

A loud curse made Carver swivel. Moseby was engrossed in a four-way conversation with Bob Swaine, Gloria Loo, and Brigham Merkhinn. Carver moved in closer and eavesdropped.

"I'm only saying," Merkhinn said, doing his best to control himself, "that there's always a time for change. For the GGBC it is now. I'm not denigrating Bob Swaine's merits, and I'm certainly not going to say that he hasn't done a superb job. He has, and I don't know many of the board of directors that say he hasn't. But—"

"Yes, there's always a but," Gloria Loo said. "You don't know how demoralizing it has been for us. We don't know if you and your crowd are trying to take over the company for yourselves, or if you even have the good of the company at heart."

Gloria Loo was a striking Chinese dancer, with radiant dark eyes that flashed like a Fourth of July night. She stood with arms crossed, as if warding off anything Merkhinn might say. She wasn't about to be convinced.

"Gloria, you know what we want," Merkhinn said. "We want to bring in fresh blood. We want that director from New York, Leon Van Doorn."

"There's no doubt Van Doorn is very good," Loo said, "but we already have an internationally known and respected director. Swaine."

Swaine smiled self-consciously, one hand holding a cocktail.

"I'd like to think," Merkhinn said, consciously reflective, "we are taking into consideration the feelings of everyone. That includes the choreographers and the musicians and the stage crew. So you see, there is more to all of this than just the performers. It's a question of the total needs."

"Bullshit," Swaine said heatedly. "It's a question of egos. You guys don't like the publicity and fame that I get."

"Perhaps, but we also don't like the idea that the media think the company belongs to you, that it's your ballet company, your private expression of self. It is not. It is operated and owned by the directors. And furthermore . . .''

Carver knew there would be more, but he moved away.

At one of the buffet tables he mixed himself a weak Wild Turkey and soda. Sipping the liquor, Carver saw Joyce Kiltering with several other dancers, one male, two female. She turned away, apparently finished with her part of the conversation (or perhaps she was bored?), and went to a set of panoramic windows. She stood there, one elbow cupped in her hand, sipping a water-clear drink. Vodka? Gin? Tequila?

"Go ahead," a female voice said to him, "talk to her."

Gloria Loo stood close to Carver, grinning a sly smile. She had a wineglass in her hand. He looked at her, and then at Joyce Kittering. Loo must've finished her argument with Merkhinn. Obviously.

"Don't be shy," Gloria Loo said. "You've been looking at her most of the time you've been here. Get her out of your system."

She tipped her wineglass in salute, smiled again, and walked away. Carver hesitated only a few seconds before heading in Joyce Kittering's direction.

"Hello," he said.

She looked at him and smiled thinly.

Well, at least she hadn't walked away. He was still *enpointe*.

"Don't you find the party interesting?" he asked, silently cursing himself for such a banal opening gambit. "Or uninteresting?"

"Actually I hadn't thought about it. It seems to be the sort of thing you might enjoy."

"Oh, gee whiz. You can really cut, Joyce. I don't think I've given you any reason for that. Judging from that remark, you must think I'm really shallow."

"I wouldn't know, honestly," Joyce said, gazing out the windows at the clear night sky.

"Honestly, dishonestly—what difference? I've wanted to get acquainted with you.

"I don't understand why."

"What is that supposed to mean?"

"Surely it's obvious. You came into the theater with Burck and his boyfriend. You were seen going into the dressing rooms with Don Terman. And you seem to be on excellent terms with Myron Moseby and his boyfriend. I'd say that speaks for itself."

"Well, I'll be damned," Carver blurted. "You think I'm homosexual."

"Aren't you?"

"No," Carver said, and explained his confrontation with Terman. "So that's all there is. All part of the writer's life. But this makes me curious . . . how do you feel working with gay dancers?"

"I'd never had any of them hit on me before. And besides, you're a reporter, and there's been a lot of strain in the company over bad publicity. Very few of the dancers want to see Bob Swaine kicked out of the company."

"I know about that. Is this guy Van Doorn any better?"

"Of course not. He's a good choreographer and director. Actually, I've heard rumors that the reason he's being considered by Merkhinn is because he can take orders, that he doesn't make waves. That's off the record. I never said that."

"Van Doorn stays out of the limelight, is that it?"

"So I've heard. Which probably means that someone else wants to be the grand wizard of the company, taking all the bows, getting all the plaudits."

"Yeah? Who?"

"It's just an opinion," Joyce said, regretting her words. "I wouldn't want you to write anything that would get me into a lot of trouble. I don't want to start all over again, with another ballet company."

"You could always move to New York, Joyce."

"Hah hah, you have a droll sense of humor, Bascombe."

"Call me Carver. Please."

"You're really trying hard, aren't you?"

"Pour oil on me. I can loosen up. In time. Under other circumstances."

"You are persistent. Still angling for an invitation."

"Sure. Doesn't dinner sound romantic?" Carver rolled his eyes and laid a hand alongside his cheek, looking insincere. "Checkered tablecloth? Dripping candle in a Chianti bottle? How about it? Hmmm? If only to prove I'm a straight male."

"I don't know. Proving you're straight isn't everything."

"Then it's something else. What?"

"You're a little old, aren't you? Over thirty?"

Carver admitted he was over thirty. But not by much.

"I like men who are my own age, not so old," she said.

"I'm not that old." Carver said.

"I also like my men to be athletic and well built. You're a bit on the thin side for my taste."

Carver grumped.

"But you're persistent, I'll say that," Joyce said. "I don't know if I like that or not. But . . . I'll take a chance."

"Tomorrow, then. After rehearsal."

"All right, Carver. Now you can get me a glass of water."

"What?"

"I'm drinking water. You can fetch me another glass of it. With ice and a bit of lemon."

"Oh, sure," Carver said, as he remembered wondering whether it was gin, vodka, or tequila. "Don't move. I want to find you again."

He maneuvered his way to the buffet and filled a water glass. Carrying the glass, Carver looked over the heads of the crowd and saw Burck and Meaghler in an alcove. Meaghler was prodding a finger at Burck's chest. Burck's face was blank, resolute, and he shook his head at whatever point Meaghler was making.

Angling back to Joyce, Carver saw her arguing with Deborah Canby. Deborah apparently said something angrily, shoved Joyce aside, and jerked open the sliding glass doors to the terrace.

"What was that all about?" he asked, and gave Joyce her glass of water.

"You're the journalist," she replied. "Why not go and see?"

He heard the unmistakable sound of a challenge. Carver slid open the door and stepped onto the terrace. Damn, it was cold. He hunched himself, sliding his hands into his pants pockets.

He scanned the well-lit terrace and heard a long retching sound. The air was filled with a familiar sour smell. Carver walked past several large urns, following the heaving sounds and the smell. He saw Deborah Canby bent over a low ornamental urn, clutching the rim. She was throwing up into it.

TEN

Gentle, cold winds blew over the penthouse. Leaves from potted shrubs skipped feebly over the tiles. A cloud passed over the rising moon. The breeze carried a curdled smell from the woman huddled over a decorative urn.

"Are you all right?" Carver Bascombe asked, hurrying to Deborah Canby's side.

She whirled, a linen napkin in her hand, apparently to keep her dress from getting soiled. She seemed more guilty than startled. "Sure, yeah, I'm all right," she said, dabbing at her mouth with the napkin. "It's nothing, really. I'm okay. Truly."

There was something odd about her response—and there was something strange about the way Joyce had challenged Carver to follow Deborah Canby onto the penthouse terrace. And Carver thought he had it figured out.

"You do this often?" he asked.

"What do you mean?" Deborah replied, nervousness shading her words.

For this evening Deborah wore a lowcut burgundy velvet dress. Her light-brown hair, almost without color, was loosely framed around her face in casual curls. Multicolored eyeshadow hid rather than enhanced her dark glossy eyes. She was nervous, which matched her thin yet muscular body. There was hardly any fat on her, the skin stretched taut over her cheekbones, the cords of her neck prominent.

"Bulimia," Carver said, playing his hunch. "Ballet dancers often worry abnormally about their weight. It's known that a few eat and then deliberately throw up what they've eaten. Are you going back for seconds, Deborah? Or thirds?"

"None of your business, faggot," Deborah said, pushing Carver aside and striding away.

She pushed the French doors open and glared at Joyce Kittering as she swept past. Carver followed Deborah inside.

Joyce followed Deborah with her eyes, a bemused look on her face. She turned to face Carver. "Well, did you get something for your story?"

"Not really. She has a real problem."

"Actually, she thinks you do."

"Yeah?"

"Deborah is the one who noticed you going backstage with Don Terman."

Carver nodded, but said nothing.

"So, don't you understand? Deborah was the one who spread the word that you were gay."

"And she doesn't like gays," Carver stated.

"No, she doesn't. Deborah has a real problem there."

"Add that to her weight problem. She must be a fun person to know."

"I really wouldn't know, Carver. Our personal lives don't mesh. Deborah goes her way and I go mine."

"I'd like to know more about how you go," Carver said. He took out his notepad. "Any objections to an interview?"

"No, Carver, I've no objection. But not here. I should never have come to this party. Actually I'm not much of a party person. And two in one week, well, it really hurts my concentration onstage. I'm not really in the mood for an interview. It can wait until tomorrow, can't it?" After all, your article is really concentrating on Joel Burck. He's the star."

"Okay with me."

Carver looked around the crowded room and saw Burck chatting with Brigham Merkhinn and Graham Maltby. He didn't see Bart Meaghler anywhere. He smiled at Joyce and asked her for her address and phone number. He jotted the information into his notepad. He really wanted to take Joyce Kittering home, but that wouldn't work out. Don't press, Carver cautioned himself.

On the other hand . . .

"Look, Joyce, you said you're not enjoying yourself— why don't I take you home? I'll see if Burck is ready to leave."

"I'll say one thing, Carver Bascombe, you are one persistent man."

"Yeah."

"All right," Joyce said, and grinned. "Why not?"

Carver thought her laugh was lovely, laying loosely in her throat, almost as though the sound came on tiptoe, like a child learning to dance. He told Joyce he had to find Joel Burck, to let him know he was leaving. Besides, he hadn't been paying attention to Joel Burck's whereabouts.

Carver and Joyce found the dancer talking with Brigham Merkhinn and Graham Maltby. The two GGBC directors ceased their conversation when Carver approached. He thought they had a guilty look, and wondered what the conversation had been about. The three men greeted Joyce Kittering with studied politeness.

"We were talking over the long-range future of the company," Maltby said when Carver Bascombe asked him bluntly.

"I think," Carver said, "that the readers of *Dancer's Life* might find your speculations interesting."

"Actually we have nothing to say for publication," Merkhinn said.

"And I would like to go home," Joel Burck said.

"The party is just rolling," Maltby said.

"Yes, it is," Burck agreed, "but I do have a headache. Bart and I were having something of an argument earlier on. And arguments don't sit well with me. I sent Bart on

97

ahead to get the car." Burck looked at his watch. "He's been gone some time. He should have returned by now."

"Maybe he left you high and dry," Maltby said.

Burck compressed his lips, barely concealing his rising irritation. Carver again sensed an undercurrent; he tried to make eye contact with Burck but failed. Burck turned away, as if looking for someone else to talk to. Maybe it was a love triangle?

"Joel, I'm taking Joyce home. Bart might have left angrily, left you and me to get home in a cab. I'll drop you off at your apartment." He leaned in close and whispered, "Mike will be there again."

"Yes, Bart might very well have done something like that out of spite. Bart was . . . was in one of his moods."

Yeah, Carver thought sarcastically as he put an arm through Joyce's. He'd bet on that. He'd seen how much liquor Meaghler could put away. If not an alcoholic, he was damned close.

They had to take several detours around knotted groups of dancers and musicians. In a few minutes they were on the sidewalk. Meaghler's Mercedes-Benz was at the curb, the engine running.

"Oh, my god," Joel Burck said.

On the driver's side the window was starred with a hole. Dark flecks spattered the windshield. In the streetlights the flecks looked red. Bart Meaghler was behind the wheel, his head slumped back. He did not move.

"My god," Burck repeated, the words squeezed from his throat.

ELEVEN

"There is nothing," Lieutenant Arnold Applegate said emphatically, "absolutely nothing, Bascombe, to indicate that Joel Burck was the intended victim, that Meaghler was not the target. Nothing at all, do you understand me?"

"The overcoat," Carver said, trying to sound reasonable and calm.

Difficult at best, Applegate's patience was thin, and becoming thinner.

Shortly after his arrival, Applegate had sent two detectives and several uniformed police to Moseby's penthouse. The police took statements concerning Meaghler's last living moments. A few of the guests had seen him leave, taking a camel-hair overcoat from the closet. Others had previously seen Meaghler and Burck arguing, but several guests testified that Joel Burck had not left the party.

Downstairs the homicide lieutenant had taken charge. The fingerprint experts did their job; the police photographer snapped three rolls of 35mm film.

Joyce Kittering and Joel Burck stood under the apartment building's glass-and-chrome canopy. She had an arm around Burck, comforting him. Burck's head was down on his chest, and he was pressing a balled-up handkerchief to his swollen eyes. His cheeks gleamed wetly, and he hiccuped spasmodically.

Perhaps because of the chill there were few curiosity seekers. The police kept the dozen or so bystanders away from the crime scene.

The coroner had pronounced Bart Meaghler dead. He had given his estimate of the time of death—the past half hour or so—and driven off. His white-coated assistants loaded the body into the blue morgue wagon.

A tow truck was in the process of hooking up the Mercedes. The tow-truck driver looked at the bullet-shattered windshield and the blood and shook his head. Whatta life.

Sergeant Applegate and Carver Bascombe stood near the car. Gusting winds tugged at their clothes; Carver kept his hands in his pockets. The tarry smell of asphalt mixed with the scent of nearby shrubbery was carried on chilly blasts.

"So he borrowed Burck's overcoat," Applegate said. "It's a cold night, or haven't you noticed. Half a dozen witnesses at the party upstairs have already stated to my men that Meaghler arrived without a coat. So did you. Isn't that right?"

"Yeah," Carver said.

"So there you are."

"No, Burck was supposed to be killed. Not Meaghler."

"So you say. I say there's no proof."

Carver wondered if he should mention the argument between Burck and Meaghler. No, let it go. Applegate would find out soon enough. But what were they arguing about? Applegate had already made up his mind Meaghler was the probable target, not Burck; not much point in trying to convince him otherwise. However, Carver was stubborn.

"Sergeant, why would someone shoot Meaghler? What's the motive?"

"I'll find it," Applegate answered.

"What about the other killing? This morning. Ben Rosada."

"You think they're connected?"

"Only through Burck."

"If that's so, then why not try this on for size."

"Yeah?"

"Let's say you're right, Bascombe. That there is a connection between your client, Burck, and Rosada and Meaghler. Rosada is a known blackmailer and crook. He's got something on Burck, and Burck is tired of paying him off. We haven't found the connection yet, but we're looking."

"Go on."

"So Burck kills Rosada. Yes, I know, he wasn't there this morning, he was with you. So he hired someone to do it. Maybe Meaghler, his good friend and lover. Or someone else. Yes, I like that."

"I'll just bet," Carver said sarcastically.

"Yes, but maybe Meaghler doesn't approve of murder. He threatens to tell all he knows to the police. Burck arranges to have Meaghler killed."

"Applegate, do you really believe that?"

"It's every bit as good as your theory. But, see, I know you have a problem. You have a client, and you gotta go by what he says."

Carver said nothing but inwardly resented Applegate's assumption that he believed a client always told the truth. Bernie Weinbaum had told him time and time again to have an open and inquiring mind—and to figure the sonofabitch that pays the bills usually lies. Rose had offered much the same advice.

"Anyway," Applegate said, "I have to ask a few questions of your client."

He turned and walked under the building's canopy. He stopped in front of Joyce and Burck. Carver followed.

"I'm sorry, Mr. Burck," Applegate said to the grieving dancer, "but I have to ask you some questions."

"What kind of questions can you ask that make you sorry?" Burck said.

"What I meant was, I have to intrude on your grief with questions."

"Look, Officer," Joyce Kittering interrupted. "You know this man has had a hell of shock. He's in trauma. Can't these questions wait? I mean, really. Can't they wait?"

101

"Do it tomorrow, Lieutenant," Carver said. "I'll vouch for my client. He'll be available to you in the morning."

"For god's sake," Joyce said emotionally, "let the poor man get a night's rest."

Sergeant Applegate pondered this for a few moments and then agreed; he'd see Joel Burck in the morning.

Carver hailed a taxicab, and they were soon at Burck's apartment building. A familiar station wagon was parked in front. Mike Tettsui stepped out when he saw the taxi drive up. Carver paid the driver and then introduced the private detective to Joyce. She was burning with curiosity but held her questions in check.

In the elevator Tettsui suggested that he call a doctor for Joel Burck.

"You know someone good?" Carver asked.

"Sure. Remember Dr. Asawa?" Tettsui answered.

Carver nodded, recalling a case some months before when he and Tettsui had a client that needed discreet emergency treatment. Dr. Asawa had helped a guilt-ridden woman after she had botched a self-imposed abortion.

"Call him," Carver said.

In the apartment Tettsui telephoned Dr. Asawa. He then went through the apartment, checking it out. Burck sat facing the windows and stared at the night sky. Carver turned on a table lamp. Burck had been silent during the taxicab ride, and had said nothing in the apartment. Carver thought the man's silence almost eerie.

Joyce Kittering sat in a chair and looked at Carver Bascombe. Actually, she gazed intently, the next best thing to a stare. Tettsui finished his recon and turned on a floor lamp near the bar; he poured himself a Perrier. They waited for the doctor.

Carver turned and saw Joyce watching him. "Something on your mind, Joyce?" he asked.

"Yes, Carver, there is," she replied in a hoarse whisper.

"What's the problem?"

"You, you're the problem."

"What about me?"

"What kind of a journalist are you? You talked to that police detective as though you were some kind of friendly enemies, and then you bring me here and there's another detective waiting for you and Joel."

"A private detective," Carver said softly.

"That's what I mean," she said, her voice still hoarse and unsteady. "Where did he come from?"

"It was an arrangement."

"See, you're not answering me. You're pretty good at avoiding a direct answer."

"I'll tell you all about it . . . tomorrow."

"What the hell is this 'it' you're talking about?"

"Be patient," Carver said.

"And you know, there's a way you have of ordering people around. You really have a way with people. I'm not sure I like it."

At that moment the doorbell rang. Tettsui moved smoothly, clicking off the floor lamp. Carver walked swiftly, his motion flowing and deliberate. He took up a position next to the door. He glanced at Tettsui, who held an automatic pistol at his side. Carver hadn't even seen the man draw the weapon.

"Who is it?" Carver called through the door.

"Dr. Asawa. You called me."

Carver opened the door, and Tettsui returned his 9mm Heckler & Koch to his waist holster. Tettsui briefly introduced the doctor to Carver and Joyce, and then to Joel Burck.

The doctor was short, with a wiry body that he used economically, as though he had once been clumsy and had trained himself to be nimble, like a tightrope walker's apprentice. As Dr. Asawa shook hands, he brushed a shock of gray hair from his eyes.

Dr. Asawa spent a few minutes with Burck, checking the dancer's pulse and his eyes. He finished the examination and turned to Mike Teltsui.

"It is as you say, the man is exhausted and under great stress. Physically he is as perfect as I have seen in some time, but his trauma is considerable. I shall give him something to sleep, and a prescription for the next few days.''

The doctor injected Burck with Diazepam.

''That will do for tonight,'' he said. ''If there is further need, then I would suggest he see his own doctor.''

''Will he be able to dance tomorrow?'' Joyce asked.

''No, I should think not,'' the doctor said, repacking his medical bag. ''He should get as much rest as possible.''

Mike Tettsui helped Joel Burck to the bedroom. Dr. Asawa left, and Carver went to the bar and mixed himself a bourbon and soda. Tettsui returned to the front room.

''I'll sleep here again, Carver,'' he said, ''Burck was almost asleep as soon as he hit the bed. I helped him off with his clothes and covered him.''

''Thanks, Mike,'' Carver said. He turned to Joyce. ''I'll take you home. My car's downstairs.''

''I can take a cab.''

''Don't be belligerent. I don't mind the drive.''

''Maybe I don't want you to drive me home.''

''All right,'' Carver said tersely. He was in no mood to put up with her. ''I'm leaving anyway. I'll take the elevator with you.''

She nodded, forcing herself to remain silent. On the street, Carver again suggested he drive her home. Joyce again refused and began to walk away. Carver caught up with her in several strides and took hold of her arm.

''There isn't a cab until you get to Van Ness. A half mile at least. Don't be stubborn.''

Joyce breathed heavily, frosty clouds issuing from her mouth; the night was cold. Reluctantly she agreed, and fifteen minutes later Carver parked on California Street, near Laurel Street. Joyce had not said one word. He noticed a late-night coffee shop down the block and invited her for coffee. Joyce refused. She climbed out, and he watched her go into her apartment. Not a word. After a brief time a light came on in a ground-floor window. Carver shrugged and headed for Fillmore Street.

He parked the Jaguar in the Hi-Valu service station. He locked the gates of the mechanic's bay and then headed for his office-apartment.

He felt used up. He felt helpless. There was no way he could have foreseen Meaghler getting shot instead of Burck. He had to believe that was the way it happened, otherwise he had to doubt that Burck was in danger. He was bone-tired, and he had a lot to think about.

Carver changed direction and went into a neighborhood bar.

"What'll you have?" the bartender asked.

Carver ordered a straight double of Wild Turkey. A handful of men and several women were at the plain wooden bar. Three of the five booths were occupied. The bar had no hanging ferns, no decorative upscale lighting, no jukebox, and no video games. In the rear was a pool table; the light over the table was out.

"Hi, Carver," one of the men greeted him.

Another couple nodded at him. He acknowledged them with a negligent wave of his hand. Carver paid for the drink and carried the glass to one of the empty booths. For a long time the glass was untouched. Carver slumped into the seat and slid his feet out of his shoes; he rubbed one foot over the other.

Just to damn many people to watch, too many to question. A fucking mess. Carver took a drink of the bourbon. Yeah, this was one case that had him in turmoil. He hadn't been able to foresee Meaghler's death. No one could.

Deep down inside the animal stirred. The hunter. Carver Bascombe felt it but did his best to ignore it. Who was he hunting? Who was he kidding? At this moment he had nothing. Not exactly an unknown situation. History might repeat itself. Often does.

Platitudes didn't help. Not when he had confronted two deaths in less than two days. Why not just fall apart like any normal human being? Just walk away from it. Go to bed and sleep for about a week. Let the cops find the killer. Eventually even Applegate will stumble onto the right clues. But that wasn't the way Carver worked; no, he had to remain cool, unruffled.

Who was he kidding?

Find the killer. Nothing else would satisfy Carver. Whoever the killer was, he gave off a spoor that stung the hunter's nerves. The stalker deep inside bristled in anticipation, snuffling and smelling the air.

TWELVE

"Hey, Cahva," a voice said, interrupting Carver Bascombe's thoughts.

"Hello, Jimmy," Carver said to Jimmy Bowman, the owner of the Hi-Valu station.

"Was I comin' in at a wrong-o time-o?"

"No," Carver said, gesturing for Bowman to sit opposite. "Nothing important."

Bowman put a bottle of beer down and wriggled into the booth. "How's the case workin' out, with the dancer man?" he asked.

Carver shrugged and finished the last remaining bourbon in the glass. He signaled to the bartender for a refill.

"We don't see you much in here," Bowman said. "But like I say, when a man ain't fox huntin' then there's nothing like the sociability of one's own company in a bar."

"Do you really say that, Jimmy?" Carver's voice was tired.

"Sure. It sounds good, don't it? Kinda like something Phil might come up with."

"Phil?" Carver said. "Who's Phil?"

"Why, Phil Ossofer," Bowman replied, and laughed. "When I can lay a bad joke like that on you, you must be all twisted around in your head. Anything you want to talk about?''

The bartender brought Carver's drink. Carver drank a taste and then gave a brief rundown on what had happened since the morning. Bowman shook his head; all he'd done was two tune-ups, pump a lot of gasoline, sell around forty quarts of oil, and check the profit sheets of his two other service stations. Ordinary stuff.

Someone else had killed two human beings. Busy, busy.

"A real head-bustin' problem," Bowman said sympathetically. "Maybe I got some advice for you. Wanta hear it?''

"Jimmy, I can use all the help I can get.''

"See, I obviously am no detective, but man, I been around. I seed all kindsa shit, all kindsa people. Now most people, they're all right. Know what I mean? I mind my own business, but I like to think I sort of look out for the other guy.''

"Right, Jimmy, right," Carver said offhandedly. He drank the bourbon down to the halfway mark.

"So what I mean, some guys, and some foxes too, they ain't right in the head. I've seen some real strange-o's, real weirdo's, flake-o's, nutso's. An' one kind, they don't give a damn about anyone. They're not communicatin' with the human race. No feelin's, no nothin'.''

"I agree, Jimmy. So what's your point?''

"So you got some guy, maybe a woman, who's just killed two people and is trying to kill another one. The first victim just got in the way, and the second was a mistake. Does the killer care? Is he off in a corner pissing and moaning?''

"Are you asking . . . ?

"Nah, it's just a question out in the air. So the kinda guy you are looking for is a nutso—one of those pathological misfits. A guy with no feelings, except for himself, not really, really caring about anyone else.''

"A sociopath," Carver said.

"Yeah, one of those. So you don't have to ask a lot of

questions of all them suspects. All you gotta do is find the one who's real conceited, real arrogant, real self-centered. And I mean real!''

Carver looked with wonder at Jimmy Bowman.

"Jimmy, you've hit it. But it's not that easy. We're dealing with a lot of artistic and creative types. These people can be very temperamental. But I think you've helped. Damn if you haven't. Let me buy you another beer.''

"Don't say I never turned down a free beer. Or anything free, for that matter. My mom never raised no fool.''

"Definitely not,'' Carver said, signaling vigorously to the bartender for another round. He felt a hell of a lot better.

Joel Burck woke to ashen gloom. The ceiling was a dark gray patch. His bedside clock read 3:40. His eyes felt heavy and scratchy. God, he thought, it just isn't possible. Bart couldn't really be dead.

But the blood had been real. The bullet hole in the windshield had been real. His loss was real too. An ache filled his chest, and his heart beat irregularly. Or was that all imagination, something the mind uses when it can't accept the unthinkable?

No, the bed was empty. No imagination there. No quiet evenings together, reading, listening to music. No walks around the city, no nothing, not a thing. Bart Meaghler was gone. Gone.

Lying in the darkness was far easier than thinking about facing the morning, with all the little reminders—the smell of Bart's cologne, the way he liked his raisin-bread toast very dark, his habit of doing housework in his bare feet. God, all the little things, so many of them. So many.

Someone had killed his friend. Someone Burck knew. Someone in the company. Someone who knew what kind of overcoat Burck wore to Moseby's party. Was Carver Bascombe correct? Had someone meant to kill him, and shot Bart instead? Was this true?

Why, why, why did he listen to Moseby? Hire a detective? No! He would rather Bart were alive.

Bart was dead. The fact was so final, so horrifying, that the mind merely turned the thoughts into meaningless words.

Burck turned his face to the wall. He jammed his fist against his mouth. He could feel the tears beginning again.

THIRTEEN

The next morning Carver was up before seven. He had slept fine, better than he thought he would. Yeah, he felt good. Deep down the little bastard hunter was jumping up and around, snapping teeth, ready to follow a spoor, throw a spear, notch an arrow, load six into a .357.

Carver made coffee, ate a bowl of hot cereal at his desk, and read the morning paper. Oh-oh. Nothing like murder on page 1.

Travel Agent Shot

Late last night the body of Bartholomew Meaghler, a local owner of a well-known travel agency, was found shot on Nob Hill, in front of the Dolores Court Apartments.

Police were summoned to the scene, where they found the victim behind the wheel of his automobile. The vehicle was parked, with the engine running, in front of the apartment building. Mr. Meaghler had been attending a party in the penthouse of Myron Moseby, a wealthy art dealer.

The incident had been reported to the police department by Carver Bascombe, a local private detective, who had been at the

same penthouse party. The report came to
the homicide bureau at 10:42 p.m.

The investigating officer in charge, Detective Sergeant Arnold Applegate, said . . .

Hell! Damn it! Carver cursed. He had been afraid of
this. Now everyone would know he was no journalist. His
job was going to get tougher. What the hell would Joyce
think? As far as she was concerned, Carver Bascombe was
some kind of liar. Damn!

He read further. Applegate stated he was looking for
Bart Meaghler's enemies, if any. There seemed no motive
for the killing, not as yet. The police would continue their
investigation blahblah and blah. Mostly blah. The column
also stated that Mr. Meaghler shared an apartment with
Joel Burck, one of the principal dancers of the GGBC, and
so forth, and so on, et cetera. More blahblah.

Meaghler's older sister, Mrs. Carole Asquith, his only
surviving relative, had been notified and was making the
funeral arrangements.

No motive . . . good god.

Disgustedly, Carver dropped the paper onto his desk, as
if maggots had suddenly crawled over it. He turned on the
office radio to a classical station. He went over the reports
that the college kid had collected on many of the top
members of the GGBC. With half an ear he heard a radio
commercial for the upcoming gala premiere.

He looked up when he heard Rose Weinbaum opening
the office's outer door. She stepped in, taking off her coat
and floppy cap. She glanced in through her open door at
Carver, and at the cup of coffee on his desk.

She went into his apartment and emerged with a coffee
cup. "Good morning," she said finally. "Or is it?"

He told her the latest events. Rose had heard most of it
on the morning newscast. She had her problems also.

"About Burck," she said. "I haven't been able to dig
up a damn thing."

"What do you make of it?" he asked.

"At first I thought I might've run into one of those

federal witness programs, you know, where the government takes a witness and gives him or her a new identity, a new career, a new home.''

"I'm familiar with the program."

"I'm still working on that, but it doesn't look as if that's the case here. A new career in the ballet? Impossible. I presume you want me to keep checking."

"Keep checking, Rose."

"Any ideas where I can continue with this checking you so blithely command?''

"What?''

"I've used most of my resources. I'm out of ideas. I can use sources out of state, but it gets expensive. I know a cheaper way to go.''

"What's that, Rose?'' Carver asked, almost without interest.

"Just go up to Burck and ask him point-blank. Just who the hell are you, and where did you come from?''

"Just like that?''

"Yeah, just like that. Saves a lot of time, the direct approach, the blunt attack, the forthright interrogation.''

"Yeah,'' Carver said without enthusiasm.

The man had just lost his friend and lover, and someone was trying to kill him. Probably still in shock. Badgering the man did not seem a reasonable method.

"Rose, I'm still trying to figure out who is trying to murder Burck and why.''

"Maybe it's one of those cases where a killer fuddles things. He has a motive to kill one, but kills a few others he doesn't have a motive for, thinking the cops won't figure it out.''

Carver cocked an eye at Rose. "You, my dear lady, have finally gone around the bend.''

"It's only a suggestion.''

"Okay, but keep trying to get something on Burck's background. Remember he's young, twenty-eight. Don't you know someone on the local Selective Service board?''

"That's good, boss,'' Rose said. "I don't, but I know someone who does. I'll call in a marker or two.''

"I've had some thoughts. Want to bounce them around?"

"We've nothing else on the fire. No clients. You're all caught up with the security inspections for your commercial clients. Let's hear it."

Carver spent a few minutes telling her what Bowman had suggested in the bar.

"We're dealing with someone with a fantastic ego. And someone who is very cautious, Rose. I'm going out on a limb, playing a hunch, but . . . I'm eliminating the musicians and the directors."

"Okay, boss, I'll bite. How do you figure that?"

"Someone is trying to kill Burck. But not at first."

"What do you mean?"

"All the accidents were deliberate. But the first one, the glass in the slippers, wouldn't kill Burck. Obviously the one who did that knew Burck wouldn't die from that. It would cripple him. Prevent him from dancing."

"Okay, Carver, I see that," Rose said.

"So the glass in the slippers came first. Then the elevator. Then there was the accident with the damaged tire, and then finally the attempt to run Burck off the Twin Peaks road. Then he was shot at."

"I get it. The killer has gone from attempts to incapacitate Joel Burck, at first to cripple, and then to attempted murder. Each succeeding act became more forceful, more violent. It was only a matter of time before killing Burck was the next logical step."

"Yeah, that's the way I figure it," Carver said, sipping his now cold coffee. "Killing Burck wasn't the original intention."

"Of course."

"Now the process of elimination. The glass in the shoes. Would a musician put glass in a dancer's shoes?"

"Possibly. But not probably."

"Would a businessman, one of the directors, try to cripple a dancer in that fashion?"

"Possibly."

"It's a hell of a lot more possible that a dancer would

put glass in another dancer's shoes. Ruin his feet. If the hate were strong enough."

"Okay, Carver, let's go on that assumption. So which is it—a male or female dancer?"

"Take your pick."

"Hmmm. What do you do next?"

"Now we need a motive. That's what I'm hunting for."

He lapsed into bright thoughtfulness. Rose went into her office.

Carver picked up the folder of GGBC personnel and headed for Burck's apartment. Sergeant Applegate was going to question Burck, and Carver wanted to be there before the homicide detective.

Mike Tettsui opened the door and said hello. He put the gun away. Tettsui had a paper napkin tucked into his shirt and was drinking orange juice. He reseated himself at the breakfast table and continued eating sausage and scrambled eggs.

"Anything new, Mike?" Carver asked, pouring himself orange juice. "Burck all right?"

"He seems all right, Carver. Anyway he's up, almost dressed. I offered to make his breakfast, which apparently is something Meaghler did most of the time, and he just about broke into tears again. Other than that, considering the options, he's all right."

Joel Burck walked into the kitchen. He looked terrible. A gray face with deep eye sockets does not harmonize well with lemony sunlight. He would have looked more natural loitering near a sewage treatment plant.

Carver asked how he was.

Burck grunted and sat down opposite Tettsui; his arms hung from his shoulders lifelessly. Did he want orange juice? He shook his head slowly. Coffee?

"Tea," he said, barely audible.

In a few minutes Carver had tea ready. He began to pour it into a cup.

"In a glass, please," Burck said softly.

"What?" Carver said, the teapot hovering over the cup.

"Please, Carver, in a glass. In the cabinet."

Carver shrugged and poured the tea into a tall, thick glass. Burck sipped the brew steadily.

Mike Tettsui had said little. He pushed his empty plate aside. "What now?" he asked Carver.

"We talk with Applegate. Then I want you to stay with Joel for the rest of the day."

"Can do. I got a good night's sleep. I like earning money while I'm sleeping."

"Worth every penny," Carver said. "I want to see some people, and maybe a hunch or two to check."

"You have an angle?"

"Sort of, Mike. I've got Rose gathering info. She has the telephone number here, and she might call."

Carver motioned for Tettsui to come aside. He told him his theory, and that he had to play the hunch.

Joe Burck had drunk about half his tea when the doorbell rang. Carver opened the door and admitted Detective Sergeant Applegate, he of the closed, one-track mind.

"Hello, Michael," Applegate said to Tettsui. "What are you doing here?"

"I'm the second team."

Carver offered Applegate coffee and he accepted. He leaned against the kitchen countertop and began to question Joel Burck.

"Mr. Burck, I'd like to know what you and Bart Meaghler were arguing about at the party last night."

Burck merely moved his head back and forth. No, no.

"Come on, Mr. Burck," Applegate demanded. "You want to find the one who killed your friend, don't you?"

"It was personal," Burck answered finally. "Personal."

"I see," Applegate said, implying he didn't. "Do you know of anyone you might consider an enemy of Mr. Meaghler's?"

"No, I certainly do not," Burck said, his voice unemotional. "Bart was well liked by everyone. As far as I know he had no enemies."

"Sure, that's why someone put a friendly bullet in him."

"That's crap," Carver said flatly.

116

"You think so?" Applegate asked. He drained the cup of coffee. "You really think so, Bascombe?"

"You're repeating yourself," Tettsui said, almost slyly.

"I suggest you stay out of this, Michael," Applegate ordered.

"He was not supposed to die," Burck said calmly. "I was supposed to be killed."

"You've been listening to Bascombe," Applegate said. "Too damn much."

"No, it's true," Burck said. "I know. Carver was right."

"Hard to believe, but I'll bite. He was right about what?"

"The overcoat."

"We're back to that again, are we?" Applegate said. "Well, Mr. Burck, you may know a lot about dancing, and you may have lived with Mr. Bartholomew Meaghler for a few years, but that doesn't mean you knew much about the man. He had a police record."

"That's impossible," Burck said heatedly.

"It's not a long record, certainly not as long as my arm. More like my pinky finger. Your friend served six months in the San Mateo County jail about seven years ago."

"For what?" Carver asked.

"Nothing heavy, Bascombe, I'll say that. Drunk driving, hitting a fire hydrant. A third offense, by the way, and he was already on probation. And here's the kicker, Bascombe—it was the same county jail where Ben Rosada did some time."

Applegate looked smugly at the three men. An unexpected bull's-eye.

"So, Mr. Burck," he said. "What do you think? Do you know anyone who might have hated Meaghler?"

"I have to reply the same, I know of no one."

"All right, then I suppose you'll have to know . . . my investigators have supplied me with information from guests at the party about your argument with Mr. Meaghler."

Burck looked at Carver and then lowered his eyes. Carver realized that Joel Burck had probably been withholding information from him. But was it important information? Applegate seemed to think it was. Carver glanced at Tettsui, who moved his shoulders in a half-inch shrug.

"You were arguing about money," Applegate said. "Good old green stuff. Nothing high and mighty, no great intellectual argument, not jealousy, just plain old money. Meaghler needed it, according to witnesses within hearing range, and he asked for it, practically demanded it of you, and you refused your friend."

"I have nothing to say, Sergeant," Burck said.

"What a relief," Applegate said sardonically. He looked at Carver. "Aren't you going to interrupt and give me some legal hocus-pocus about the man's rights?"

"Not me," Carver said, as innocently as he dared. "You've got the stage. Strut your stuff."

"So my next step was to find out why Meaghler needed it. After all, he had a lucrative business. He had an expensive car and shared a luxury apartment."

"You're a tough one," Tettsui said quietly. "And long-winded, too."

"I'm getting there, Michael, the pièce de résistance," Applegate said. "We looked real close at the deceased, and we came up with another factor in Meaghler's personality. He liked to gamble. A few thousand on the horses, a few thousand at the Reno gaming tables, a few thousand here, a few there. All adds up. Isn't that so, Mr. Burck?"

"Yes, that is so."

"Bartholomew Meaghler owed a lot of money to gamblers. Around twenty-five thousand. More than he could raise. He tried to borrow most of it, if not all of it, from you. And you wouldn't give it to him."

"No, I wouldn't." The words were tainted with regret.

"So that's where we stand in the investigation. Last night Mr. Meaghler was most likely shot and killed by gamblers."

FOURTEEN

In the sunlit kitchen, the four men were silent for a moment.

"Is that what you've got?" Carver finally asked. "A gambling debt? And you think—no, you believe—some gamblers rubbed him out."

"We have other evidence," Applegate replied, again very smugly, "that suppports that theory."

Carver shrugged; with Applegate there was simply no room for discussion. Carver had a few counterarguments that could punch holes in Applegate's theory, but his own oxygen intake was important; he didn't want to waste his breath. Sure, Applegate was a good homicide investigator, and eventually he'd realize that Burck was the intended victim, but in the meantime . . .

He didn't dislike Applegate; he was simply frustrated by the detective's narrow view. He was glad to see Applegate leave.

"At least the cops have a theory," Tettsui said. "I suppose it's possible. Gamblers might have killed him over a bad debt."

Carver made a derisive sound.

"I gather you don't buy it, Carver."

"You can't collect money from a dead man. Gamblers might lean on him, but they won't kill the golden goose."

"Then perhaps they used Meaghler as an object lesson."

"No," Carver said. "Breaking a leg or giving a bad beating is just as effective."

He reached for a telephone and called his office.

"Carver Bascombe's office," Rose answered in her sexy, throaty voice. "Investigations in confidence. Mrs. Weinbaum speaking. May we help you?"

"Rose, it's me. I need you to run some checks."

"Go ahead," she said, apparently ready with a notepad.

"First, get whatever you can on a jail rap for Bart Meaghler and Ben Rosada."

"Got it," Rose said without comment.

"Second, Meaghler was a gambler. See if you can dig up any information on gamblers he owed money to."

"That last bit could be tough, boss. You might do better talking to Jimmy Bowman. He's into that scene."

"I thought of that. But I want to see what else we can get. Keep trying, Rose," he said and hung up.

Carver dropped another coin into the slot and tapped numbers.

"Hi-Valu, you got the boss."

"Jimmy, this is Carver."

"Ho, Cahva, what's doin'?"

"You were a big help last night, and I could use more of the same."

"Light the fuse, friend."

"You're familiar with the gambling scene. Those in it."

"Yeah, that's true."

"That man, Meaghler, the one who—"

"I read the papers, Cahva. Drop it into low, my man."

"He was heavily in debt to gamblers. I'd like to know who."

"I can try. Might know in a couple of hours. Give me a call, okay?"

Carver thanked his friend and hung up. Mike Tettsui had heard one side of the conversation, but it was enough. Carver asked Tettsui to watch Burck and to see that the dancer got plenty of rest. Tettsui nodded and poured a cup of chocolate (with a sedative) for Burck. Carver left a few minutes later. He drove to the theater, where the security guard remembered him from the day before.

As he walked across the lobby Carver heard music. The orchestra was rehearsing *A Midsummer Night's Dream*. He paused and listened. Not bad. He went into the auditorium. The orchestra was finished with their rehearsals, and the dancers filled the stage. Another rehearsal was about to commence. The dancers would go on and on, often for ten or twelve hours.

John Guiterez was at the piano, playing some time steps for general warming up. Several ballerinas were going through a routine involving *en diagonales*.

Few male dancers were on stage, and Carver did not see Bob Swaine or Vassily Visikov, the crippled choreographer. Near the wings, wearing street clothes, were Joyce Kittering, Don Terman, and Eric Hudson. Carver wanted to speak to them all, but not at the same time. But would they speak to him?

Walking up the aisle toward him was the Chinese ballerina. He remembered her name: Gloria Loo. She carried a flight bag containing her ballet gear. Carver moved aside to let her pass, but she stopped and looked at him. A lopsided smile creased her face, as though listening to an inner joke.

"Well, we still haven't been properly introduced," the woman said. "I'd hoped you'd get around to interviewing me, but I guess that was all some kind of undercover story. I'm Gloria Loo."

"Carver Bascombe," he said, shaking her hand.

A smell of perspiration hovered between them. Rings of sweat made dark half-moons under her breasts. Night-black, Gloria's hair was pulled back in a severe ponytail.

"I'd like to hear your reasons for playacting," she said, "if it's no big deal."

Carver shrugged.

"Deborah Canby says you're another homosexual." Gloria cocked her head at him and hooked a thumbnail under her teeth. "Is that true, or was that part of the act?"

"That's something Miss Canby assumed."

"That's a good trick, Carver, not answering a direct question."

"Apparently."

"You're really a private detective?"

"Yeah."

"And monosyllabic."

"Yes," Carver replied with a laugh.

"That's good," Gloria said, joining in with a pleasant chuckle. "I like the strong silent type, and I don't find you unattractive. As a matter of fact I think you're rather rugged-looking. Yes, tall, dark, and handsome. But not too handsome. But definitely dark. Do you think I talk too much, Carver?"

"Yeah, a bit."

"That's one of my failings. But then you're quiet and I'm not. Isn't that what they say, that opposites attract?"

"I've heard that," Carver said.

"Ah, you sound as though you have business else-where. What kind of business do you have here in the theater as a detective?"

"Looking for Brigham Merkhinn."

"Shot down in my tracks. Another evasive answer. That's a habit I don't find all that attractive. But, Mr. Merkhinn? He's in his office upstairs, probably trying to find more excuses to get rid of Bob Swaine."

Carver nodded and turned to walk back to the lobby.

"I'll go with you," Gloria said and hooked an arm through his. "I noticed you took my advice. You finally talked with Joyce Kittering last night. Are you attracted to her? I gotta admit she's very pretty." She waited for him to reply, but he was silent. "Okay, Carver. I can't take a hint, but I understand all about pregnant silences and pauses. One just trundled past."

They went through the big double doors, and she pointed the way to the stairway to the mezzanine offices.

"Why not ask me out for dinner?" Gloria asked. "Or for drinks, or a walk in the park. I like to go to the planetarium occasionally. Or fish for bass, or something?"

"You're a brash woman, Gloria. Not such a bad thing—sometimes."

122

"And besides, you've got the hots for Joyce Kittering. I saw how you looked at her onstage just now. Well, that's your hard luck. I think I'm a much more interesting woman."

She grinned and walked away. Carver went up the carpeted stairway. Outside Merkhinn's office he heard voices raised in anger. He stepped in without knocking.

A nervous secretary was putting papers into a filing cabinet. She glanced at Merkhinn's private door and dropped several papers. Behind the closed door, a familiar voice cursed loudly, and somebody hit something. A hand or fist on a desk? Somebody was having one hell of an argument. Carver picked up the fallen papers and handed them to the secretary.

"May I help you?" she asked, looking nervously at Merkhinn's office door.

From the shouting, Carver figured there were only two men. Brigham Merkhinn and what sounded like Bob Swaine.

"Who's winning?" Carver asked, and walked rapidly into Merkhinn's office. Two men, Swaine and Merkhinn, were facing each other, with Merkhinn keeping his leather-topped desk between himself and the angry choreographer. Neither of them was aware of Carver's presence.

"It's your idea," Swaine shouted at Brigham Merkhinn, gesturing openhandedly. "And everyone knows it. It's no good denying it, or changing it."

"This company," Merkhinn answered heatedly, "is not your toy! It's not yours to do with as you please! I refuse to be put constantly in a position where I have to explain conditions with which I do not agree! Conditions and plans I did not want. And, goddamn it," he said, his voice bellowing, as if to get his point across by sheer volume, "plans I would never have agreed to!"

"It's a great idea," Swaine said, still shouting, "and you have no power to prevent it. I still have artistic control of this company."

"I'll be glad when you're out!"

"Hey!" Carver shouted, his baritone cutting into a space between yells.

They turned jerkily, surprised.

"What the hell," Swaine said as he recognized the black man standing at the closed office door.

"Who let you in?" Merkhinn asked loudly.

"No one, I just walked in."

"Then, Mr. Bascombe, you can just walk out," Merkhinn ordered.

"No," Carver said, and settled himself loosely into a green leather chair. He placed his hands on the armrests. He smiled benignly at the two static men.

"Bascombe, I don't know what your game is," Swaine said between clenched teeth, "but I don't like it."

"Questions and answers. Like what the hell was all that shouting about?"

"It's none of your business, Mr. Bascombe," Merkhinn said. He ran his fingers over his head in an attempt to smooth what little hair he had. He placed his hands flat on the desk.

Merkhinn had recovered nicely. Perhaps that's what made him a good executive. Swaine, on the other hand, thrust his hands in his pockets, as if he was fearful he might hurt someone. Probably Carver Bascombe. Swaine turned and paced and turned again, facing Carver. He was still unsettled. Perhaps that's what made him a good choreographer.

"According to this morning's paper," Merkhinn said, "you're identified as a private investigator. Is this true, or have the media once again engaged in hyperbole?"

"No error," Carver replied.

"Then you are not writing a story on Joel Burck and on the ballet, particularly this company."

"No."

"Shit!" Swaine said loudly. "What the hell is this?"

"Haven't you read the paper?" Merkhinn asked Swaine. "Or listened to the news?"

Swaine shook his head, silent for once.

"You do know about Bart Meaghler?" Carver asked.

"Sure, I was at the party. So were you."

"The morning papers identified me correctly. I'm not a journalist. I'm a private investigator."

"Damn it!" Swaine blurted. "It has to do with Joel Burck. You came in with Burck, so that's got to be it. But what the hell you could be doing for Burck I don't understand."

"What were you and Mr. Merkhinn arguing about?"

"Nothing secret there," Swaine said. "Merkhinn didn't like my plans to—"

"That's none of Bascombe's business," Merkhinn said, "so just shut your mouth!"

"Fuck you," Swaine said, his words low, almost coy. He turned to Carver. "You know about the performance on Alcatraz?"

Carver nodded.

"Well, I never bothered to get Merkhinn's permission to have the ballet performed there. As if I had to! I don't have to tell Merkhinn anything. Until he boots my ass out of here, I'll run the artistic end of this company the way I think best."

"It won't be your windup toy for long," Merkhinn said angrily.

"All right," Carver said soothingly, "the two of you can pick up where you left off—after I leave. Mr. Merkhinn, I understand that you were within earshot of Burck and Meaghler at the party. I'd like to know what they were arguing about."

"Money," Merkhinn said.

"Gambling debts?"

"Yes, how did you know that? Did the police tell you?"

Carver lifted both hands and turned them over.

"Burck wouldn't loan Meaghler the money," Merkhinn said. "That's what I heard."

"I'll be damned," Swaine said, getting interested.

"So you were the one," Carver said to Merkhinn, "who told the police about the argument."

"Me and several others. I was chatting with several of the dancers and Graham Maltby."

"Who were the dancers?" Carver asked, taking out his notepad.

"Hey, Bascombe," Swaine said, "are you working with the police? Or are you asking these questions for your own purposes?"

Carver ignored the question and turned to Merkhinn. "Who were the others you were talking with at that time?"

"I think Swaine has a point, but I'll admit I'm consumed with curiosity. Let's see, I was talking with Bellini, Terman, Overman—he's a musician, I don't think you've met him—and Maltby, of course. Oh, and Eric Hudson."

"Do you recall anyone leaving the party at that time?"

"Certainly. Meaghler. I saw him leave Joel in a huff."

"Did you see Meaghler take a coat from the foyer closet and leave?"

"Well, I didn't see him take it, but I caught him out of the corner of my eye as I took a glass of champagne from one of the servers. And yes, now that I think of it, he had on an overcoat. A pale tan sort of thing."

"Did you see anyone leave just before Meaghler left?"

"No," he said. He paused thoughtfully. "I don't think so. Until you and Burck and Joyce Kittering left. And no one after that."

"Did you notice anyone returning to the party?"

"I don't recall seeing anyone, coming or going."

"Okay," Carver said, and then turned to Swaine. "Did you see anyone? Leaving or returning to the party?"

"No, I didn't. I certainly didn't see Meaghler leave."

"Mr. Bascombe," Merkhinn interrupted, "if it's true that Meaghler was in debt to gamblers, isn't it likely that they killed him. Because he didn't pay up."

"That's the police theory," Carver said, "but I don't buy it. Well . . . thanks. I've got enough for now. You two men can go back to screaming and yelling."

"Nah," the choreographer said. He chuckled and rubbed his chin. "I think we've had our daily outburst. Very soon Merkhinn and the other directors can just relax. They won't have old Bob Swaine to kick around anymore."

Carver suppressed a laugh and left the office.

FIFTEEN

The Thunderer greeted Carver as he returned to the auditorium. The set designers had added blocks of red stripes, slats of blue, and stripes of white, all coming down and crisscrossing as if the flag were a loony dancer. A single oblong of stars on a field of blue danced on high.

The stage lights were low, and the dancers bobbed, pirouetted, and leaped, carrying dozens of fireworks sparklers. Quite an effect.

Joyce Kittering was not dancing this rollicking number. Carver made his way to the side entrance into the wings. There was a hustle and bustle that seemed different. The dancers were more on edge.

He found Joyce in the semidarkness of the wings doing warm-up exercises. Her rhythm of *battements tendus* and *batte ments tendus engagés* was slow, graceful, languid, like water rippling over smooth stones. Her eyes were slits, almost closed. Carver detected a slight flutter of the lashes.

Even over the roaring jocularity of *The Thunderer*, he heard the rustle of Joyce's tutu, the swish of her leotard as her legs scissored open and closed. He watched with fascination for many minutes. She slowly stopped and looked onstage at the ongoing comedy dance. She plucked a towel from the rack and began to dry her face. She stopped and realized someone was watching. She turned.

"Hello, Joyce," Carver said.

She closed her lips tightly, then turned and began to walk away.

"Hold it," Carver said, reaching her quickly and taking her arm.

"Take your hand off me," she said grimly.

"I'd like to explain," Carver said. "I told you last night that I would. I meant what I said."

"No, I don't want to listen," she replied, jerking her arm loose. "You lied to me, Carver."

"Sometimes that's part of the job."

"I don't like your job. What kind of work is that, a private detective? Spying on people, guys hired to bust up unions, all kinds of industrial sabotage. I've read enough about that stuff."

"It isn't like that," Carver said. "Not with me, anyway."

"Keep your voices down, you two," Eric Hudson said, stepping in. "You can't compete with John Philip Sousa. Not allowed."

"Carver Bascombe is a lot of trouble," Joyce said angrily, "and I don't want any part of him. And this is none of your business, Eric."

"Joyce, you're so strong-willed," Hudson said. He turned to Carver. "Give her a year or two to cool off."

"I need to talk to Joyce," Carver replied, and casually switched on his tiny recorder. "And to you too, Hudson."

"Of course, Carver, I'm at your service. I think that's what I am. What service am I offering?"

"Eric, this concerns Bart Meaghler. And Joel Burck. What affects Burck might affect all the dancers."

"I see, I see. Go ahead, ask your questions.

"Where were you during the approximate time Meaghler was shot?"

"We answered those questions to the homicide detectives. Couldn't you get the information from them?"

"The police and I barely seeing eye to eye."

"Don't talk to him, Eric!" Joyce demanded, her arms folded defiantly.

"It won't hurt to be helpful, Joyce. I think I was talking with you . . . although I'd had a few drinks, actually quite a few, so my memory is somewhat clouded."

"Not then, Eric," Joyce said, angrily biting off each word. "We were talking just before I talked with—him." She looked at Carver, her eyes narrowed, fingers drumming on her arms. "Bascombe is an engaging conversationalist. Not witty, not sexy, but interesting. I suppose most liars are like that. Some kind of occupational hazard, I expect."

"Actually," Hudson said, frowning in thought, "I do remember standing near Bart and Joel. An argument, something to do with money that . . . I think, yes, Bart owed some money, and he wanted Joel to help him. Something like that, anyway. I really didn't pay attention."

Joyce nodded slowly, still frowning, looking at Hudson. She tilted her head and looked at Carver.

"Actually, Eric," she said slowly, "I don't recall you standing around Bart and Joel at all. But I remember hearing the argument when I was getting myself a glass of water. I passed by Bart and Joel. I didn't see you at that time."

"What about that, Eric?" Carver asked.

"As I said, I did have a bit too much to drink. I know I heard the argument between them, but I suppose it's possible it was an ongoing thing, and I heard a later version. I remember . . . I was talking with Merkhinn. Actually, he was doing all the talking. Actually, arguing. The same old, tiresome thing. Getting rid of Swaine. Mr. Maltby was there. And Bellini . . . couple of others. At least I think there were others.

"That's the problem with drink," Hudson continued ruefully. "It robs you of time and space." He looked at Carver. "I'd check a few other people, just to be sure. I'll take your word for it, whatever you find out. I'd kind of like to know where I was myself."

"Eric, do you recall if anyone left the party, say ten to

twenty minutes before the guests were informed about the death?''

"Can't say that I did. The police asked us that too."

"How about seeing someone return to the party?"

"No, sorry," Hudson said, shaking his head.

"That's all, I think," Carver said, and wrote several entries into his notepad. "Joyce, I'd still like to explain."

"You just don't take no for an answer, do you?" she said. "It's still no. N-O." Joyce stomped away to the elevators.

"I'm afraid, old man," Hudson said, "that you've an uphill battle ahead of you. Somehow I don't think you're very good at this sort of thing. Romance, I mean."

He grinned and walked away, humming a melody from *The Thunderer*.

Damn! Carver thought. He wasn't getting anywhere with Joyce. It was certainly not for lack of trying. He turned off the pocket recorder.

What he really wanted was an overall plan of Moseby's party, where everyone was, minute by minute. With a blueprint like that he might find the hole in time that the killer used to go downstairs and wait for Joel Burck, shoot him, and return to the party.

Carver was convinced the killer had been at the party. Although some of the members of the ballet company were not there. Notably Vassily Visikov.

He left the theater and drove to Sutter Street, where he parked his car on the parking roof of the Moseby Art Gallery. He checked the alarm system on the Jaguar and locked it.

The gallery was plushly carpeted, with spotlights singling out paintings and drawings on the walls. Moseby specialized in early twentieth-century masters, such as Picasso (of course) and Braque, along with Max Beckmann and Oscar Kokoschka. Moseby had some personal favorites tucked away in back rooms, among them works by Otto Dix and Eugene Berman.

Moseby also had several walls hung with American artists—some of the better-known Action Painters of the postwar period, and some of the trendier artists. Some of the artists he enjoyed for their artistic merit, others only for their monetary merit.

One painting was for personal vanity: a full-length portrait of Moseby in a striking pose, assured, haughty, painted by Frank Ashley.

"Ah, Carver," Moseby said as he saw his friend admiring the portrait. "What brings you here today?"

"To see Leroy."

"About what, might I inquire, dear boy?"

"Come along," Carver said. "That'll save me repeating myself."

Leroy Dolny was the manager of the gallery but actually spent much of his time promoting the more contemporary items for sale. He also acquired paintings for the gallery, often traveling to other cities for that purpose. He had a good eye for the unique, and often spotted trends before the high priests in New York City.

Dolny was pleased to see Carver. The three men talked about the tragedy of Meaghler's death for an appropriate time. After several minutes Carver came to the point.

"Leroy," Carver said, "you have a gift, though not as great as the photographic memory of Sergeant Ernie Ludlow."

Moseby and Dolny groaned at the mention of the homophobic homicide detective.

"All right," Carver said, "I'm sorry I brought him up. Anyway, Leroy, you have a fine memory. Tell me what you remember about the party last night. Who was where, and when."

"I see," Dolny said. "You're trying to reconstruct the period of time between when Bart Meaghler left the party and when he was reported murdered."

"Yeah," Carver replied. "You got it."

What counted to Carver was that Dolny had stayed close to the front door and the buffet tables, checking on late arrivals and overseeing the food supply. He also had a good overview of the large front rooms. In a short time, Dolny had recalled fairly clearly where many of the guests had been.

"Unfortunately, Carver," Dolny said, "there's more than one exit from the penthouse. There's a door off our master bedroom, and there's always the fire escape off the terrace."

"Naturally, dear boy, we've told the police what we could. Of course, Leroy didn't draw a timetable."

"No," Carver said. "Applegate should be able to figure out something like that for himself." He looked at the sheets of paper containing names of guests and times. Not much use, really. "So several people did leave, and several latecomers arrived after Meaghler had left. Mostly orchestra musicians, I see. And Alice Boygen, one of the prima ballerinas."

He folded the papers and tucked them inside his jacket. He asked to use the phone, and called Jimmy Bowman.

"Bad news, Cahva," Bowman said. "You don' wanna mess with this guy."

"Okay, you've warned me. Who did Meaghler owe the money to?"

"Molerath."

"Jee-zuss," Carver said, the word a snakelike hiss.

"Yeah, you don' wanna fuck with that guy. He's broken a lot of bones on a lotta guys."

"But that's usually all he does. He's never killed anyone."

"Yeah, Cahva, but Meaghler owed the guy over twenty-five K. He might get very nasty over that kinda dough. His hoodlum enforcers might get carried away with enthusiasm."

"How do I get to him?"

"Not easy, but you might try seeing Murray the Goose. Remember the Goose?"

"I remember, Jimmy. Okay, thanks."

"Hey, watch out for yourself."

Carver hung up and thought for a time.

"I doubt if that was good news," Moseby said.

"No," Carver said, "but it might lead somewhere. I'd tell you—"

"No, dear boy, I've been involved with you in several of your cases, and I know several of your traits. You don't tell anyone anything until you're positively sure. Makes for interesting suspense, but most likely avoids lawsuits."

Carver grinned. He thanked both Moseby and Dolny and left. Under normal circumstances he would have enjoyed wandering around the gallery studying the art work. Not now, since he had at least one more stop.

"What kind of a car?" the young man asked, stroking his straggly mustache.

"A late-model black sedan, probably reported stolen night before last," Carver said.

A warm wind blew across the police storage lot, fluttering Carver's trench coat. The man behind the glass window was uninterested in the black detective's problem; there were simply too many cars in the lot that had been towed in.

"Without a license plate," the young man said, still fingering his mustache, "or some kinda identification number I don't think we can help you, bud. Just too many cars out there."

"A lot of cars that had been reported stolen?"

"Yeah, sure. Alla time."

Carver thought there was a slim chance that the car that had tried to kill Joel Burck had been abandoned and then towed in. And that the owner hadn't already claimed it. There was a long chance the killer might've left fingerprints.

All long odds, since the killer-thief might have wiped the car down. Also the car might have been abandoned in one of the other Bay Area counties. Carver had to try.

"How about me just walking around to see if I might spot the vehicle?"

"Well . . ." the man said doubtfully. He looked over his shoulder, as if he might be under surveillance. Two policemen in the front office were paying no attention. The man shrugged. "Sure, take a look. You sure can't steal anything."

Carver used fifteen minutes walking between rows of cars. If the car was here then it had to be badly scraped in a particular pattern. Many of the autos were clean, while others were totaled, ghastly wrecks, images of death on the streets and highways. Many cars had windshields and side windows smashed; the vandals probably wanted the stereo components or the contents of the glove compartment.

After a half hour Carver had scrutinized every car. Nothing. Not one black car with bad scrapes only along its left side. Nothing.

Carver thanked the guy at the window and left the impound lot. As he walked to his car two men moved in alongside. One clutched Carver's arm, a crushingly painful grip. The other pressed in close to his left side. Checking to see if he was hot?

"No gun," the guy on his left said.

Carver moved fast.

Not fast enough.

SIXTEEN

The guy on Carver's left reached out and crushed a fistful of fingers around his throat.

"Don't be a wiseass, Bascombe," the man with the bruising grip said. "We just want to talk."

Both men were shorter than Carver. The man holding his arm had a problem; smelling his own sickly-sweet, overripe-prune breath probably caused him to squint. Crease lines radiated from around pale eyes—it looked like a child's drawing of two dying daffodils.

The other guy dropped his hold on Carver's throat. He wiped his hand on a handkerchief. Then blew his nose. As an afterthought, Carver figured, not wanting to waste a motion. Large protuding teeth kept the man's lips apart, which was probably all to the good; if his lips were together they'd resemble slimy oysters.

"We gotta talk," bad breath said.

"Yeah," oyster lips said. "There's a luncheonette up the street. We'll go there."

"A little public, isn't it?" Carver asked. "I didn't think Molerath liked bad publicity."

"No, we don't mind numerous people," the guy with the teeth said. "And what's a 'molerath'?" He snickered, his bivalve lips hitching a ride under his nose.

"Me, personally," bad breath said, "I like people. I'm

into humanity, the mix a all kindsa types. Real inerestin'. Like, I bet you're a real inerestin' sorta guy, Bascombe. So we been told, anyway."

"Mind getting your hand off my arm?"

"Sure, Bascombe," the fetid one replied in a harsh voice.

Fresh blood ran into Carver's arm when the man let go; the arm tingled; and he had to force himself not to rub at it.

"Balsanek," the foul-breathed man said, pointing to the man with protruding oversize incisors.

"And he's Krieb," the man named Balsanek said.

The restaurant catered to the many blue-collar workers in the area. At the counter were bulky men in work-stained coats, oily gloves jammed into their back pockets. Several booths were still empty; noontime was about a half hour away. Krieb motioned to an empty booth, next to a plate-glass window. The view of Potrero Avenue was just magnificent—all kinds of trucks and buses and cars, and several run-down service stations on opposite corners. A three-legged dog limped past. Terrific scene.

Carver slid into the booth, and Krieb and Balsanek sat opposite.

"Well, guys," Carver said, "I guess you wanted to talk to me about something?"

"Yeah," Krieb said, squirming his bulky body to get a good seating posture.

"That is correct," Balsanek added. He sat upright, while his partner hunched over the table. "We must talk, and we shall do that as we eat."

"Yeah, we're on a expense account," Krieb said. "We coulda ate in some fancy joint, like the Fairmont or somethin', but we hadda grab you when we could."

"Yes, Mr. Bascombe, you exited the ballet theater very fast," Balsanek said, "and we didn't think detaining you in the art gallery was advisable. We had to take you as the situation warranted."

"That's what I said, Balsanek," Krieb said.

Obviously they weren't going to talk until they had

ordered. Krieb favored the T-bone steak and potatoes, with soup and salad, and he'd see about dessert afterward. Balsanek, the thinner man, ordered a tuna salad and a chocolate milkshake, real thick.

"And make it with chocolate milk," he told the waitress, "and chocolate ice cream and chocolate syrup."

Carver ordered a cup of coffee.

"You oughta eat somethin'," Krieb said, "you're too thin for your own good. Even though I could tell you got a strong arm. I don't think I'd like to take you on, macho-like one on one, as the greasers say."

Carver said nothing, but recoiled slightly at Krieb's breath.

"So what's it about?" Carver asked.

"What do you think it's about?" Balsanek replied.

"I could take a chance with a wild guess, but I think you'll tell me when you're ready."

"Smart," Krieb said. "We were told you were smart." He picked up the fork in front of him and inspected it. He inspected the knife and spoon and called the watiress. "Lady, this fork is dirty, see that bit of egg, prob'ly left over from someone's breakfast and the dishwasher didn' get it off. Get me a clean one."

The waitress threw him a tired look, but took the fork and began to walk away.

Krieb reached out and took her arm. "Tell you what, lady, bring me a clean set of utensils, a knife and a spoon. Okay? Sure, go on." He gave her the other pieces, and then turned to Carver. "One thing I can't stand is dirty silverware."

The waitress returned with Carver's coffee and a new set of implements. Krieb checked the pieces and was satisfied. They waited. Carver drank a mouthful of coffee, Balsanek cleaned his fingernails, and Krieb sucked air between his teeth. Finally the waitress brought their orders.

The two men ate, and Carver drank his coffee. Whatever it was these guys wanted, they didn't want to bust up Carver. He figured they were the types that wouldn't worry too much if they had been ordered to break both legs or put a bullet into each kneecap. Patellacide.

As Kireb mopped the last of the gravy with a mangled piece of wheat bread, he looked at his partner and nudged him.

"Yeah, Bascombe," Krieb said, "now we talk."

"I've been ready for hours."

"Don't be such a . . . yeah, you really are a wiseass."

"It's like this," Balsanek interrupted. "We want you to do a job for us."

"For you?" Carver said, allowing a small bit of absurdity to taint the two words. "Really? Honest and true?"

"Gee and shit," Krieb said. "A wiseass."

"Oh my, a sagacious rectum," Balsanek said. He stared at Carver. "Just listen and remain quiet. It's about Meaghler."

"He owed a certain someone a lot of bread," Krieb said.

"You can't collect from a dead man," Carver said.

"Shut up," Krieb said. "We know that. We want you to find out who offed him."

"Me?"

"You, Bascombe. We can't go to the cops, can we? Besides, if they find the killer, then he's in jail where we can't get to him."

"It's for our image," Balsanek said. "We don't want our customers to think we go around killing people just because they owe us money. Why, that'd be crazy! What are we, some species of abnormal animals from television cops-and-robbers shows?"

"I'm going to take the fifth," Carver said.

Balsanek snickered.

"So here's the deal," Krieb said, wiping his mouth of the remains of his lunch. "You find out the killer, and then you report to us."

"The police have a good chance to get him."

"Fair enough. But we want you to keep us informed. Each and every step of the way. And when you get him, or when you know the cops know who he is, then you let us know. We'll take it from there."

"You know I can't do that."

"No," Balsanek said. "We know you *shouldn't*. A different thing altogether. You're a lawyer, even though you don't practice. So you know there's a lot of stuff you shouldn't do. But that's not the point. You *can* do it. Maybe you shouldn't, but you can do it. I think you're a person who can do anything if you want to do it badly enough."

The waitress stepped over, writing the bill on a pad.

"You're going to kill the guy," Carver said flatly.

The waitress looked startled for a moment as she put the bill on the table.

"Maybe," Krieb said. He winked at the waitress, who had backed up a step. "We're TV writers, an' we're talking about a plot." He faced Carver, waggling his fingers in some kind of big-time-producer parody. "So the guy is trapped, so we don't know how to get him outta the trap. He's a bad guy, so maybe we should kill him off. What do you think?"

The waitress gave them a nervous grin and left to stand near the cash register. Krieb grinned, and Balsanek cocked his head at Carver.

"I think you two guys are nuts, and you can tell Molerath I said so."

"Oh, we don't know about that," Krieb said. "And like Balsanek said—what's a 'molerath'?"

The two men slid out of the booth. Balsanek left the tip and paid at the register. Carver remained sitting, drinking the last drops of coffee. He watched as the two men left the luncheonette and walked out of sight around the corner. He followed and saw them get into a late-model dark sedan. He jotted the license number into his pad. More for insurance than anything else. Carver was certain he'd see the two men again.

He returned to Burck's apartment.

Mike Tettsui opened the door. "Meaghler's sister is here," he said.

"How's Burck?"

"About the same. Still in shock. Hasn't eaten much."

Carver nodded and saw a woman coming from the guest bedroom. Tettsui introduced Carole Asquith. Mrs. Asquith was several years older than her brother. Carver guessed she was a couple of years short of forty. Not a bad-looking woman either. Whoever Mr. Asquith was, he apparently had an eye for beauty. Mrs. Asquith wore a dark business suit, which made her look like some kind of female politician competing in a man's world. Dress for success, Mrs. Asquith!

Pushing her luxuriant dark brown hair into place, she shook hands with Carver. Unlike her brother, Carole Asquith did not engage in lengthy conversations or meandering monologues.

They sat in the front room, where she ignored the view.

"The funeral arrangements have been made," Carole Asquith said, her voice a pleasant soprano. "Tomorrow afternoon. I don't know how many of his friends will be at the funeral. I haven't seen much of Bart in the last few years."

"I'm sure there'll be a lot of people there," Mike Tettsui said.

She nodded, with some reluctance. Carver guessed that her brother's homosexuality had been an uncomfortable fact of life with his family.

"I didn't know your brother very well," Carver said. "And I don't know much about his family." He hoped his prompting her might lead to more information about Joel Burck, but it was a long shot.

Carole Asquith talked in short sentences, with many long pauses between. Since becoming an adult and coming out of his own closet, few of Bart Meaghler's friends had ever met his parents. Even Joel Burck had never met Meaghler's parents. Carole and her husband, Lawrence, had met Joel, but Larry had a difficult time accepting his brother-in-law and his male lover.

She went on in this vein, saying little about any of her brother's virtues. She thought he seemed a relatively happy man, although he drank too much, and was a success in the travel agency business.

She finally had nothing more to say, her grief a black sponge soaking in her depression. In answer to Carver's question, she told the two private investigators that she was staying at a hotel a half block from Hallidie Plaza, close to the cable car turntable.

"I'm staying the night here," Carver told Tettsui.

Tettsui grinned and said the couch was really very comfortable. He'd be back in the morning. They'd all attend the funeral the next afternoon. Tettsui offered to drive Carole Asquith to her hotel. She accepted, and the two of them left the apartment.

From a hall closet, Carver selected several blankets and a couple of pillows. He dropped the bedding on the couch. He turned off most of the lights and then went into the kitchen and poked around. He was hungry, realizing he hadn't eaten anything since breakfast.

The refrigerator and freezer were well stocked, and the cabinets bulged with canned and packaged goods. No starving here. Carver went to Burck's closed bedroom door and knocked.

"Come in," Burck's voice said.

"Are you hungry?" Carver asked when he stepped in.

Burck was sitting in bed, the counterpane littered with books and magazines and several sheets of paper and envelopes. The young dancer was pale, his pale brown hair neatly combed. His eyes were still puffy, but that was expected. He seemed in control, and Carver sensed a lack of tension in Burck, as though an ashen fog had evaporated.

"Yes, Carver, I could eat something. I feel up to it."

"How about a steak? Baked potato and some vegetables?"

"Yes, that would be all right."

"You want it in here?" Carver asked, indicating the bedside table.

"Yes, please. And Carver . . ."

"Yeah, Joel?"

"There are some matters I wish to discuss with you. Very soon."

"Is it about the killer?"

"No, not really."

"Okay, then it can wait. Whenever you're ready."

Carver returned to the kitchen and took several sirloin steaks out of the freezer. In a short while the other items were baking. Looking at Burck's music collection, he selected several records and put Delibes's *Sylvia Suite* on the Bang & Olufsen turntable.

Building a nest of kindling in the fireplace, Carver put a small oak log on top and lit the kindling. He sat at the windows and watched the sky darken, listening to the music.

When the steaks were finished under the broiler, he brought a tray into Burck's bedroom. Carver ate at the dinner table. The stake was fine, medium rare. He was a helluva cook.

He flipped through his notes and compared the whereabouts of various members of the ballet company at Moseby's party with those at Eric Hudson's party the night before. Yeah, he was narrowing it down. There weren't that many. Carver went back several pages and compared his own recollection of who was where at Moseby's.

He hadn't noted anyone leaving, but that meant little. There were those exits out of Moseby's apartment: one exit out of Myron's bedroom, and another from the kitchen pantry, which was a tiny elevator to bring groceries and such.

And of course, there was the fire escape. Which recalled Deborah Canby on the terrace. Carver thought about that incident. Was there a possibility that she had seen someone go down the fire escape? Or was there a possibility she was there as a lookout, and used the bulimia idea as a cover? He wanted to talk to Deborah Canby.

SEVENTEEN

Mike Tettsui arrived promptly the next morning. Carver whipped up scrambled eggs and set out breakfast for three.

"You seem better this morning," Tettsui said to Burck.

"Yes, I'm much improved. I've had a great deal to think about, and I have come to some decisions. I think they are important decisions, but time will be the judge."

"Anything you want to talk about?" Tettsui asked, aiming his question first at Burck and then looking at Carver.

Carver shook his head and remained silent.

"I'm going to the theater," Carver announced as he finished his meal.

Tettsui would stay with Burck, as he had yesterday. The dancer seemed at peace with himself; a small smile played at the corners of his mouth. Had the Great Answer to Life come to Burck in a dream? Hardly likely, thought Carver as he let himself out the door.

Again he was conscious of the posters on the telephone poles advertising the premiere of the new ballet. Their proclaimed date seemed to batter at Carver. The date was two nights away. Would Burck be alive to dance in Visikov's new ballet? Could Carver keep him alive?

Once again the guard recognized Carver.

"There's no one inside," the guard said. "No rehearsing in the theater today."

"Where are they?" Carver asked.

"Mr. Swaine wanted the dancers to practice at the rehearsal hall. Around the corner, in the old Victorian. The stage crew is breaking down the sets and flats. Getting ready to ship them over to Alcatraz."

"Is Vassily Visikov still inside?"

"Yeah, Mr. Bascombe. In his office, probably. Upstairs."

Carver thanked the man and went inside. On the curved mezzanine he heard music from behind a door. He opened the door.

Vassily Visikov was seated in a recliner chair, one arm thrown over his eyes. Benjamin, the spectacularly muscled young man who pushed the wheelchair, sat nearby in a straight-backed chair. In opposite corners, a set of JBL speakers filled the room with music from John Guiterez's ballet score.

Benjamin reached over and tapped Visikov's foot.

"We got a visitor, Mr. V," Benjamin said.

Visikov shook his head, moving his right hand in time with the music. Benjamin looked at Carver and shook his head. Carver understood the gesture: he had to wait until the music ended.

Carver went to the stereo set and lifted the needle. No time for niceties. He turned to face Visikov.

"Why did you do that " Visikov asked brusquely.

"You want me to throw him out?" Benjamin asked.

"No, Benjamin," the crippled choreographer said. "I don't wish violence to intrude on my creativity."

"I haven't had a chance to talk with you," Carver said.

"Talk with me?" Visikov asked, genuinely puzzled. "I understand that you are not the journalist you once proclaimed. That you are, if the newspapers are to be believed, a private investigator. What could you possibly want from me?"

"The police are chasing down the wrong street."

"I still do not understand. You have no official capacity in the investigation of that unfortunate man's death."

"What I want to talk about, Mr. Visikov, must be for you only."

"I see," Visikov said. He rubbed a hand over his unshaven cheek. He turned to Benjamin. "I think I will take a chance on Mr. Bascombe."

"I don't think it's so good an idea, Mr. V."

"I'm sure it will be all right. Put me in my chair, Benjamin, please—and then you may leave us in private."

Benjamin nodded and lifted the choreographer out of the recliner and into the wheelchair. The motions seemed effortless. Then Benjamin went, reluctantly, pausing at the door. He clamped his teeth, forcing himself to remain silent. He stared at Carver. A dangerous man. Benjamin closed the door solidly behind him.

"Go ahead, Mr. Bascombe," Visikov said, "ask your questions."

"I understand that you were not at Eric Hudson's party . . . and not at Moseby's."

"Yes, that is correct."

"Why not?"

"Surely it is obvious."

"I'll tell you what's really obvious. That guy, Benjamin, can pick you up like a pillow and carry you anywhere. You could attend any party you might be invited to, and it wouldn't matter if Benjamin had to carry you up twenty flights of stairs. He'd be glad to do it. But Eric Hudson's party was at a single-story house on Twin Peaks. And Moseby has an elevator. So why didn't you go?"

"I—"

"Why not, Mr. stuck-in-your-wheelchair Visikov? Why the fuck not!"

"How dare you! What do you think you are?"

"A worried-sick man. Two men are dead."

"Two? What do you mean?"

"Two men have been murdered. One guy that worked in Burck's building, and Bart Meaghler, Burck's lover."

"I'm afraid I don't see the connection, Mr. Bascombe."

"I'm going to level with you. First, how important is Burck to your ballet?"

145

"He is very important. Of course there are other men in the company who could dance my ballet, but there is something about Joel Burck, some wonderful charisma that he occasionally projects when he dances. He is the best in the company to perform my ballet. He is the premiere male dancer—as far as I am concerned. And he could be greater yet. Not many dancers have had this persona. Yes, only a handful in history. Nureyev. Baryshnikov. Nijinsky."

" 'Nijinsky is dead,' Burck said to me recently."

"Yes, he would say that," Visikov said softly. "Of course."

"Yeah. And *he* wants to stay alive. And I think you're the only one who doesn't have a good motive to want Burck dead."

"What! Burck dead? I don't understand what you are saying."

"The story goes like this," Carver replied, and proceeded to take several minutes to explain the "accidents" and the attempts on Burck's life. He related Burck's hiring him. Then Carver gave his reasons for narrowing his suspects to only four or five.

Vassily Visikov was clearly shocked and angered. "But you do not suspect me?" he said.

"No, I don't. And not Benjamin. For the same reason I don't suspect the musicians. They have nothing to gain. A dancer's death can only benefit another dancer. Or the directors who are against Bob Swaine. I could be wrong, of course."

"There is the possibility that someone has a neurotic homicidal complex against the homosexual element. Thus Meaghler, and Burck."

"I'd thought of that. But if that were the case, then the killer would have had better chances against a dozen of the male dancers, and several of the lesbians."

"Yes, I see your point. And why would the killer strike only those in the ballet. Homosexuals are all over this city."

"You've got it. The killer has to be someone in the

Golden Gate Ballet Company. It's too concentrated around Burck.''

"But I could have a grudge against Burck.''

"Even if you did, you'd have to rely on Benjamin to do your dirty work. Your wheelchair would be conspicuous if you tried to do these things by yourself.''

"I see,'' Visikov said, rubbing his chin. "So where does that leave us? With your suspicions and no proof.''

"I need an ally in the company. I need someone who can keep his eyes open. I need someone above suspicion. Because I need to lay a trap.''

"Ah, now you interest me. You want to plan the moves, like the schematics in a ballet?''

"Something like that. I want to force the killer's hand. And I want him trapped, with no way out. And a good place would be—''

"On Alcatraz!'' Visikov exclaimed. "Of course. Brilliant! There is no way for the killer to escape. Once on the island, he could only swim or take a boat.''

"And you can help me.''

"You are a most intriguing person, Mr. Bascombe.''

"Call me Carver.''

"I shall need Benjamin. Would that be all right? He is my right hand, like a son.''

Carver went to the door and signaled Benjamin to come in. Vassily Visikov related Carver's story, and what was needed.

"The problem, Benjamin,'' Carver said when Visikov had finished, "is that I can't be everywhere at once.''

"Yes, I get it,'' Benjamin said. "So you want me and Mr. V to be your seeing eyes?''

"Just watch. Watch everyone. Anything out of the ordinary. And thanks to both of you.''

He went down the curving, plush carpeted staircase and crossed the lobby. He became aware that someone had stepped in behind him. Benjamin? Carver began to turn— and a fist slammed into his neck. Another punch to his kidneys. He felt himself fall, and then he was suspended in air. He felt as if he were cargo floating in a gantry net.

Carver was dragged into the darkened auditorium. He opened his eyes, dimly aware of seeing the carpet passing beneath him. He felt as though his head had connected with a brick. Or a brick had connected with it. Or something. Anyway it hurt.

They held him by the armpits, one on each side. Carver figured that out. Good. Swell. Fine. He wasn't unconscious. The powers of reason were not dimmed, nor were they scrambled eggs. Carver shook his head as the two men hauled him onto the stage. They dropped him onto the floor. He heard them step away from him.

The floor felt smooth and cold. He pushed himself to a sitting position.

"Feeling all right, are you?" a voice asked.

EIGHTEEN

Carver looked into the deep shadows of the curtained wings. Don Terman walked onstage—the black dancer who had made a pass at Carver.

"I'm glad my friends didn't hurt you," Terman continued, walking to the middle of the stage, his movements a gliding motion. "I didn't want you bruised even the teensiest bit."

Don Terman had dressed himself in black: tight-fitting slacks, turtleneck sweater as smooth and shiny as sealskin. As he walked, his black-laced shoes clicked metallically. Tap dancer's shoes. With taps.

"Yeah?" Carver said, flinching at the quaver in his voice. He pushed himself into a standing position. "Why not?"

"Oh, because of something you said to me. Do you remember?"

"Yeah, I remember," Carver answered, taking deep breaths.

"You slapped me," Terman said, and rubbed his fingertips up and down the side of his face. "Did you really mean that if you hurt me, I wouldn't dance for weeks?"

"I might have overreacted."

"Oh, I'd say that. But I think of myself as a fair man. I'd like to see if you could hurt me enough. I said you had

149

a good-looking, rough quality. I do wonder if you're really rough. Do we understand one another?''

''Yeah. You want me to work you over.''

Terman laughed. He faced Carver, about six feet away, and bobbed languidly on the balls of his feet.

''I'm not a masochist, Carver,'' he said mockingly. ''If I may call you by your given name? Or would you prefer that we converse on a formal basis?''

Carver turned and looked at the two men who had dragged him into the auditorium. He recognized them as dancers in the company. Which of them had rabbit-punched him? The tall white dancer or the stocky black one?

''Are those two guys going to stay out of it?'' Carver asked Terman.

''I told them it was between you and me. I'd have sent you a proper invitation, but I thought perhaps you might not accept.''

''Right,'' Carver said.

Terman looked at his two friends and told them to stay out of it.

''Of course, Donny,'' the tall one said. ''We're the watchmen.''

Terman nodded and went up on his toes. Oddly menacing.

Carver stepped back, legs apart, his hands at his side. Waiting. Terman moved lightly forward, a fast *glissade*, arms *en bas,* then whipped a leg at Carver's hip. Carver rolled away from the attack, drifted quickly into a spraddle-legged stance, his head erect and centered over his body. The next kick hit him hard in the upper arm.

He hadn't even seen it.

Carver ignored the paralyzing pain and moved back, one leg stretched behind him, ready to block. Fat lot of good it did; Terman hit him in the chest with the ball of his foot. Another kick knocked Carver to one knee. Breathing hard, Carver twisted around, his fists raised in the classic X-shape, his left arm in front of the right.

He blinked his eyes and saw a blur of motion.

Damn! Terman was fast, and fought with his feet. Carver

recognized the technique. Savate! Yeah, a dancer might learn to use that French kick-boxing style very well.

Pretty stars! And emerald lightning bolts behind his eyes! Carver rolled, feeling the unyielding floor under him. Yeah, he was on the floor. Good place to be. All he had to do was stay there and he wouldn't be kicked.

Forcing himself, Carver got up, went into a hunched-over stance, and studied Terman's eyes. Shifty black bastard. Carver was ready for it.

Terman flicked a leg, a feint, Carver saw his eyes move, and he moved out of range of the other foot. Use the vision of the sphere, he commanded himself. Terman snapped another front-jab kick. Carver blocked it with a move of his right hand, caught a fold of cloth in his fingers, and let the movement carry Terman away. He smashed his other fist into Terman's exposed groin. Then stepped back fast, into a neutral stance.

Hey, not bad for a guy over thirty. Against a very physically fit twenty-five-year-old. Press the attack.

Out of the neutral position he moved swiftly. He brought the imaginary sphere of attack movements into the air space occupied by Terman. One-two! Simultaneous jabs into Terman's chest and a spear thrust into the man's back.

Carver deliberately held his punches back. He didn't want Terman so injured that he couldn't dance. Another set of punches, each in a brief arc of movement. Damn, one hand went into thin air. Couldn't get it right every time. Terman was fast.

Terman moved back, shaking his head. The dancer had difficulty breathing. Carver's spear thrust with outstretched fingers had bruised his neck; his throat felt like someone had poured acid into it.

More moves, and Carver caught most of them on his forearms. A low block. A right inside scooping block. Terman's legs flew at Carver's face and flailed at air. Carver jiggled and jangled, first to one side, then other. Always looking for the perfect opportunity to hammer Terman down.

Terman moved as Carver feinted, drawing the dancer in, and went into a high front kick. Carver saw Terman's knee go up and realized his own hip was exposed. He ejected his breath forcibly, causing his ribs to close tight as a shield for his kidneys. Swiftly he moved in at the dancer—and Terman's kick slid by.

Bad move! By Terman. Carver whipped both hands out simultaneously and punched both sides of Terman's rib cage. The dancer's leg movement carried him around and he fell to the floor. Terman gasped for breath, holding his side.

Carver moved back fast, pivoted on one foot, and faced the two dancers who had carried him. Just in case they wanted a fraction of the action.

"Stop this!" a woman's voice screamed. "Stop it!"

Carver peered into the dimness of the auditorium. Two figures came running down the aisle and vaulted onto the stage. They were Joyce Kittering and John Guiterez. She was in street clothes, a warm cinnamon skirt and pleated ivory blouse. The composer wore slacks and a very expensive iceberg-blue cashmere sweater.

"What the hell are you doing?" Joyce demanded.

She stood with hands on hips, her chin jutting defiantly. Did she really expect someone to sock her on the chin, Carver wondered.

"Settling an overdue account," Carver replied.

He walked offstage into the wings. Joyce and Guiterez went to Don Terman and helped him to his feet. Carver paused at the two dancers flanking him. The taller one shrugged.

"Fair and square, Donny said," the man said. "And I'm afraid that's what he got. Go in peace, brother."

Carver sat in a backstage chair and tried to meditate into rhythmic breathing. He closed his eyes, eliminating everything in his mind, as if he were a garbage truck dumping sewage. Zen and the art of trash ejection.

"Carver, what the hell was that all about?" Joyce asked.

"Donny thought we had a score to settle. His idea, not mine. How about lunch, Joyce?"

"No, Carver, not now. Perhaps later," she said, probably sensing the disappointment in Carver. "John and I just came in to pick up some clothing. We're on the way to the cemetery.''

''Why? Meaghler wasn't your friend.''

''Because,'' John Guiterez said, stepping into the scene, ''Joel asked us. I suppose he was afraid there wouldn't be too many people at the grave.''

''John, I think it's more likely that Joel needs friends around,'' Joyce said. She looked at Carver. ''Are you going?''

''Yes, I am,'' Carver said.

Don Terman and his two friends walked backstage. Terman breathed raggedly, glowering at Carver—then a thin smile flickered briefly over his face. He nodded at Carver and gave him a slow wink. Terman put his arm around the tall white dancer, and the three men headed for the stage exit doors.

With narrowed eyes, Joyce looked at Carver, studying him for a brief moment. She turned to John Guiterez.

''John, would you mind getting my gear? It's on my dressing table.''

''Sure, Joyce, I'll be glad to,'' Guiterez said, and walked toward the elevator.

''I want to see you later,'' Joyce said to Carver. ''I think it's important.''

''Then tell me now.''

''No. I guess I still don't trust you. We'll talk after the service at the cemetery. Would that be all right? I need someone to give me advice.''

Carver nodded and kept silent. He sensed Joyce was very agitated and trying to remain composed. Not doing too good a job, he thought. She wanted to wait, then he'd wait.

John Guiterez returned, burdened with parcels. Joyce thanked Carver, and she and Guiterez left by the same backstage exit used by Terman and his friends. Carver sighed and remained sitting, going over several points that had been bumping and colliding in pockets of his mind.

He finally stood and moved backstage, further into the darkness. He remembered seeing a first-aid box on the wall. He found it and removed bandages and antiseptic. A

153

few yards away he went into the men's lavatory. He wrinkled his nose at the odor of sweat and urine and clogged drains.

At one of the sinks, Carver took off his coat and then his shirt. Another custom shirt ruined. Blood had seeped into the fabric from his shoulder and his chest. Carver washed the blood from his bruised torso, and then covered the scraped areas with thin bandages.

The door to the lavatory opened and Carver turned. No one else was supposed to be backstage. He caught a whiff of something rotten. Cabbage?

"Pretty good stuff there, Bascombe," a familiar voice said.

"Thanks, Balsanek," Carver said, shrugging into his jacket.

"I'm Krieb," he said. "He's Balsanek."

"Yeah, I forgot," Carver said.

"Bullshit," Krieb said, his breath making Carver wince. "You just like to mess around with us."

"Yeah."

"Are you all right?" Balsanek asked.

"Sure. You saw the fight."

"We saw it."

"You didn't want to stop it?"

"Nah," Krieb said. "You were doing just fine. We're just keeping tabs on you. We don't like to interfere with other people's fun."

"He could've kicked the shit out of me. Would Mr. Molerath have liked that?"

"Ah, well," Balsanek said, "if you were in jeopardy then we might've interfered. Although I doubt if . . . anyway, what's a 'molerath'?"

Krieb laughed, and Carver gritted his teeth.

Carver maneuvered past the two men. "You two can stay," he said airily. "The men's room suits you."

"Very jocose," Balsanek said. "Very like a clown. Just keep looking over your shoulder. We'll be around."

NINETEEN

A warm wind ruffled the leaves scattered over the cemetery. The sky was a gemstone blue. Clouds were almost motionless, gliding slowly and serenely, like albino stoics.

A lovely day in Colma, city of monument carvers and cemeteries.

Green shadows and 24-karat sunlight shafts lay across the grassy knolls. The soft breeze carried the muted mutterings of a minister at the head of a casket. A soft sweet fragrance drifted from a large bouquet of flowers adorning much of the casket.

About two dozen people were clustered around the casket. Meaghler's sister, Carole Asquith, stood with her head bowed, the hem of her black dress blowing slightly in the warm breeze.

Next to her, Joel Burck stared ahead. A group of gay men, friends of Bart Meaghler's and Burck's, stood apart gazing at the flower-bedecked coffin. Among them were Myron Moseby and Leroy Dolny. The youthful minister read from the Bible.

A distance away, Carver Bascombe stood in the sunlight near an oak tree. He had changed into a dark gray three-piece suit, with a light gray shirt and a somber tie. Carver couldn't hear the minister's words, but had attended enough funerals to guess the contents. Ashes to ashes, dust to . . .

that sort of thing. Yeah, everybody has to go. What was the old gag? No one gets out alive.

Over one hundred yards away, beyond myriad granite crosses and tombstones, stood two men. Carver had noticed them several minutes ago. He rubbed his chin, then walked slowly to his car in the nearby parking lot. After checking the anti-theft alarm, he opened the trunk.

Several cars away Mike Tettsui stepped out of his station wagon. He walked over to Carver. They nodded wordlessly to each other; Carver had found what he wanted and moved into the shade of the nearest tree.

After leaving the ballet theater, Carver had returned to his office and changed clothes. He had brought Rose Weinbaum up to date. She informed him there had been nothing new in the past history of Joel Burck; Carver told her to keep at it. Then at Burck's apartment he had related to Mike Tettsui the incidents concerning Terman, and the two thugs, Balsanek and Krieb. Mike Tettsui had followed Carver and Joel Burck to the cemetery.

"Think that's them?" Tettsui asked.

"Um," Carver grunted.

He leveled a small pair of prism binoculars to his eyes. "Uh-hunh. He'd thought so. Balsanek and Krieb. What were they doing at the cemetery? What the hell did they want? Keeping tabs on Carver?

"That's them," Carver said.

"What the hell do they want?" Tettsui asked.

The words sounded like echoes to Carver. He handed the binoculars to Tettsui.

"I've seen better gorillas on a *National Geographic* TV show," Tettsui muttered as he studied Balsanek and Krieb.

The minister had completed his words, and several of the crowd began to walk away. Joel Burck and Carole Asquith remained at the site. Joyce Kittering detached herself from the crowd, made a friendly see-you-later gesture toward John Guiterez and Bob Swaine, and began walking toward the parking lot. She angled toward Carver Bascombe and Tettsui.

Carver lowered the glasses when he saw her. She kept

coming, and finally stopped facing him. Her hair caught the sunlight, creating a ruby halo.

Carver said hello, and Joyce said hello. Tettsui said hello, and then walked back to his station wagon, leaving the two of them alone.

"Carver, I've changed my mind about listening to you," she said. "I just felt that I haven't been fair. I apologize for mouthing off like I did. I guess I was still in shock. And I guess I was scared, too." She turned away, her hair ruffled softly by a gentle wind. A warm caress. "Seeing Bart Meaghler like that in his car . . . all that blood." She shuddered and faced Carver. "Now I'd like to hear you out."

"Right. Let's walk to your car, but I have to keep an eye on Joel."

"Why."

"That's one of my reasons. Burck hired me as a bodyguard."

"Oh? Why?" she asked. Her brows crinkled in thought. "It couldn't have been because of Meaghler. You were at the theater before that."

"Several attempts have been made on Burck's life, Joyce. They were made to look like accidents—but they weren't. And two men have been murdered."

"Two?"

"Meaghler was the second."

"My God!" Joyce said, her eyes widening. "What are the police doing about it?"

"They think the two are unrelated. Two different, isolated cases."

Joyce and Carver stood next to her car, a two-door sport sedan.

"All right, Carver," she said, "I've heard that you've been making comparisons. Timetables and that sort of thing, where— "

"Who told you that?"

"I heard it from Merkhinn's secretary. Marcia is a friend of mine."

"Damn!" Carver said bitterly. "How did she find out?"

157

"There's an intercom in Visikov's office. Merkhinn gave her standing orders to leave it open. Marcia told me he likes to know what's going on everywhere in the company. Merkhinn is a nosy bastard, and we think he has a lot of the offices bugged."

"Damn it!"

"He thinks he's some kind of a spider, weaving a web. It's all part of his idea to get Bob Swaine out of the ballet company. Anyway, about your timetable chart, where everyone was supposed to be at the party. I'd like to see it."

"I don't think that's a good idea, Joyce."

What was the use, he thought, since there wasn't conclusive evidence that pointed to one person?

"I might . . . have something that might help you protect Joel. But only if I see how you've worked it out."

Carver nibbled at a knuckle.

"You've been trying to get me to have dinner with you," she said. A faint kindliness came—and went. "Let's meet somewhere."

"Fine," Carver said, smiling inside.

"All right," Joyce said, and laughed.

They agreed to meet at a popular restaurant in North Beach. The United States Cafe.

"I'll follow you into town," Carver said.

Joyce thanked him and got into her car. Carver got Tettsui's attention and pointed to Joel Burck. Message understood: Tettsui was to drive Burck back to the apartment. Carver climbed into his Jaguar and followed Joyce out of the cemetery grounds.

Other mourners got into their cars. Carver saw Joel Burck get into Tettsui's station wagon along with Carole Asquith. He was momentarily separated from Joyce by a car driven by John Polivitch; the composer seemed intent on getting somewhere in a hurry. Carver pressed the accelerator and was soon behind Joyce Kittering again.

She took the scenic route, up Guadalupe Canyon Parkway. Carver followed as Joyce drove her car along the twisty road at high speed. The sport sedan swooped around the curves, often straddling the center line. Carver shook his head at her erratic driving. What the hell was Joyce trying to do?

He drove in his usual expert manner, wheel held at arm's length, listening to the engine's revs, ready to drop the transmission into a higher or lower gear. He kept a close eye on the car ahead.

Guadalupe Canyon Parkway snaked over the top of San Bruno Mountain. Beyond the metal guardrails were steep drops into rock-strewn ravines.

Joyce's car skidded across the center line, the car's rear end threatening to swap places with the front. Carver clamped his teeth together; she was in trouble. He stepped on the gas and tried to pull alongside.

He could see her now, peering frantically over her shoulder, to see if he was still following, Carver guessed. Her eyes were wide, white, and her mouth was open. Joyce ducked her head, apparently trying to get the car into a lower gear. Her hands whipped at the steering wheel, which seemed to have a life of its own. Or was Carver exaggerating her actions in his mind?

No. The car ahead went straight for the guardrail on the opposite side. Something was wrong with her steering! Damn it, Joyce, get your brakes on, Carver commanded silently, and futilely. Pull the emergency! Throw off the ignition switch! Anything! Get that damned car stopped.

The car hit the guardrail, with metal screaming and sparking in the daylight. Carver winced at the sound. He saw Joyce struggle with the wheel, and the car swung madly back, fishtailing and sliding. He tried to get around her. If he moved fast enough, maybe, just maybe he could get ahead of her and let her connect with his rear bumper. Then maybe he could use his own brakes to slow both cars. Worth a chance.

Carver stomped on the accelerator, gauged his distance carefully, aware that the wildly careening car ahead could suddenly smash into him. He moved alongside Joyce; he saw her ashen face, the white spots of fear on her knuckles.

Then another car came around a curve. Straight at him.

Carver slammed on his brakes and jerked back behind Joyce's car as the oncoming vehicle roared past.

No good. He had to try again. Had to try on the right side. Carefully he sped up . . . and was frozen at the sight of the next curve. Joyce's car slithering over the center line. Moving across the oncoming lane of traffic. Joyce fighting to keep the steering wheel to respond.

He saw it happen. The sport sedan slid broadside in the wrong lane. Then a tire burst. The sedan flipped over. And over. A tire tore loose. Sailing in the air. Was it Carver's imagination, or did he hear a terrifying scream?

Later he wasn't sure; it seemed impossible that he heard anything over the screech of metal, the pounding chassis against the asphalt road, the rending of the guardrail.

He stomped on the brakes. Out of the corner of his eye he saw Joyce's car disappear over the edge into a rocky canyon. The Jaguar slammed to a stop. He jumped out and ran to the guardrail—as a dense gray cloud of smoke billowed up from the canyon.

He slid down the steep shale incline, gasping for breath. God! Look at that! The car was upside down at the bottom. The top crumpled, windows shattered, one door twisted open. Flames licking out from the engine. Smoke! Damn! Damn! Give him the strength and the speed and the time!

The flames licked at the grease around the motor block, and then the car burst into fire.

TWENTY

County firemen rolled up the canvas hoses and stored them in the red fire trucks. One of the firemen nudged his friend and nodded at the disheveled black man sitting disconsolately on the broken guardrail.

"Heard he saw the whole thing," the fireman said. "Friend of his."

"Yeah?" his partner said. "Thought the woman was white."

"She was—but who could tell after all that."

They looked at the charred vehicle, all twisted steel and iron and plastic. Joyce's car had been hoisted onto a low flatbed truck. Blobs of fire-foam dropped off the contorted, blackened body onto the roadway. The firemen continued reeling the hose.

For over a hundred yards, dozens of burned-out highway flares marked the asphalt with ashen spots. Using red flags and bright flashlights, uniformed county sheriffs kept the traffic moving. Parked close together in the center of the chaos were sheriffs' cars, a car from the arson detail, other fire trucks, and a fire marshal's sedan.

An ambulance and the Medical Examiner's car were parked at the broken guardrail. Two attendants leaned against the ambulance, smoking cigarettes; their work was done.

The man from the arson squad walked away from Carver; bad news wasn't easy to digest. The deliberate tampering with the woman's car was obvious; it didn't take a trained investigator to see the cut brake lines, the tampered steering mechanism.

The county Medical Examiner walked over to Carver Bascombe.

"I'm sorry," the ME said.

Carver nodded. He was numb, didn't know what else to do; a nod seemed as bad a response as a scream or a furious outpouring of curses.

"Are you going to notify her parents? or . . . ?"

"I didn't know her family," Carver said huskily. "The police can take care of that."

"Well . . ." the ME said, not knowing what else to say.

Carver guessed she was about fifty, and though she may have seen many violent deaths she still had not become cynical and blasé.

"She had friends where she worked," Carver said. "I'll tell them about it."

Death diminished him. John Donne said it. Was it true? Or . . .

"Sorry," the ME said again, and put her hands on Carver's shoulder.

Perhaps death did diminish him. Tens of thousands of people in the world—God knows how many—died every day. Carver didn't exactly feel diminished by all that. Or did he? Was that the reality? Many deaths diminishing the living? Until they too died, diminishing others.

The ME and Carver remained at the guardrail for a time, staring down at the canyon and the fire-blackened rocks.

"What do we do now, Krieb?" Balsanek asked.

Krieb shook his head. He didn't know. What the hell, they were behind Bascombe when the dame's car went out of control. Went over the cliff. Shit, what a mess.

The two men were back about half a mile, their car parked off the shoulder, out of sight of Carver, the firemen, and the police. Especially the police. Balsanek had a pair of field binoculars and watched the action down the road.

"He's moving," Balsanek said. "Bascombe. Getting in his car."

"Okay," Krieb replied, stifling a yawn. "Let's go."

They got in their sedan and followed Carver, maintaining a respectable distance behind. They tailed him all the way to Russian Hill, and parked a block away from Burck's apartment building.

Carver pulled on the parking brake, checked the burglar alarm, and headed for the apartment building entrance. He noted without interest Tettsui's station wagon parked across the street.

As he rode the elevator, he forced himself to snap out of his funk. Come on, he'd seen death before. Sure. It's always a lovely sight, he thought sardonically. One second, a human being, living, breathing, then seconds later just a bundle of chemicals and tissue. God, he was morbid.

Damn it, he had a right to be morbid. One more death in this case. And it might've been prevented. Oh yeah? How? He was such a smartass, how would he have done that? Seen into the future? How could he guess that someone would saw partyway through the brake's hydraulic lines? Then tamper with the steering column? What was he, some kind of mind reader?

His job was to keep Joel Burck alive. He was doing that just fine. If anyone had tampered with the Jaguar, the alarm would have gone off.

Why kill Joyce Kittering? Carver didn't know. So take a guess! Joyce either knew something, or the killer thought she did. No accident, like with Meaghler. Until he knew different, Carver had to assume Joyce was going to tell him her suspicions, something that might point the finger of guilt.

Anything was possible. Anyway, tampering with her car was deliberate. No doubts there. The arson squad had been quite emphatic about that.

Deep down, squirming with anger and frustration, the animal-thing, the hunter-ferret, the prowling stalker kicked and scratched. Oh, the huntsman reared up. Bristled with mental activity. Every survival sense trembled. Wide were its eyes, polished were its claws, sharp the killing tooth. Carver knew the primeval creature well; a reliable friend that lurked deep.

Carver entered the apartment. Tettsui and Burck had already heard the news on the radio. There was little that Carver could say; he had liked Joyuce, despite the various misunderstandings.

"You want to talk about it?" Tettsui asked Carver.

"Not now."

Joel Burck went to the wet bar and mixed several drinks. His own thoughts were jumbled and sad, his eyes swollen and red. He would miss Bart terribly. But it was over. Nothing he could do. Bart wouldn't come back. Never. Nevernever. He choked back a sob, catching it in his throat.

With trembling hands he brought a drink to Carver, who took it wordlessly. The solitude in the apartment was almost palpable, a depressing, heavy membrane, like the skinned hide of a forest deer. Burck muttered something and went to his bedroom. He closed the door softly.

Mike Tettsui turned on several lamps, and then started a fire in the fireplace.

Carver gazed out the window; he watched the sunlight dim and the early evening shadows lengthen. Was he going to brood for days? Or was he going to dig himself inch by inch out of this pit?

"Come on, Mike," Carver said to Tettsui. His voice was husky, as if he hadn't used it for a time. Carver brought out his attaché case. He spread the contents on the dining room table. "We've got work to do."

"Where do we start."

As Tettsui worked on the fire, Carver told him more about the case, and they discussed the timetables.

Tettsui leaned on the table and looked at the papers.

"Carver, I don't think you can reduce what few facts we have in this case to a few charts. We're dealing with humans, and one of them has a screw loose."

"Yeah," Carver said, and sighed. "You're right. It's what Jimmy Bowman said—we're dealing with a fantastic ego. I've eliminated the musicians and the directors, and most of the dancers—at least in my own mind. Maybe I'm hunch playing."

"Sure you are. But what the hell else can you do? It's just sitting-and-waiting time. This killer is waiting too, and we can't outguess—"

The telephone rang, interrupting Tettsui's words. Carver picked up the phone.

"Carver, this is Rose."

He recognized the throaty, sexy voice, and pantomimed her name to Mike Tettsui.

"What've you got, Rose?" Carver asked.

"It took a bit of doing. Had to call in a few markers, but it's good. That stuff on Meaghler's and Ben Rosada's jail sentences. I'd say Applegate was blowing smoke."

"They weren't in jail?"

"Sure they were, boss—but not at the same time. I'd say there was no way Rosada and Meaghler could have met. Rosada was released two months before Meaghler went in."

"Good work, Rose. I'd say Applegate was playing games, creating tensions, manipulating emotions. Good try, too."

"There's more," Rose said urgently. Her voice became even huskier. "Hang on to your socks."

"Go," Carver said.

"I've found out about Joel Burck. And it's . . . well, just listen. I had a private investigator back east check around. A friend. Irene Papazian. She's damn good. And it's going to cost us."

"Yeah, so?"

"Irene went digging, went deep, around New York, checking vital statistics, birth records, stuff like that. She just called in. Joel Burck—he told you he was twenty-eight?"

"Yeah?"

"Not true. He should be twenty-nine, almost thirty."

"Rose, why would he lie about his age? What difference could one year make?"

"There's more. According to state records, Joel Burck was born twenty-nine years ago, in Bayonne, New Jersey. Fourteen months later, two months after his first birthday, baby Joel contracted scarlet fever— and died."

TWENTY-ONE

Detective Sergeant Arnold Applegate put down the telephone. He cursed under his breath. Damn it. If there was one thing he detested, it was changing directions in a case. Perhaps—no, he couldn't weasel out of this one: Bascombe had been right all along.

He looked at the telephone, wishing he had never picked up the goddamned thing. Another dancer from the Golden Gate Ballet Company—dead. The arson squad had reported that Joyce Kittering's vehicle had been tampered with. Deliberately. Her death was no accident. No doubt about it.

He picked up the report from the motor vehicle traffic detail. He wished he'd never seen this either. The report had arrived a half hour before the telephone report of Joyce Kittering's accident.

Applegate sighed. He reread the report: a black late-model sedan had been found abandoned near Bernal Heights. It's right side had been badly damaged. From the manner in which the scrape marks had been inflicted, the vehicle had been in motion at a high speed at the time of the accident. From the overlay of deep scratches, the car had hit another object several times.

The black sedan had been reported stolen three nights ago, just before midnight. The owner was a Mrs. Jennifer

Ordway, a well-off woman who lived in an expensive apartment on Crestmont Drive, near Buena Vista Heights.

Was this the car that had sideswiped Joel Burck? Applegate wondered why he was being so cautious. Of course it was the car. All the evidence pointed to Burck having told the truth about a car trying to run him off the road.

He had to go by the book. According to the book, one coincidence is negligible; two a detective never ignores. Someone was definitely trying to kill someone in the ballet company.

In all probability Bascombe had been correct; it would appear that Joel Burck was the intended victim. No. Applegate shook his head. No point in hedging. Bascombe was right, and Burck's life was in danger.

Again Applegate cursed; now he'd have to apologize to Bascombe. And to Joel Burck. Fortunately there were procedures for such eventualities. The department wouldn't have much of a black eye from the media. By moving quickly, Applegate could keep tabs on Burck.

And keep tabs on Carver Bascombe.

He picked up the phone and called the traffic detail.

"Bellamy here," the officer at the other end said.

Applegate identified himself and told the officer he was calling to gather more information about the damaged black sedan found on Bernal Heights.

"What about it, Sergeant?" Officer Bellamy asked in a bored manner.

"I want to know why it was just found, why it hadn't been reported sooner."

"These things happen, Sergeant."

"What kind of things, Bellamy?"

"We got a report that the car had been there for a couple of days. A black-and-white cruises that area every day, but they never saw it."

"Why not, may I ask?" Applegate said.

"It was hidden. There's an unpaved road that follows the crest of the east ridge. Lots of trees, pepper trees and weeping willows. Real bushy sort of trees. The car had been driven under one of those trees.''

"I understand.''

"A neighbor had seen it, but they don't talk to the cops much up there. Not since one of the neighbors got arrested for growing an illegal substance in his vegetable patch. Anyway, this neighbor talked with others of his ilk, and finally reported it to us. Mostly they just wanted it towed awy, get it out of the neighborhood. An eyesore, they said.''

"Okay, thanks,'' Applegate said. "I get the picture.''

He stood, shoved some papers into a drawer, and put the black-sedan report into a file folder. He walked across the room to where one of his superiors sat behind a scarred desk. "Lieutenant, got a minute?'' he asked.

The lieutenant looked up. He was a man of medium height, with thinning hair but with a luxuriant bandit mustache.

"Yes, AA,'' he said, one of the few detectives who got away with using Applegate's initials.

"I got a problem with Bascombe.''

"Which Bascombe?''

"Your buddy, Carver,'' Applegate said, and told the details of the case in a few minutes.

"I see,'' the lieutenant said. "What about Ben Rosada? Wasn't there anything there to work with?''

"We looked and looked. We couldn't find a thing. I was already coming to the conclusion that Rosada was linked only to Burck—because of what Bascombe told me. Now I suppose we have to find someone who hired Rosada. But the problem is Bascombe—how do I handle it?''

"You'll find he's not vindictive. He really has an instinct for digging around, getting the goods on badasses. He'll cooperate fully with you.''

The lieutenant took the stolen-sedan report and studied it. He turned and looked at a large map of the city hanging on a wall. He went to it and gazed fixedly at one part of it. Sergeant Applegate followed him.

"Notice something, AA?" The lieutenant asked.

"What's that, Lieutenant?"

"Where the car was heisted, on Crestmont Drive . . . and where it was found?"

"What about it? Those are two different parts of town, miles apart."

"So it would appear. But . . ."

The lieutenant drew a pencil line from Buena Vista Heights to Twin Peaks, where he marked a spot, and then to where the car was found.

"See?" he asked Applegate.

"God. Yes."

To Applegate the name of one possible suspect stood out. At least it was a possibility, a very strong possibility. Killers often make at least one stupid mistake.

"Obviously not conclusive," the lieutenant said, as though he had read Applegate's mind, "but indicative of further investigation."

"Yes, yes it is," Applegate replied enthusiastically. "I'll see Bascombe in the morning. I think Joel Burck should be safe enough until then. He's got Bascombe and Mike Tettsui guarding him."

Applegate stared at the map and the penciled lines. Damn, it was so easy it was embarrassing. And Bascombe had no way of connecting this up. There were several things he had to do.

He called the police laboratory and asked for a complete cleaning of the black sedan, paying particular attention to any fibers and hairs they might collect. He would send down the paperwork for a fiber analysis and hair and folicle analysis within the hour.

"This is going to take time," the lab technician said. "A couple of days anyway. We're backlogged at least that much. Might even take three days."

"Or four?" Applegate said sarcastically. "Or more?"

"Yeah," the technician said.

Applegate itched with frustration. A couple of days! More, maybe! There was nothing he could do, except tell the tech that this was an emergency case.

"Sergeant, that's all we get," the tech said.

Applegate hung up. Okay, so it would take time. At least he could keep his eye on Bascombe and Burck and one possible suspect. One false move and the suspect dancer would get hammered on the spot.

TWENTY-TWO

Carver opened the bedroom door without knocking.

Joel Burck was in the same position: knees up, head down. The music on the stereo was a Bach organ toccata. Burck looked up, his eyes red-rimmed. "Yes, Carver?" he asked.

"For a corpse you look damn good."

"I don't know what you mean," Burck said, his brow knitted.

"I just received some information. You were supposed to be dead twenty-eight years ago. You're buried in New Jersey."

Burck narrowed his eyes and pushed out his thin lips. What he had dreaded had finally occurred. On the other hand, he had already made up his mind to inform the ballet company; surely he should speak truthfully to Carver Bascombe.

He lowered his eyes and breathed heavily. After a moment he looked at Carver. Yes, it was time. "You want answers, then," Burck said.

"Yeah, you're right about that," Carver said.

"Then it is time. You want answers," he said heatedly. "Then that is what you shall have. You will understand. Answers, not tears. You will understand much, and what Bart meant to me."

Burck wiped his eyes with the back of his hands and swung himself off the bed. He hurriedly put on his coat.

"In a brief time you will know much," he said, speaking rapidly, determinedly. "What you do with it is your affair, but tomorrow night, after the benefit premiere, everyone in the ballet company shall know."

"Why not tell me now?" Carver asked.

"I could, but I have made my decision. Allow me my small moment of melodrama. This decision did not come easy. I would like you to respect my wishes."

"You're paying the bills, Joel."

"I thought perhaps we had a better relationship than merely one of employee and employer."

"Yeah," Carver said softly. "There are a lot of questions, and I don't have any answers."

Burck hurriedly packed a set of leotards and several pairs of ballet slippers into an overnight bag. He wiped a handkerchief over a thin film of sweat below his straw-colored hairline.

"I cannot prove it," Burck said, turning to Carver, "but I do not believe that the answers to your questions are related to the attempts on my life."

"Why not let me be the judge of that?"

"Come," he said, grabbing Carver by the arm. "You want answers? Then answers you shall have. Come!"

Burck hustled Carver to the front door. Carver shrugged out of Burck's grasp. He told Mike Tettsui to be bright and early: tomorrow was the big day. The three men left the apartment. Tettsui drove off in his station wagon, and Carver followed Burck's directions to an address several blocks from the Golden Gate Ballet theater.

During the drive, Carver went over the obvious. The paper trip. His client, some six years ago probably, had used a technique known as the paper trip. He had taken the identity of a dead child, a young boy who would have been about Burck's age if he had lived. That child was named Joel Burck. The routine from that point was fairly simple: a request for a birth certificate to the county in the state where the boy had been born; then a passport in

Burck's name, and then a driver's license, using the passport and birth certificate as identification. From then it would be a simple matter of establishing the new identity.

Let's open the Pandora's box of inquiries.

Big question: why?

Big question number two: who was Joel Burck really?

Carver parked a block from the given address, the closest parking available. Burck pointed to a three-story building, with a formidable windowless first floor of stone. The second floor was encircled with industrial wire-screen safety windows. The third floor had more conventionally spaced wire-mesh windows.

Burck stepped out and used a key to unlock a heavy door. When it creaked open, Carver realized the door was solid, metal backed. Carver didn't see any other doors, and figured any exits were around the back of the building.

"Come," Burck said. "You are so anxious."

He went up a steep flight of stairs to a second floor. He unlocked another door and clicked on the overhead lights. He stepped into a barren room. Or almost barren room; off to one side were several straight-backed ladder chairs, a television set, a VCR, and a bookshelf containing videotapes.

The windows, which Carver had seen from outside, were clear and clean. During the day they must burst with light. Carver took note of several other doors and wondered where they led.

"Wait," Burck said, and pointed to a chair near the windows.

Carver sat, his hands on his knees, and watched as Burck donned his leotards and his ballet slippers. Red. Bright red slippers. He then stepped into a resin-box near the stage.

"Not many people know of this place," Burck said to Carver. "It is my private rehearsal hall. I come here to be alone with myself, to practice, and to wallow in nostalgia." He rubbed his feet in the resin. "Of course Bart knew of its existence."

"Did Joyce Kittering know about it?"

"Yes, she did. And Bob Swaine. But none of the others. Certainly I did not show any of the directors."

"What makes you so sure Joyce or Swaine didn't tell others in the company?"

"Why would they? They gave me their word."

Joel Burck took a videotape from the shelf, inserted it into the VCR, and turned on the TV set. He went to the far end of the room and waited.

An arrow plunged into a target bull's-eye. On the TV. Carver recognized the emblem of a British film company.

With the rise of the music came the title of the film. *The Red Shoes*. Carver had seen the famous film about ballet many times. What the hell did this have to do with Joel Burck?

As the music continued, Burck waited. Apparently for an appropriate moment. Then he began to move. Long, gliding turns, wonderfully lithe pirouettes. Carver was mesmerized. Burck continued, his moves assured and graceful. And yet somehow different.

"Do you like this, Carver?" Burck asked loudly as he danced. The words were forced out with the effort to speak and dance at the same time.

"Very much, Joel," Carver answered.

"Yes, *The Red Shoes*. A favorite of mine."

"Yeah, it's a great movie."

"Bart . . ." he said, choking on the word, "Bart loved it dearly."

Burck shook his head, his eyes closed. He danced, sweat flipping from his face as he leaped and turned. Carver's attention was diverted to the TV screen. The film had cut to the next dance episode; the tape had been edited, the story narrative deleted, leaving only the dance routines.

"For a long time," Burck said, "I was quite taken with Moira Shearer in the film. So lovely. But it was Robert Helpmann that I truly admired."

Carver nodded, watching, wondering where this was going.

"I first saw this film when I was a young boy," Burck

said. "It was already old then. It made a great impression upon me. But," he continued, eyes on some distant time past, "perhaps a great impression is an inadequate way to describe my youthful feelings and emotions."

"I get the idea," Carver said.

"I fell in love with the idea of dancing. Everything I thought about, my whole young life, revolved around dancing the ballet. I breathed it, I lived it, I dreamed it. I was consumed by the dance."

He continued to glide, from end to end of the hall, on tiptoe, sometimes arms elongated, then akimbo, twirling slowly, majestically.

"The dance," he said, breathing hard. "I wanted to dance on the stage, with the ballet. I studied with the best, and I danced, and I danced. Hours at the barre, days—even nights—weeks. Months and years, Carver. As with all would-be dancers. Constantly studying, exercising. And then—a childhood dream that came true. Do you understand, Carver? Do you see the difference?"

What was the difference? Carver asked himself. He studied the dancer's turns and leaps.

Burck's dancing style was different from the style he used with the Golden Gate Ballet Company. True, the differences were subtle, and Carver's knowledge about ballet techniques was not sufficient to see all the differences, but he saw the major ones. What Burck was doing at this time seemed old-fashioned, classical, as though from another time, another place.

Was this how the ballet was danced in the nineteenth or eighteenth centuries? He began to see what Burck was showing him, what he was telling him with the movements of the dance. Right, Carver said to himself, he got it. So what did he do with it? And what did it have to do with someone trying to murder Burck?

He heard a door open.

Wasn't the building locked? He couldn't remember seeing Burck relock the front door, but didn't the latch lock itself when it closed?

Footsteps.

On the stairs.

Carver reached instinctively under his jacket . . . and stopped. He wasn't wearing his shoulder holster. He saw the door to the studio begin to open. Joel Burck had not noticed.

Two men stepped into the rehearsal hall. Carver didn't recognize them. At first, in the bright light, he thought the two might've been Krieb and Balsanek. But they weren't. They were both of a size, and stocky, wearing brown shoes and gray overcoats.

"So, Mr. Burck," one of the men said as they moved into the middle of the hall, "we have found you."

Joel Burck stopped his dance. He looked at the two men, then at Carver. He shrugged. Well, what had to happen had happened. He had waited for a long time. Six years. Bart had . . . oh, Bart, he had warned him, warned him it would happen. Nothing could be put off forever.

Carver stepped in and faced them. "Out," he said. "This is private."

"That is no concern of yours, black man," the one doing the talking said.

"You're not cops—"

But that was all Carver said. A movement to his right. A blur of an arm. Nighttime came on fast. He swayed, trying to get a hold on the sudden, blotting pain. But there was nothing. Only the long fall.

TWENTY-THREE

The interesting thing about floors is how they reminded Carver of his childhood. Was that the way with most people? Was it because of the time babies spend crawling? Some kind of affinity with floors and rugs? Kind of friendly, actually.

Carver opened his eyes. He didn't think he had been out for long. Maybe only a few seconds. Just long enough to consider the philosophy of the floor. He looked carefully through slotted lids, half expecting to see the corpse of Joel Burck stretched out. On the floor.

He heard voices—foggy, distant, gray voices. He breathed slowly, taking in large amounts of oxygen. Fresher down here on the floor. Carver opened his eyes fully.

The voices.

"There will be no trouble," a deep voice said.

"We will welcome your return," a mellow voice added. "Everyone will welcome you."

"No," another voice replied. Burck's voice.

The dancer stood near the silent loudspeakers. The two men sat on reversed chairs, arms hanging over the backs. One smoked a cigarette.

"There will be no reprisals," the deep voice said. "Things are different there. A new chairman is in command."

"I like it here," Burck said.

"It is not your home," the deep voice said sympathetically. "You are not trully happy here. You cannot be."

"I was not happy in the Soviet Union," Burck said flatly. "I have no family there."

"But you are afraid, are you not? Afraid of being found out?"

"No . . . not anymore."

"Why then did you conceal your identity from the Americans?"

"My reasons are my own. You cannot coerce me to return."

Carver listened for several more minutes, the conversation going over the same ground again and again. The two men with Burck alternated with their gruff questions and pleading statements.

So, Carver said to himself, Burck was a Soviet dancer. A defector. Was that the big secret? Who were these two guys? A couple of Russian choreographers? No, that wasn't funny. Those two guys couldn't dance a two-step without asking permission. Or was that Carver's own prejudice speaking? Yeah, probably.

He breathed hard and rolled onto his elbows. The three men at the other end of the dance hall looked at him. The one who smoked a cigarette walked over to Carver and stood over him.

"You are awake, black man?"

"Not a bright question," Carver said.

He got to his feet. He felt fine.

"Nothing like a brief snooze—on the floor," Carver said, brushing his hands over his clothes, "to make a guy feel like . . . well, to feel like dancing. I can thank you for that."

"I apologize. I felt you were going to interfere with our work."

"I would have. I'd like to try."

"Ah. You want to fight with me?"

"No," Carver said, walking toward Joel Burck. "I've changed my mind."

He didn't think the two men were dangerous to Burck.

179

If they were they would've done something by now. What a euphemism—something. Burck was alive; they hadn't killed him. Which meant they probably weren't going to. They looked capable of murder. Looked like they might enjoy it, or at any rate feel indifferent about it.

"You're a Soviet dancer," Carver said to Joel Burck.

"Yes, or rather I was. Now I am an American dancer."

"You could've told me, Joel. It would have been confidential. But I should've figured that out. There was something about your speech patterns—as if English wasn't your native tongue. Anyway, I don't think we can keep it a secret."

"No, I don't think so either. It's all right. Bart wanted me to speak out long before this. But I could not."

"Why not?"

"Please, I would rather speak to you of this at another time."

"Right," Carver said. He turned to the two Russians. "You got anything better to do?"

"I think you still want to fight," the second man said, lighting a fresh cigarette from the butt of the other. "Yes, I think so.'"

"Not me. I'm an American. I only tackle you KGB guys when I'm outnumbered ten-to-one."

"Very amusing, black man. We are not KGB."

"No?"

"*Nyet*. We are cultural attachés."

"Over at the consulate on Union Street?"

"*Da*. That is where we work."

"But you're not KGB? You went looking for Burck on your lunch hours and found him, all by yourselves?"

"*Da*, that is so."

"Yeah, sure," Carver said sarcastically, and turned to his client. "Come on, Burck, or whatever the hell your real name is. Let's go. You've got to be in shape for the big opening tomorrow night."

"Yes, Carver. Let us go. Tomorrow will be a big night. I shall tell the world who I am during the premiere. I will face the Immigration Department after that."

"I like a bit of drama too," Carver replied, and elbowed his way past the two men. "Pardon me, boys, you're blocking the way."

The first blast tore a huge hole in the middle of the dance floor.

Flames licked through the ragged hole, and black clouds boiled up.

Carver pushed Burck back, and the two Russians fell to the floor. All four men scrabbled backward. Carver looked fast for another exit.

"Any other door?" he yelled at Burck.

"Yes!" the dancer yelled back.

The second blast blew in the front door to the rehearsal hall.

The light fixtures swayed. Crackling flames raced along the polished floor, melting wax in its path.

Carver grabbed Burck and pushed him to the rear door. The two Russians followed. They were all yelling at once, giving directions, trying to figure out what had happened, how they could get out, and where the other door led to.

Carver pulled open the door and a sheet of red flame illuminated the hall. But there might be enough space to reach the stairway. The only problem—

"Goes up," Carver yelled, pointing to the stairs.

"Yes," Burck said, "But maybe—"

"A way out off the roof!"

Part of the ceiling gave way, and wood and metal screeched. Overhead several beams groaned as the fire ate at them; one bent and then fell with a roar to the dance floor. The wide windows blew out from the heat and built-up pressure. A bonfire ahead of them; an inferno behind. Zero choice.

Throwing his coat over Burck, still dressed only in thin leotards, Carver jumped into the hallway and ran for the stairs. Burck followed. The two Russians stalled in the doorway, backing away from the flames eating at the walls and linoleum in the hallway.

"Come on!" Carver yelled as he paused in the middle of the stairs. He snatched his hand off the railing. Hot! His breath gagged in his throat as searing heat reached deep into his lungs.

Was this another of Burck's "accidents"? Deliberately set? Or was it just an old boiler or something going up? Didn't seem likely. He'd bet it was another attempt to kill Burck. Yeah, he'd bet his life.

The old paint on the walls was a feast for the fast-food flames. The dry, termite-ridden molding cackled gleefully as it was consumed by the fire. Smoke rapidly obscured the hall.

Carver jumped off the stairs and leaped across the hall. He grabbed the Russians and shoved them into the hall. "Run!" he yelled at them, and went after them. Joel Burck had climbed to the third floor and opened a door.

Then every light fixture went out.

"Damn it," Burck yelled. "There's more fire up here!"

Carver yelled back, "Understood! Worse on second floor!" He didn't want to consider the first floor. And as good as the Fire Department was, the firefighters might not get to them in time. They had to save themselves. He reached the third floor.

A rending, screeching noise made him look up. A mistake!

A heavy, fiery beam collapsed over Carver, one end smashing to the floor. The other end caught on the far wall, smashing through plaster and lathe. Carver was pinned under the beam.

He beat at the flames with his hands, tearing his clothes in a desperate attempt to get out from under. He heard someone scream. God! It was himself. One of the Russians kicked at the beam, and it moved a few inches. Carver twisted and managed to force himself into the wider angle between the floor and wall. He could smell his hair smoldering.

The second Russian joined his comrade, and the two men rolled the beam off Carver. They reached down and hauled Carver to his feet. He swayed, shuddering.

No time for that. Had to get out.

Carver choked, spewing discolored phlegm onto the

floor, and stumbled through the thick gray smoke. He dropped to all fours and crawled fast. He grabbed his handkerchief from his pocket and pressed it to his face.

The two Russians had thrown off their coats.

"Where is water?" they yelled at Burck. "Water faucets? Drinking fountains? Toilets?"

Burck didn't know; he'd never been to the third floor.

Carver grabbed the dancer. Forget the water. What about the roof? Any way up there?

Burck didn't know. Carver looked down the stairs and grimaced. The flames were crackling and spitting bright sparks. He looked around, the only light coming from the flames. The third floor was crossed with several hallways, with doors opening to offices and storerooms.

There had to be a stairwell that went to the roof. Had to be! Down at the other end. Carver yelled for them to follow him.

The four men stumbled down the hall, all crouched over, their hands touching the warm walls. Carver heard glass shattering. All around them were the sounds of splintering and loud popping as floors and walls were split asunder. The smoke grew thicker, roiling and curling around them.

They could barely see their hands in front of them. Carver pulled Burck down onto the floor, where there was a chance to get what little oxygen remained. The floor felt hot, and the floorboards quivered under their hands.

The building seemed to be shaking. Death throes.

The two Russians lumbered alongside the wall, feeling their way. Soon all four had found a door, which might lead to the roof. What then? Carver wondered. Maybe they could find a fire escape or get to an adjoining roof. Maybe.

The door was stuck, and one of them, it was hard to tell which in the dense smoke, kicked it open. A blast of super-hot air blew in, pushing the oily clouds back. For a moment. With a sucking whoosh, the clouds rushed forward, refilling the void, blotting out everything.

Someone managed to hold the door open. All four rushed onto the sooty, smoke-filled landing. From below rose a tower of fluttering, licking flames. The stairwell was a fiery pit.

The men staggered through the dark smoke to the ascending stairs. Something—a stair or a floor perhaps—gave way. One of the men stumbled, arms flailing. He toppled, clutching a banister. Wood tore loose. The man fell. Screamed. The three survivors huddled against the hot wall.

TWENTY-FOUR

"Goddamn, look at that," Krieb said.

"Damn, it was sure fast," Balsanek said.

"Like a box of matches," Krieb said. "Lights up the sky real pretty."

"Yes, a three-alarm conflagration," Balsanek said.

"Hey, a fire is a fire," Krieb said, "don't give me any of those big words."

"Think any of them can get out?"

'Well, they sure as hell ain't out yet," Krieb said.

"We certainly have an excellent viewpoint."

"We gotta move the car," Krieb said.

"Yes, I agree," Balsanek said. "Especially since I hear fire engines."

"That's 'cause you got good ears," Krieb said.

"Look—now the whole building is burning."

"Yeah, it's too bad," Krieb said.

"Yes," Balsanek agreed, and turned on the ignition and pulled away from the curb. "We'll never find the perpetrator of that one."

"Molerath ain't goin' to like this."

"I agree," Balsanek said.

The roof exit door flew open; black and gray and white vapor rolled over the roof. Three figures staggered out, choking and coughing and cursing. Flames streaked the night, and the smoke clouded the stars.

Carver Bascombe made his way to the edge of the roof. He looked down, and then to the right and left. No fire escape on this side. Yeah, that figured. They're usually on the back side, leading down to an alley or a parking lot.

The other two men joined him. Joel Burck gasped, breathing hard. The Russian stood swaying, looking dazed, perplexed. Their clothing was torn, rank-smelling with smoke.

Carver's Brioni slacks had several pockets hanging by a thread; one pant leg was slashed at the ankle. On Burck, bare skin showed through holes in his scorched leotards; he still wore Carver's jacket. The Russian's clothes were a mess, holes burned in his pants, his overcoat ripped, and his suit dark-stained with soot.

They heard the fire engines, but Carver knew the roof was only minutes from burning out from under them. They had to find the fire escape. And the only way was through the dense smoke piling up.

On the street the first fire engine, siren screaming, turned the corner and braked to a stop near a streetlight.

"They'll be too late," Burck said.

Carver nodded and told the two men to follow. He groped his way to the far side, where the burning building adjoined a four-story building. If the Fire Department couldn't contain the blaze, all the connecting buildings would go up. And they would have been fried long before that.

More sirens. Obviously more fire trucks and firemen.

A *whoosh!* A booming noise. A truck-sized chunk of the roof disappeared, collapsing into the fire below. Flames began licking around the large hole where the roof door had been. The smell of burning tar and hot gravel filled the air.

Like giant canary wings, the flames licked up, showering the darkness with sparks and tinder. Through the engulfing haze, Carver looked at the roof of the adjoining building. Not too far up, only about ten, maybe twelve feet. He was over six feet. He could boost Joel or the Russian up to the roof. Maybe they could get a rope or—

A thick rope fell from above and flopped at his feet.

"Grab it!" Balsanek yelled.

In minutes the three men—Carver, Burck, and the Russian—were on the roof of the next building. Krieb and Balsanek showed them the way down the stairs to the next street.

They stood on the corner, Carver, Burck, and one big Russian, with torn and blackened clothes. Carver felt conspicuous, and detested the spasms that passed through his body from time to time. But then, Burck had the same terrors. Carver held himself around the elbows, gritting his teeth.

"You guys want to hang around?" Krieb asked.

"There's going be a plethora of reporters," Balsanek added.

"Yeah, a lot of them," Krieb said, "and right now there's dozens of firemen, and a fire marshall. You wanta hang around for them?"

"It's up to Burck," Carver said, teeth chattering.

"No, Carver," Burck said, "I do not wish to see anyone."

"How about you?" Carver asked, turning to the Russian.

"*Nyet*. There is nothing anyone can do for Pyotr."

"You'll have to report it to your superiors," Carver said.

The Russian nodded, and stared squint-eyed at Burck. Carver wondered; was the Russian going to make one last appeal to Burck? The Russian then looked at Krieb and Balsanek, and without saying anything, not even "thank you, you saved my life," walked away.

Carver figured the Russian had parked a car nearby. It seemed unlikely he and his partner had taken a taxi.

"Who was that guy?" Balsanek asked.

"Nobody you want to know," Carver said. "And thanks. For the rope."

"Actually, I think Mr. Molerath would've wanted us to save your lives," Balsanek said. "Otherwise we might

187

never find out who killed Mr. Meaghler. He thinks you have as good a chance as anyone. The same previous reasons apply for not going to the police."

"Yeah," Krieb said. "But we woulda done it anyway."

The two men walked to their car, which was parked down the block. Carver waited until they drove off, and then he and Burck walked around the block to where they had parked the Jaguar. Before getting in, Carver brushed most of the dust and grime from his clothes. They drove off, and several blocks away Carver stopped at a telephone booth. He called Mike Tettsui, who agreed to meet them at Burck's apartment.

TWENTY-FIVE

Tettsui listened to the bare bones of Burck's story, and to Carver's narrative about the fire. He was fascinated by how quickly Burck's malaise had altered. Strange how a life-threatening situation can change a person.

Ah well, Tettsui thought, that's one of the balms of nature. A person must bend, like the bamboo or the willow in the storm, or break. Burck seemed alive again, though still dampened by the loss of his lover. In Western culture men like stalwart oaks are admired, but strong trees break in a storm. Better to be flexible, open-minded, than to remain adamant, close-minded. Such a philosophy of arrogance leads to unhappiness and inner turmoil.

He chanced a slight smile at himself. Good—neither Bascombe nor Burck had noticed.

Carver caught the tiny flicker at the corner of Tettsui's mouth. What amused Tettsui? he wondered.

He and Burck had arrived at the apartment before Tettsui. Burck used the time to change out of his burned and torn leotards. Carver washed as well as he could; he really wanted to return to his apartment and change into clean clothes, but—

"So, the Russian drove off," Carver said, completing the story, "and Molerath's guys drove off, and we drove off. Finis."

"Okay," Tettsui said, "and you think the fire was deliberate?"

"I'd bet on it. The killer tried to get us both this time." Carver turned to Burck. "You were going to tell me about your defection, how you got to the United States."

"I'm glad that I am alive to tell you, Carver," Burck said. "You saved my life. Until that happened, I was not sure that I wanted to go on living. But when I was dancing *The Red Shoes,* I knew I wanted very much to live. I would have told you everything then, but those two countrymen of mine intruded."

"Right. Tell us now."

"My real name is Burganin," the dancer said. "But I will still call myself Burck."

For the next fifteen minutes Burck told them of his life as a young boy, his coming of age in Odessa. He soon knew he was different from other boys. Slowly he realized he was a homosexual, a despicable thing in the USSR. More so than in the USA. His life was a hell, particularly when he wanted to dance in the ballet. His father was against it.

That part of the young dancer's story was told haltingly, with slow breathing. His parents died in a fire in the country cottage they lived in. Burck was sent to Moscow, to study in a stage school for dancers. There were no other family members, no uncles or aunts. He studied hard, sublimating all his energies and emotion into the regimen of the ballet.

By age nineteen he was a young ballet star, not famous, not singled out as yet for stardom, but a damned fine dancer. Then, when he was twenty-two, he met an American—Bartholomew Meaghler, a devotee of the ballet. Meaghler was seven years older, a successful businessman in the international travel tours business.

The two men became friends, and Meaghler used his tour business know-how to smuggle Burck out of the Soviet Union. The Russians never knew what happened to one of their up-and-coming young dancers. Burganin had simply vanished.

Once in the USA, Meaghler went through the process of building papers for Burck, including getting a passport, driver's license, credit cards, a job record in his travel agency. There was a slight problem with Social Security, but not too difficult, since Burck was only a few years past age seventeen. Difficult, but not impossible.

As for his appearance—a new hairline, a darker color hair, and a small amount of plastic surgery in a young man can drastically alter his looks.

"Then we came to California," Burck said, continuing his story. "Bart's company headquarters were here, and he knew a lot of people."

The dancer changed his style of dancing, vigorously learning the faster, energetic expression of the American ballet. Difficult, yes, but not impossible; after all, it was still dancing.

"It wasn't difficult to get me into the Golden Gate Ballet Company," Burck said, winding down his story. "Not with the amount of money Meaghler and his friends, such as Myron Moseby, put into the budget. Not that it would do me much good if I couldn't dance, but that was not the case."

"Definitely not," Carver said.

They made plans for the next day, and Carver left. Tettsui stayed with Burck. Carver drove to his office and parked the Jaguar in the Hi-Valu station. God, he was tired. He ached and ached; his skin felt as if someone had taken a nut-grater to it.

Carver walked slowly down Fillmore Street toward his office. He didn't pay much attention to the dark-windowed limousine following slowly. As he reached Pine Street, the long automobile pulled ahead and nosed to the curb.

"Bascombe," a voice called softly.

Carver stopped, noticing the car for the first time. Balsanek stepped out from the front passenger side and opened the rear door. The movement was almost a cliché, but Carver understood it well enough. He climbed in and seated himself. He looked at the man sitting opposite.

Dark, expensive suit and topcoat. Large cigar. Smell of

Chanel for men. White shirt, bright in the darkness of the limousine. Tight curls framed a large face. Light eyes behind horn-rimmed glasses.

"You know who I am?" the man asked.

Carver nodded.

"Good, Mr. Bascombe, then we can dispense with the prelims. How is the case going?"

Carver shrugged.

"I think you know more than you let on," the man said. "I know about the death of the dancer, Miss Kittering. My guess is she knew too much. Do you?"

"What?" Carver asked.

"Know too much?"

Carver shrugged.

"Don't make her death personal, Mr. Bascombe," the man said. "Leave these matters of retribution to . . . to others." He blew a soft cloud of armotaic smoke. "That's all I wanted to say. You seem intelligent enough not to have this repeated. I dislike redundancies. Rest assured, someone will pay for this."

"Yeah," Carver said, feeling too tired to argue.

"Yes, someone will die," the man said, and turned his eyes forward.

The meeting was adjourned.

Carver climbed out and watched the car drive off.

In his apartment Carver peeled out of his torn and smoke-stained clothes. Gingerly he removed his bandages from Don Terman's lesson in savate. He rubbed alcohol onto his scrapes and bruises and turned on the hot water in the shower. He was going to stand under the hot water for a long, long time.

Soon the bathroom was filled with a unique smell. Hot metal pipes, hot tiles. Squishy melting soap. And the moist feel of enveloping steam. Aaaah! Carver felt good, and getting better.

The jets of hot water felt fine beating on his battered body. He was going to be stiff later. Freshly clothed and bandaged, cuts and scrapes sterilized, Carver was putting on a clean shirt when the doorbell rang.

Not another visit from Molerath? No, and not Krieb or Balsanek either. He opened the frosted glass door. Detective Sergeant Arnold Applegate stood there. Without a clipboard, Carver noted. What did Applegate want?

He gestured the detective into his office. He finished buttoning his shirt and pulled on a cashmere sweater. Applegate faced the desk and Carver seated himself gingerly. He ached all over, his muscles felt bruised, his bones gritted against each other.

Yeah, this was the life. On the brink. On the cutting edge. On the burning bridge. He wouldn't have it any other way. Sure.

"What's on your mind, Sergeant?" Carver asked.

"Interesting office you have," Applegate said, ignoring the question. "I understand you live here, too."

Carver pointed to the solid wood door next to the desk. Applegate peered inside for a few seconds, then closed the door. He went around the room, touching filing cabinets, looking at the framed license and the law degree. He ran a finger over the top of the TV and wiped the dust off on his pants. He looked at the stereo tape setup.

Carver slipped his feet out of his shoes. His feet hurt and his toes felt as bruised as pitted prunes. He looked at Applegate and rubbed one foot over the other. Hmmm; nice.

"Good stuff, Bascombe," Applegate said, and sat in the chair facing the desk. He took out his pipe and filled it, letting time pass. He went through his pockets and used his pipe lighter. Finally he was satisfied the pipe was drawing well.

Carver remained silent during this community playhouse exhibition. But there was something about Applegate he couldn't quite put a finger on. Something was different.

"I was told," Applegate finally said, "that you and I could talk. That you had a mine open to . . . well, an open mind."

Carver looked at the homicide detective with interest.

Yes, there was definitely something different in Applegate's manner. He rubbed his feet together, feeling good.

"Sergeant, you've changed your mind," Carver said, trying out his hunch. "You think the killer is after Burck. Don't you?"

"Yes, Bascombe . . . I have to admit you've probably been right."

Carver was silent. He had half expected this, but still—he had to be cautious in his reply; he might alienate Applegate, and there was never an excuse to make a cop an enemy. Not without extreme cause.

"Something tells me," Applegate said, "that I'm going to jump off a high board. The bureau received a report from the Fire Department—about Joyce Kittering's car."

"Yes," Carver said, and gestured for Applegate to continue.

"Her car was sabotaged."

Carver nodded. Tell him something new.

"And we got a report from the auto-theft bureau," Applegate continued. "The black sedan was found."

"The one that tried to run Burck off the road?"

"Yes, that one," Applegate admitted. "And there were no fingerprints. It had been wiped clean. Not exactly something the usual car thief does."

"Right," Carver said, keeping his voice neutral.

"There's more to it than that."

"Oh?"

"Do you want to cooperate, or do you want to try working this out on your own?"

"Work together? A city detective and a private detective? My, my. What would the City Hall crowd think?"

"No, I mean are you going to step aside, so that the department can conduct its own investigation in the proper manner?"

"Quite a mouthful, Sergeant," Carver said. "But I don't think we can cooperate. I already know who the killer is, and all I need is proof, the kind that will stand up in court."

TWENTY-SIX

Gray slotted shadows crept across the office ceiling. Carver felt good, damned good, even though his stomach gave out grumbling hunger signals.

His session with Applegate had been satisfying. There was not a chance that Carver was going to let Applegate step on his shoes. Not a chance that Applegate was going to let things slide; he couldn't. Applegate had the power of the Police Department; he was investigating homicides, and he took his job seriously.

Carver had his own job: protect Joel Burck. There was nothing that said he had to reveal all he knew about Burck. But if the police ever got curious, they could find out Burck's real identity easily enough.

If Rose's lady private eye on the East Coast—what was her name? yeah, Irene Papazian—if she could find out about the Burck paper trip, then so could the police.

That wasn't the problem. The problem was finding the killer before the premiere tomorrow night. Carver wondered if Applegate believed him when he said he knew the identity of the killer. He chuckled, sounding ominous within the shadows in the fall night.

Carver switched on several lamps and turned on the stereo tape deck. Tchaikovsky's *Swan Lake* drifted languidly into the air. Nice, very pleasant; soothing to the ear, to the mind. He went to the old corkboard and pinned up several of his timetable charts.

So who is the killer? Don Terman? Not likely; he was seen by Swaine and Merkhinn. One of the directors, Graham Maltby? Not likely. Gloria Loo? She didn't seem to have an alibi. Deborah Canby? She had been on the terrace. Was she using Carver as an alibi? How about Eric Hudson? He didn't seem to have an alibi either.

What about Bob Swaine? No, too many people had seen him at Moseby's. A good alibi. Damn it, even Carver had seen him; there was no way for the choreographer to be in two places at once. No, Carver still leaned heavily on the dancers. Eric Hudson. Deborah Canby. Alex Bellini. Alice Boygen. Possibly Billy Jones.

From an ornamental puzzle box in his desk Carver removed several cigarette wrappers and a stash of grass. He rolled a joint and lit it.

He sighed. Yes, the killer's name was there on the wall. Now Carver had to draw the person out, had to trap him, and do that without getting Joel Burck killed. A good trick, he figured, if he could do it.

He fiddled with the micro-recorder and played back several tapes. What was he looking for? What would he do . . . what would he do if he were the killer? He certainly wouldn't make waves, would he? Bring attention to himself? Wouldn't the killer try to be as innocuous as possible?

Who fit that bill? In the darkened office, Carver listened to the tapes again. Yeah, someone who didn't take the side of Bob Swaine, nor against him. Unless Swaine was the killer. No, forget that.

But there was something . . . something on the tape. He rewound it and listened again. Yeah, a strong possibility. Now, how would he prove it?

Plenty of police would be on hand at the premiere. But Carver had other ideas. Slowly, what he wanted took shape, and the idea grew strong in his mind. Would Burck go for it? Would Vassily Visikov?

He prowled about the office, in time with *Swan Lake*. Oh, yeah . . . the idea was good . . . the plan was . . .

dangerous . . . but mostly for Carver . . . and Applegate might not like it . . . but it had to be tried. . . .

A knock on the door. Several sharp, staccato sounds. He mashed the cigarette butt on the floor. The light from a forty-watt bulb outside in the hallway cast a silhouette on the frosted glass. A woman's dark shape. Rather tall, too, Carver thought as he turned the knob.

"Hello," Gloria Loo said, holding a brown paper bag. "I thought you might be in." She hefted the bag. "I took a chance."

"What if I hadn't been here?" he said, smelling the aroma of spicy foods.

"Then I'd have cried and eaten it all to repress my disappointment."

Carver stepped aside, gesturing Gloria to come in. "I was just thinking about you," he said without elaboration.

"Were you?" She asked, setting the bag on Carver's desk. "In what way? Real nice, I hope, because that's the way I like to think about me. Especially if it's someone I like."

She looked around the office and sniffed the air. And smiled. "Nice office," she said, running her fingers along the stereo deck. "Nice other stuff, too. Not bad equipment. You really ought to think about getting one of those compact disc machines. Lovely sound."

He offered to play something other than *Swan Lake*. Gloria declined, saying she thought the music fitted the mood.

"What's through here?" she asked, pointing to the door next to Carver's desk. "More office space? Or storage space, full of old files and stuff?"

"My apartment."

"Really?"

Carver assured her he lived on the premises.

"Golly Moley, with a bed and everything, I'll bet," she said.

He didn't deny it.

She opened the door and stepped in. She looked around, with Carver leaning against the doorframe.

"I've got plates in the kitchen," he said, "and glasses and utensils."

Gloria smiled at him, then rummaged in the kitchen. She set plates and utensils on Carver's desk. She had found a candle in the kitchen and lit it. She stuck it on a saucer and positioned it in the middle of the desk. She turned off all but one of the lamps.

The candle threw flickering shadows around the walls. Carver sat facing Gloria Loo. She opened the packages and filled two plates with Szechuan beef, snow peas, asparagus, and rice.

"Go ahead, Carver, eat."

Carver was quite satisfied and said so.

"I'd like it better if I'd made it myself," Gloria said. She looked at him. "But I bet you're wondering why I came to see you. I want to talk."

"Go ahead," Carver urged.

"I know you feel bad about Joyce."

He said nothing.

"But I think you need someone. I know I do. I liked her quite a bit. It's hard . . . hard to realize she's missing, that she's dead." She lowered her eyes. "Am I making any sense? Am I getting through to you?"

"Yes," he said.

"I said you need someone," she said almost in a whisper. "Especially now . . . after Joyce. I want it to be me." She looked at him again. "Is that so terrible?"

"No."

"If you're the kind of man I think you are, then . . . hell, I'm not doing a very good job of this."

A faint wetness made her eyes glisten. She smiled, almost shyly.

Gloria Loo pushed her chair back and removed the dishes and took them into the apartment kitchen. Carver sighed, feeling strange, as if his inner thoughts had been pleasantly invaded. He looked at the empty chair opposite him. She had been gone for quite a while.

He went into the apartment. The lights were out, with

only a soft streetlight glow coming in from the windows behind the bed.

Gloria Loo was in his bed, the covers around her knees. The rest of her was probably as naked as her upper body.

"I thought this would prevent a lot of time lost," she said. "Right? Or wrong?"

"Right," Carver said, unbuttoning his shirt.

TWENTY-SEVEN

The curve was sensual, an erotic contour, running from the foot of the bed, up along the sheet-covered leg, and undulating over the thigh. Then it continued down briefly to the waist and climbed the short distance of her arm—where the sheet ended. The rest of Gloria Loo's curves were bare shoulder and neck.

Carver had been watching Gloria for about twenty minutes. To waken her would be a sacrilege, a defiling of tranquillity. No, let her dream on.

Gloria finally wakened. She sniffed, and Carver brought two steaming cups of coffee on a tray. She sat up, holding her cup in both hands.

She was beautiful, and unconscious of her loveliness. A very natural woman. Look at that, Carver thought, the way she sits there, naked from the waist. Hmmm, lovely.

Gloria Loo looked at him. A wine-red robe covered his lean, muscular body. A rugged-looking man, she thought. Even with scars and bandages; maybe even because of them. Was she turned on by the scars and bruises? Did they make him seem dangerously attractive?

She smiled, knowing he was watching. Yes, she found Carver sexy. Scars or no scars.

This man was a constant surprise. Tough and tender, cool and passionate, often grim, but definitely playful—

under the right conditions—under the covers. Carver Bascombe was more than all right.

"How about some breakfast?" he asked.

"Where?"

"Here."

"Sure."

"Right."

"Oh, man of few words," Gloria said, and laughed. "Give me a minute to dress, and I'll be out of your way. I don't want to learn my way around that teeny kitchen."

"Agreed."

"What a relief to have someone agreeable."

"Who isn't?"

"Well, Merkhinn, for one. He's always in the middle of Machiavellian machinations."

"Yeah," Carver said. "Joyce . . . she told me Merkhinn has a lot of the offices bugged. Likes to play spider."

"I can believe that. He tried to bribe me into spying. Told me I could get better dancing roles when he took over the company. All I had to do was betray my friends. I turned him down, of course. Maybe that's why I'm not a prima ballerina. But hell, if that's what it takes to succeed, then I'll just stay where I am."

Carver rubbed a finger along his chin and said nothing. Gloria began to dress, and Carver used the time to call Mike Tettsui; he asked him to drive Joel Burck to the theater.

"Oh, and Mike," Carver said, "wear your gun."

"Like that, is it?" Tettsui asked.

"It's like that."

Carver hung up, and then from a cabinet he removed a wrapped cardboard package. Very important, he thought; it'd give Burck confidence. When Gloria was dressed, he went into the kitchen and prepared breakfast.

She turned on the radio in the office and listened to the news; the report of the fire near the GGBC theater barely held her attention. A charred body had been found in the ashes. Carver heard it in the kitchen, and listened with mild interest; he was not mentioned in the newscast.

Good, he thought.

An hour later, satisfied with orange juice, eggs Benedict, and coffee, Gloria and Carver parked near the GGBC theater. On the street were three chartered buses, engines idling. Temporary banners on the buses carried the theater name and logo.

Inside, the lobby was a sea of dancers, production assistants, musicians, costumers, and publicity people. Friends laughed and shouted at each other. There was a lot of amiable jostling amid the serious babble of chatter.

Overnight cases, bulging with costumes, had been piled everywhere; assistants put the bags on handcarts and rolled them out to the buses. The smell of the buses' diesel fumes drifted in through the open doors.

The dancers had been separated into groups, with a team leader for each group. The orchestra was similarly divided. Many of the dancers wore black armbands in memory of Joyce Kittering. Brigham Merkhinn had demanded a rush change in the printed program; it would be dedicated to Joyce.

Not surprisingly, there were reporters and photographers mingling with the dancers and company directors. Camera strobe lights flashed repeatedly over the crowd. Carver saw Merkhinn talking to a knot of TV reporters and camerapersons.

"Well, Carver," Gloria said in the lobby, surrounded by the milling crowd, "I guess we part."

She thought she had never sounded more vapid, and despised herself for not coming up with better.

"Not for long," Carver said. "I'll be riding the bus with Burck."

They stood there for a moment, Gloria slowly blinking her almond eyes. Carver reached out and took her in his arms and kissed her, long and tender, his tongue gently stroking her lips.

They parted, and Gloria smiled, her eyes gleaming, all sparkly.

"Okay," she said huskily. "See you on the bus."

Carver sought out Tettsui and Burck. "Stay with him, Mike," Carver said.

Outside the theater, Carver opened the trunk of the Jaguar and removed the wrapped cardboard package he had brought from the office. He looked around carefully, checking that no one was paying attention to his actions. He unlocked the custom-built compartment and removed his holstered Colt .357 Python revolver. He dropped two filled speed-loaders into his pockets.

TWENTY-EIGHT

Using the package as cover for his weapon, Carver returned to the lobby. The Python and two speed-loaders, six bullets each, might seem excessive firepower, but then . . . never can tell, he said to himself. He found a secluded spot on the mezzanine, shucked off his jacket, and put on his shoulder holster.

He made a detour backstage, where some of the dancers were grabbing a few last-minute warmups at the barre. He wandered casually through the dressing rooms. Many of the male dancers were chatting idly as they put on leotards under their street clothes.

Carver did a mental checkoff: Eric Hudson was at the backstage barre. Alex Bellini and Don Terman were in the dressing rooms. Deborah Canby and Gloria Loo were in their dressing rooms. Bob Swaine was in the lobby, conferring with the group leaders; they were very close to boarding the buses. Billy Jones was helping load costumes.

Carrying the package, Carver sought out Burck and Tettsui. At the auditorium doors, Mike Tettsui had positioned himself in such a way as to prevent any potential sniper from getting a clear shot at Burck. Carver took Tettsui aside and told him who he suspected as the killer.

"We need proof," Tettsui said.

Carver nodded, and then motioned for Burck to follow him backstage to Burck's dressing room.

Carver unwrapped the package and handed the contents to Burck. "Joel," Carver said, "I want you to put these on—under your leotards."

"What are they?" Joel asked.

"Kelvar T-shirts and pants. Bulletproof material."

"Oh," Burck said.

The dancer took out the heavy garments from the package. In minutes he had put on the Kelvar underclothes, with his leotards and street clothes over everything.

"I think I'm going to sweat to death," the dancer said.

"It's worth it," Carver said. "Shouldn't hinder your dancing. You're strong enough to carry the weight. Except when you're dancing, neither Mike nor I will be more than a few yards away from you."

They went to Vassily Visikov's office and knocked. Benjamin opened the door.

"Mr. V has been waiting," Benjamin said.

Visikov met them, and Carver entroduced Mike Tettsui.

"This," Visikov said, "is what you are up against."

Visikov unrolled a large set of blueprints onto his covered knees. The plans were a detailed layout of the island prison. Visikov pointed to an area which he identified as the main tiers.

"This is where we have permission to stage the dance. It'll hold almost a thousand folding seats, and it's large enough to accommodate our dances." He pointed to another section. "The orchestra will be arrayed here, with the conductor's podium in front. That's where John Guiterez will conduct the orchestra."

Carver nodded.

"And this," Visikov continued, "is where the ballet will be performed. The dancers will do a rehearsal before the main event."

Carver nodded again, then turned to Burck. "I have to tell them," he said.

Burck stared at Carver for a few moments, then his eyes softened. He nodded affirmatively, his lips thin, compressed.

"Joel Burck has to make an important announcement," Carver said to the crippled choreographer.

"Yes, I rather thought he might," Visikov said. "I imagine it's about Joel's defection from the Soviet Union."

Carver and Burck stared at the man. Tettsui merely kept his hands in his pockets; yes, expect the unexpected, he thought.

"You know about that?" Carver asked.

"Of course, Carver. Do you think we are not without our resources? What would *you* think if a stranger comes to you, a man who can dance like the angels, without any references from an established ballet school or company? It was not difficult to check, and to find out his nationality and name."

"Do others know?"

"Of course. Not everyone, of course. We respect Joel's right to remain incognito. Though we dropped hints from time to time that he could probably dance even better if he so chose. Yes, I knew, and some of the directors knew."

"Like who?" Carver asked.

"Maltby, and Merkhinn. I think that's all."

Carver sighed and shrugged. Can't keep a good secret down.

"I will introduce Joel Burck," Visikov said aimably, "and he will make the announcement. Wouldn't that be preferable? It would certainly give the media plenty to write about."

"And don't forget, Mr. V," Benjamin said, "it'll sink Merkhinn."

"I suppose so."

"How so?" Tettsui asked.

"Because Burck is on Swaine's side. With news attention like that . . . well, then I assume that Brigham Merkhinn would find it difficult to topple Swaine."

"What's important," Carver continued, "is to let the media know that an important announcement will be made. That should be the last straw for the killer, the last chance to get Burck. He has to make his move before the dance premiere."

206

"You mean, to kill him?"

"Joel is willing to be the bait. He'll be as well protected as possible. I'll notify the cops, Applegate in particular, just before the ballet begins."

"Why not sooner?" Visikov asked.

"The smoking gun," Carver said.

"The what?" Visikov said.

"We need the killer with gun in hand," Carver explained. "Or bomb, or knife, or poison blowgun, or something. We definitely do not want him tied up in legal technicalities. If Applegate comes in, he'll gum up the works. He'll arrest a suspect or two. He'll pinpoint the killer by using all the available techniques of modern forensics and pathology. That could take a lot of time. Then they go to court. And with a good lawyer the killer might get off with a slap on the wrist.

"We're not going to take our eyes off the suspect. There's little danger to Joel."

"I see," Visikov replied. He looked at Carver. "Then I take it you have an idea who the killer is?"

"Yeah," Carver said. "But we can't prove it. We need a smoking gun."

TWENTY-NINE

The bay was like a sheet of smoothed-out tinfoil. Sailboats and ferryboats, and an occasional freighter, dotted the water. The afternoon was warm and pleasant.

The chartered ferryboat churned and rumbled its way toward the docking area on the lee of Alcatraz Island. Carver Bascombe strolled the ferry deck. Nearby were Joel Burck, Mike Tettsui, and Sergeant Applegate. And of course, obviously, those three guys with Applegate were cops; Carver recognized Sergeant Stein, a six-foot, over-forty, overweight buffalo.

Carver hid his qualms. What if he was wrong? No—he was sure he had figured it right. The clue had been there. The one he suspected—no, the one he knew had killed Rosada, Meaghler, and Joyce—had to fall into a trap.

Yeah, the police would figure it out eventually. But Carver wanted the killer to himself. The suspect was too egotistical, too cock-sure, to even consider failure.

The ferry docked, and the GGBC group leaders herded their charges off the boat. Vassily Visikov was wheeled onto the dock. Carver and Burck and Tettsui waited until Applegate and his men walked on ahead.

The dock was festooned with paper lanterns, vivid banners, and bright bunting. Large, colorful printed posters had been hung to welcome the evening's guests to the benefit premiere. Electricians were working on four massive searchlights that would crisscross the evening sky.

Close to the dock was the first of many wooden gun towers now empty. With much jostling and laughter, the dancers and musicians went up wide stone stairs toward the administration buildings.

Surrounded by water, the prison was constantly blown by winds. Sometimes mild, occasionally a gale. For the GGBC, the late afternoon winds were heaven-blessed, mild, almost warm breezes.

The crowd of dancers and others enjoyed the soft winds' featherlike touches on their faces. They felt fine, until they looked at the prison block looming over them.

A sad beige color gave the monolithic prison structure an ominous appearance. The building was huge, like a gigantic warehouse, three stories high. The monotonous facade was broken by symmetrical horizontal and vertical lines of barred windows.

The members of the GGBC were ushered into the building, past barred gates, steel doors, and more barred gates. As they progressed further, their chatter and laughter grew subdued. The steel doors were foreboding and grim. When the dancers and musicians were finally grouped in the main prison block they were silent.

Overhead were tiers and tiers of cells, most of them a narrow five by eight feet. Catwalks surrounded the second and third floors, with metal staircases linking the tiers. Daylight trickled in from overhead skylights, augmented by caged light fixtures.

"God, how awful," Deborah Canby said.

"Terrible," another ballerina agreed as she craned her neck, rotating slowly to take in the oppressive cell block.

Sergeant Arnold Applegate looked around and nodded affirmatively. Alcatraz prison hadn't outgrown its purpose—it had merely grown old and decrepit. The state needed more prison facilities, not less. Every cop knew that. He looked at Sergeant Stein, who rocked on the balls of his feet. The other two, Officers Kelly and Foppiano, were interested, but their eyes betrayed their efforts to maintain indifference.

A large area had been gaily decorated with bunting, banners, ballet posters, and cheerful wall sconces. Eight hundred chairs had been placed on the concrete main floor, with another sixty for the orchestra.

Overhead, spaced along the catwalks, were theater lights, and the electrical crew had several of them lit. Their task was difficult, since they would have to do the lighting cues manually. A black cable snaked down from the lighting tiers, across the slippery floor to a far rear wall. The master electricians had attached the heavy-duty black cable to an electrical panel with over three hundred amperes and many thousands of watts.

News photographers milled about, shooting atmospheric shots. Sergeant Applegate watched Carver Bascombe and Burck, but mostly he watched one of the dancers. Applegate had made up his mind he was going to arrest the suspect after the premiere. He itched to make the collar now, but forced himself to wait; after all, the suspect was merely under suspicion.

Applegate was positive the forensic technicians would match fibers, hair, and follicles found in the black sedan.

Of course that would only place the suspect behind the wheel. At the most the suspect might be charged with attempted vehicular homicide. At the least, assault. Applegate wanted more; he didn't think it would take much investigation to link the suspect with Rosada. Then it would be murder in the first degree.

After that, the law could take its course.

By now the dancers were milling about, and the musicians were lugging their instruments into the area.

"All right," Graham Maltby said in a loud, commanding voice to the dancers. "You can use the cells down there for dressing rooms. They've been fixed up for us by our own maintenance crew. Also along that passage are tables for makeup. Go to it, we want to get the dress rehearsal under way in the next hour."

The musicians took their seats. Near the podium, John Guiterez was splendid in white tie and tails. As he removed several batons from a case, Guiterez conferred in low tones with Bob Swaine.

Carver and Tettsui followed Joel Burck to one of the cells at the far end of the area.

"This looks okay," Tettsui said.

Burck nodded and began to unpack his makeup and costumes.

As time passed, the dancers grew accustomed to their prison environment. Lively chatter returned, and many went through their warm-up exercises. A portable barre had been set up far out of sight of the guests.

Ushers and other assistants worked out the seating arrangements. Soon they were treating this unorthodox location as if they had been temporarily moved into an experimental theater.

Carver and Mike Tettsui kept a careful watch on Burck. The dancer used the portable barre to limber up. Apparently casually, Carver strolled out to the front and looked over the empty chairs. A few hours from now and they'd be filled with patrons and fans of the ballet.

A significant night.

In more ways than one.

Two men walked into the area, and Carver stared at them. Yeah, he thought, in more ways than one. Now, how did those two guys get here? They were not ballet fans; definitely not.

Krieb and Balsanek.

The two men nodded to Carver, then strolled off to one side. They kept their hands in their pockets. No doubt about it. Mr. Molerath meant what he had told Carver.

Someone was going to die.

THIRTY

Vassily Visikov rolled his wheelchair in front of the empty auditorium seats. Alex stood behind the choreographer, and Brigham Merkhinn was beside Visikov. Visikov plucked at the quilt covering his spidery legs.

The dancers were assembled near the podium and the orchestra. Overhead, the electricians had all but one spotlight turned off. Visikov and his wheelchair were in the middle of the oval beam of light.

Newspaper photographers took pictures, their flash units popping intense white blossoms of light. Visikov was news. Visikov was a character.

The dancers' conversation was a muted murmur, with an occasional low laugh. Many of them—Joel Burck, Alex Bellini, Don Terman, Eric Hudson, Deborah Canby, Billy Jones, Gloria Loo, and half a dozen more—were in stylized western costumes for the *Rodeo* ballet number.

Burck was in boots and spurs, a cowboy hat, and lightweight woolly chaps. A colorful bandanna set off the drab leotards.

Carver thought the poor bastard must be sweating badly. He looked at the rows of empty seats. Not quite empty. Krieb and Balsanek were vague, dark shadows in the dim, unlit, makeshift auditorium.

Where were Applegate and the other cops? Carver scanned

the area and saw them standing a few yards away, inside the nearest prison cells. Were they watching him, or someone else? Carver couldn't see their eyes in the gloom to be certain.

Brigham Merkhinn strode importantly out in front of the assembled dancers. He cleared his throat imperiously. Then he smiled, a small, deprecating, self-important little smile.

He made an opening speech, his words smooth, almost too smooth, oily even. Merkhinn compared the GGBC with the great ballet companies of the world. And he proclaimed that tonight the patrons of the ballet would see and hear a great new ballet, composed by John Guiterez and choreographed by Vassily Visikov.

The assembled dancers and musicians applauded, the noise echoing off the foreboding walls and through the cells.

Then Vassily Visikov rapped for attention.

"My friends," Visikov said, "tonight, in a few hours, we shall be through with our rehearsals. As Mr. Merkhinn has stated, then the curtain, abstractly speaking, will go up, and you will perform several beautiful ballets. One of which, of course, will have been created by me." He looked sternly at the dancers, and ran a hand of twisted fingers through his shaggy gray-streaked hair. "However, after the rehearsals, there will be an announcement by one of your friends. A very, very important announcement. I think you and our patrons, and the various news media, will find it very interesting. Now—Swaine! On with the rehearsals."

Bob Swaine gave the dancers a last-minute pep talk. He signaled for the lighting crew to dim the lights. The auditorium went into semidarkness; late-afternoon daylight still filtered from the ceiling.

John Guiterez tapped for attention with his baton, and the music began, Aaron Copland's *Rodeo*. One spotlight flashed on, pinpointing a dancer in stylized western garb. Giving commands during the rehearsal as little as possible, Swaine guided the dancers through the opening number.

With only a few interruptions, *Rodeo* ended, and the

company took a break. Carver stayed close to Burck. In Guiterez's ballet, Joel Burck would dance the lead, the man condemned to die. Alex Bellini would dance the role of Death, and Billy Jones performed as the Interrogator. Other dancers would be performing as prison guards. Deborah Canby, substituting for Joyce Kittering, and Alice Boygen would perform in gray shrouds as sort of the dancing equivalent of a Greek chorus.

Detective Sergeant Arnold Applegate signaled to Sergeant Stein and to Officers Kelly and Foppiano. They came in close, and Applegate whispered his orders. Stay close to the suspect; watch every move. The suspected dancer was not performing in *The Prisoner*.

"Where is he?" Stein asked anxiously. "I just saw him a second ago."

"I thought you were watching him," Kelly said.

The lights dimmed and then went to blackness. The daylight no longer gave any illumination; the sun had set.

"Damn it," Applegate hissed. "Get your flashlights. Find him."

The somber, dirgelike overture began. The music swelled in a cacophony of drumrolls. The spotlights blazed on.

For a second.

A sizzling flash! The lights went out. The prison building was plunged into blackness.

The dancers were shocked into frozen attention.

Then someone began shouting, "Get some lights!"

Who had shouted? Carver didn't know. Applegate? He dug into his pockets for his penlight.

Kelly fumbled on a flashlight. He swung it around wildly.

"Watch him!" Sergeant Applegate yelled.

The homicide detective didn't mean Kelly.

Sergeant Stein pulled out a flashlight and switched it on. He swept the beam around the audience. He caught Carver Bascombe in the light. Then he hurriedly picked out Sergeant Applegate.

Two voices cried out simultaneously:

"Get Hudson!" Carver yelled.

"Hudson!" Applegate ordered loudly. "Find him!"

THIRTY-ONE

From the darkness came the sound of running feet.

A white exclamation point of flame erupted. The shot sounded like a hundred shots as the single sound echoed off the prison walls.

Several of the dancers screamed, sharp noises that sounded like humans trapped in sudden agony.

Someone gave out a strangled cry.

Several flashlights crisscrossed inadequate beams.

Showers of sparks poured out of the electrical junction box for a few seconds, then subsided.

"Over here, Carver!" Mike Tettsui yelled.

Carver Bascombe flashed his penlight ahead of him. Tettsui was pinned in the beam. Carver cursed his own stupidity. He should've guarded Burck better than this. His own ego had gotten in the way. Yeah, he just had to capture Eric Hudson his own way. Not much point in regrets, Carver told himself as he joined up with Tettsui.

"Come on!" Tettsui said, and they took off running down the hall.

"What happened, Mike?" Carver asked, the words pumping out fast.

"Not sure . . . Hudson must've rigged . . . the lights. Some kind of short-circuit. Then took a shot at Burck in the dark."

"Then Burck ran off," Carver said, slamming out the words. "I caught a glimpse of him in my light."

"He's hard to see, in that black and gray striped prison costume."

"It works for Hudson, too."

"Where're the cops?" Tettsui asked.

"Back there, I guess," Carver said.

The two men stopped. They switched off their lights. They listened. An ominous silence surrounded them in the blackness.

"Hear anything?" Tettsui whispered.

"No," Carver replied as quietly.

He tapped Tettsui on the heel with his shoe. He slipped out of his loafers. Mike Tettsui bent over and untied his shoes and stepped out of them.

The two men crept forward quietly.

The concrete underfoot had been well waxed and felt as smooth as tile.

Sergeant Applegate was lit by beams from three flashlights.

"What happened?" he asked tersely.

"The main power board was blasted," Officer Foppiano replied quickly. "Saw someone running away just after the panel short-circuited."

"We picked up a rubber-handled screwdriver near the box," Officer Kelly added. "All burned and melted. Hudson must've shoved it into the box. Blew everything. The guy was lucky he didn't electrocute himself."

"Okay," Applegate said, aiming his light down the corridors. "Let's get some order here. Kelly, keep these dancers out of the way. We'll spread out, find Hudson. Watch for Bascombe and Tettsui. They're out there somewhere."

"They got guns?" Sergeant Stein asked.

"Probably," Applegate said, and moved along a corridor. He looked up at the catwalks and probed with his flashlight. He picked out several men and a woman leaning on the railing.

"What's going on?" the woman asked.

216

"We have a problem here," Applegate said. "You're electricians, right?"

"Yes, we are. With the company."

"How long to fix the power box?"

"Depends on what happened," the woman said. "We sent Joey down to take a look. As soon as we know, we'll start fixing it."

"The box was deliberately shorted," Applegate said.

"Is that right?" she said. "If it's really blown, then it might take a couple of hours."

Applegate cursed, then told them to do the best they could, as fast as they could. He didn't answer their questions concerning what sounded like a gunshot, or why the fuse box blew up. He moved away, shining the light ahead of him.

One of the dancers, Billy Jones, hurriedly stepped out of the gloom. He carried several narrow small boxes in each hand.

"'Hey, Sergeant," he called excitedly, and identified himself. "I heard that—you talking to the electricians, y'know. You gota problem. You need lotsa light, right?"

"We do," Applegate answered.

"Then we got light," Jones said, holding out the boxes. "All you need. A terrific idea! Sparklers. From *The Thunderer* ballet. We got dozens of boxes, with hundreds of sparklers, y' know. Maybe even thousands. They'll put out a lot of light. All you'll need. For a while, anyway."

"Follow me," Applegate ordered.

Jones followed him.

"Some of the dancers are saying Hudson is trying to get Burck. Trying to kill him. That Burck is really some kinda Russian defector. Sounds real bizarre to me, y'know. Is any of that true?"

"Don't know about his being Russian—but yes, he's in grave danger. Burck might be dead already."

"Damn, I knew Hudson thought he was the best dancer in the company," Jones said excitedly, running alongside Applegate, "even the world, but I didn't think he'd flip over it."

"Just trying to eliminate some of the competition," Applegate said.

The homicide detective and the dancer loped off down the corridor.

Joel Burck moved as silently as he could. He moved from cell to cell, his eyes straining to see in the darkness. He had to keep moving. He had to stay out of the way of the killer. Hudson? It didn't seem possible. Not Eric Hudson.

With a gun! Where did Eric get the gun? Probably smuggled it in his makeup kit. Easy to do. Or maybe with his costume case.

He crept cautiously, smelling the sweat pouring from his arms and face. Burck knew one thing: He had to keep moving. He had to stay away from Hudson. Give Bascombe and the police time to capture him. Then he'd be safe—

A strong arm clamped around his neck.

Burck's defenses were quick. One hand clawed desperately at the arm around his neck. His other had clamped over the wrist of the man trying to strangle him. No! Not to strangle. A gun! Burck felt the gun at the end of the wrist he had grabbed.

Hudson's outstretched hand was a live thing, straining under Burck's clutching fingers. Relentlessly Hudson's hand forced Burck's back. The muzzle was only inches away from Burck's temple.

THIRTY-TWO

Slowly, agonizingly he struggled against Burck's strength. Hudson did not want to miss. He brought the gun closer to Burck's head.

"You've got to die," Hudson hissed between clenched teeth.

Suddenly a bright light stabbed into Hudson's eyes. His cornea responding violently to the flash. For an instant he was blinded.

Burck brought an elbow down hard, driving it into the pit of Hudson's stomach. Eric Hudson gasped and pulled the trigger. The shot echoed and echoed and echoed. The bullet plowed along Burck's chest and passed through his left arm.

Burck spun away. Twisting and dodging.

Below, the corridors seemed to be lit with strange fires, huge dandelions of fire.

Carver Bascombe and Mike Tettsui were seen as weird phantoms, lit by the flashing hot balls of sparkling fire. Dozens of Fourth of July sparklers were held aloft by Billy Jones, Applegate, Sergeant Stein, Gloria Loo, and several other dancers.

Hudson crossed an arm over his eyes. He squinted into the sun and the moon and the blackness of space. The sparks dazzled and the smoke obscured. The smell of hot metal rose to the catwalk. All along the corridor below the sparklers were strung out like gigantic fiery flowers.

Hudson blinked. What was happening? All those people? Flickering demons, all shadow and diamond-bright light. Black twisting shadows dancing over the floor, over the walls, like shifting unreal monsters.

Four or five flashlight beams reached out, as if they too were living fire, and touched Eric Hudson's face and body.

Giving a horrifying shriek, he turned and ran off along the catwalk.

The cells at his side were vertical blurs. He headed for the stairs at the far end. He caught the rail and swung himself to the next floor. There the staircase ended. There was nowhere to go.

"Give it up," Carver Bascombe called loudly. He stood with his revolver hanging by his side. Eric Hudson would be an easy shot. The distance wasn't that great. Less than a hundred feet.

Mike Tettsui held his automatic in both hands, at his chest, ready to aim and fire. Sergeant Applegate and Sergeant Stein had their revolvers drawn.

"This is the police," Applegate shouted. "Come on down, Hudson. There's nowhere to go."

Hudson swayed and clutched at the catwalk. He fired into the sparklers, one shot, two shots.

The sparklers were dropped, and burned on the concrete floor. The dancers and police ran into cells for protection. The angle was bad for Hudson to shoot into the cells. He began to run along the catwalk. He had to find a way out.

But there was no way. He knew it.

Run! Move! See how his muscles flowed! See how graceful. How perfect, unique, beautiful, like no other dancer ever. Couldn't they see that?

Hudson's steps turned into *jetés, then lengthened into grands jetés,* each leap exhilarating him as no dancing before had ever done. It was magic! He could leap higher and farther than any dancer that ever lived!

220

"See!" Hudson yelled, knowing everyone could hear him, that everyone was watching. His eyes wide, his mind transcendental. "The greatest! The finest dancer in the world!"

Carver ran following the sounds overhead of Hudson's running steps. His flashlight beam aimed at the uppermost tier. Mike Tettsui and Applegate followed him, each carrying a flashlight. Don Terman followed, carrying a fistful of freshly lit sparklers.

Carver aimed his light and caught Hudson in the beam. The dancer raced on. He had almost reached the end of the catwalk. Carver saw a small red light, about the size of a quarter, jiggle along the wall behind Hudson. The dancer had to stop.

But Hudson pirouetted, flexed his legs, and with every muscle in consummate coordination, performed an absolutely sublime *grand jeté*.

Right over the railing.

Into the air.

The coin-sized red spot followed him over the edge. The spot centered on Hudson's chest.

A single, sudden shot echoed among the corridors. Eric Hudson twisted violently, his arms flailed erratically. He had lost control of his jump. With an odd cry, as though of regret, or of disappointment, Hudson fell to the concrete.

THIRTY-THREE

Bedlam!

Nervous chatter. Questions. People milling. Circles of confusion. Who? What? What the hell?

Joel Burck came loping up, breathing hard from clambering down the staircase and running along the corridor. He pressed a hand against the bullet hole in his left forearm. The pain didn't seem bad, but he knew it would intensify. He looked at the crumpled body of Eric Hudson.

"What happened?" he asked.

"He was shot," Carver answered. He felt odd, standing in his stocking feet over a corpse.

They were surrounded by a shifting, fluctuating ring of sparklers and flashlights. The effect was strange, with wavering shadows and shimmering light. Detective Sergeant Arnold Applegate knelt down and examined the body.

Blood trickled from a single bullet hole in Hudson's chest.

"Who fired that shot?" Applegate demanded angrily.

"I don't know," Carver said, "but I saw a laser-scope red dot on Hudson's chest."

Applegate stared at Carver, biting back an exclamation. Carver beamed his light into the overhead catwalks, swinging the light back and forth, searching out the sniper.

Applegate stood with his hands on his hips and glowered. He felt helpless. Goddamn it! he thought to himself, forcing down the urge to voice the cursing. Nobody saw a goddamn thing.

He ordered Stein, Kelly, and Foppiano to search the tiers and corridors. Damn, he thought, in a half hour this place was going to be overrun with ME Wolfram, police photographers, and a forensic team. With a little luck, the ballet opening would only be delayed a half hour or so.

He cursed silently. Public relations!

Joel Burck knelt down alongside Eric Hudson. For the moment it was all he could do to look at Hudson: the man who had tried to kill him. Why? he asked himself.

Was Hudson that consumed by jealousy? That neurotic, that obsessed, that he only saw Burck as the one single stumbling block to his own eminence as the premiere dancer in the Golden Gate Ballet Company?

Perhaps. Poor Eric Hudson.

Carver stood silently, his fisted hands jammed into his pockets. Mike Tettsui handed Carver his loafers, and Carver put them on. He looked at Burck, at the dancer's wound, at the blood seeping over Burck's fingers.

"Come on, Joel," he said harshly. "You've got to have that attended to."

"Yes. There's a ballet to perform."

"Goddamn it, is ballet a part of the show-must-go-on code?"

"Yes, Carver. Merde."

The two men walked out to the makeshift auditorium. Carver's face was set, and his steps were hard and somber. Visikov and Merkhinn, and Swaine and Guiterez, and all the other members of the company were waiting.

Carver scanned the area carefully. Where were Balsanek and Krieb? Or was their job over? No point in staying around? Bob Swaine moved forward, his face pale, distorted.

"What do we do?" Swaine asked Carver.

"Go on with it," Carver answered, forcing out the words low and huskily. "Get a substitute for Hudson."

"The electricians tell me," Graham Maltby said, "that they'll have all the lights fixed in less than thirty minutes. I'm more concerned about the police."

"They can't stop you," Carver said. "In less than an hour a boatload of paying ballet lovers is going to land on Alcatraz. As far as the police investigation, their forensic technicians will be called." He jerked a thumb into the far dark shadows, where Eric Hudson's corpse lay. "Everything they have to do is back there. No one in the audience will even know what's going on."

John Guiterez, decked out in white tie and tails, looked at Bob Swaine, and Brigham Merkhinn looked at Visikov. They all turned and looked at Graham Maltby.

"Well?" Swaine asked Maltby.

"I'll check with the police," Maltby said.

"Do that," Carver said.

Maltby and Brigham Merkhinn started to walk down the corridor.

"Hold it, Mr. Merkhinn," Carver said harshly, and put his hand on Brigham Merkhinn's chest. "I've got a few words to say."

"What's the meaning of this?" Merkhinn demanded angrily, trying to push away Carver's hand.

The dancers and musicians stared at the two men. Carver dropped his hand, then curled his fingers into a fist and punched Merkhinn in the jaw. The director of the ballet company staggered, eyes glazed, and fell to the floor.

Merkhinn twitched, and then forced himself into a sitting position. His mouth was bleeding. He glared at Carver Bascombe. "What the hell?" he said, rubbing the blood from his lips.

Sergeant Applegate came up and asked the same question. He stood, again with hands on his hips, and glowered at Carver.

"Merkhinn put Hudson up to this," Carver said, harsh and loud. He looked at Merkhinn, his mouth set, his eyes narrowed. "You lied to me about Hudson at the party. You said you saw him when Meaghler and Burck were arguing. You lied. Hudson wasn't there. He was outside

224

waiting to shoot Joel Burck—but killed Bart Meaghler instead."

"No, no!" Merkhinn said, the words quavering from his bloody lips. "I never! I never told him to kill anyone!"

"I believe you," Carver said. "But you promised him the lead position as dancer in the company if he could get Burck out of the way. Maybe you suggested a series of accidents, or maybe you left it up to Hudson."

Bob Swaine looked at the man sprawled on the floor. He breathed hard, his hands bunched into fists.

"Why?" Swaine asked, the blunt word ejected like a bullet. "Why, Merkhinn?"

"He wanted to get you out of the company, Swaine," Carver said. "He knew that Joel Burck was a Soviet defector." He looked at the crowd around him, at their surprised faces. He looked with contempt at Merkhinn. "Merkhinn was one of the few. Visikov knew, and Maltby did, too. But they respected Burck's anonymity. Not Merkhinn."

"Oh, dear God," Merkhinn moaned. He put his stained fingers over his eyes. "I didn't want to believe Hudson would kill anyone." He looked at Swaine and Maltby and Visikov. "Don't you see. Swaine was taking over the company. He wasn't good for it. He was getting too much power."

Merkhinn choked, and reached into a pocket for a handkerchief. He dabbed at his lips. He moved his body until he was kneeling, as though he were going to pray.

"Please believe me!" Merkhinn cried out, tears running down his face. "See, don't you see, Burck was on Swaine's side. Burck respected and admired Swaine. If Burck ever told the news media about himself there would be a lot of . . . a lot of . . . publicity for him, and for Swaine. The company would be on Swaine's side. Then I could never get rid of Swaine. Never! Don't you see that?"

"You bastard," Swaine said. He quivered with hostility. "You told Hudson to kill Burck."

"Oh, God, no," Merkhinn whispered. "Only to put

him out of action. I had no idea Hudson would go that far.''

''And the killings . . . what the hell, just what the goddamned hell did you think when Meaghler was killed?''

''Not even then,'' Merkhinn sobbed, putting his fists to his face, his head bowed. ''I really believed it was just a coincidence about Meaghler, that gamblers had really done it.''

''What about Rosada?'' Carver asked.

Merkhinn looked blank, puzzled.

Carver realized that Merkhinn didn't know a thing about Ben Rosada. He told the kneeling man about the elevator mechanic. Merkhinn looked horrified, lost.

''And Joyce?'' Swaine demanded.

''I just didn't think it was possible,'' Merkhinn said, squirming under the eyes of the dancers. ''Believe me! I just didn't! I had to believe it was an accident. I had to!''

''You're a poor excuse for a human being,'' Swaine said, ''and I'll make sure you get tossed out of the company permanently.''

Carver looked at the pathetic figure kneeling before them. He needed to breathe air, fresh air, not air polluted with corrupted ambition. He turned and walked out of the prison building.

THIRTY-FOUR

Searchlights crisscrossed the evening sky. The banners on the dock flapped in the warm wind. The bay waters surged against the pilings and the concrete breakwater. A smell of salt and faint kelp-iodine drifted in the air.

Costumed in prisoner gray, the ushers from the ballet company lined the dock area. They watched as the first ferryboat pulled alongside.

Among the first throng to step off the boat were Jimmy Bowman and a lady friend. Carver greeted them, and Jimmy introduced his companion, a brown-skinned lovely. Then Myron Moseby and Leroy Dolny joined them. Carver perfunctorily introduced them to Bowman's lady companion.

Along with the hundreds of excited patrons, they were shown to the auditorium in the prison. Moseby wondered what was on his friend's mind; Carver certainly seemed distracted.

The assembled guests were properly silenced by the forbidding atmosphere of the prison building. Vassily Visikov introduced Joel Burck, who gave a brief speech about his place of birth. The press photographers took pictures, and the reporters scribbled the announcement. All routine. The news seemed anticlimactic, and not as earth-shaking as Merkhinn had feared.

Burck seemed ready to dance, despite the minor wounds

in his chest and arm. The doctor who had come with the police forensic team had done an excellent job patching up the dancer. But a substitute dancer would take his place in the first ballet; Burck was determined to dance *The Prisoner*.

Carver and Tettsui stood near the exit. Carver had a lot of questions still nagging at him. Was it really over? He didn't think so. Who had shot Eric Hudson?

The lights dimmed, and the opening strains of *Rodeo* filled the corridors of Alcatraz prison.

Somehow the music depressed Carver. He left the audience and left the prison building. He was drawn to the dock area by the bright lights and the lights of the city across the bay, softened by the mist.

The two chartered ferryboats were tied to the dock. They were festively, magically ablaze, twinkling with lights strung over the bridge and the railings.

He heard a faint roar of applause, and then silence. Carver continued to stand on the dock, his hands deep in the pockets of his trench coat. He didn't have to hear John Guiterez's music for *The Prisoner*. The notes were imbedded deep in his mind. He didn't have to see Joel Burck to know the dancer was doing a brilliant job.

Sergeant Applegate stepped alongside him. "How did you know it was Hudson?" he asked.

"From little things," Carver answered flatly. "Unlike the other dancers, Hudson had said he didn't care who won leadership in the GGBC, Swaine or Merkhinn. He'd go with whoever came out on top. That kind of opinion didn't jibe with his own ego, which was more than considerable. And, of course, Merkhinn lied about Hudson's presence at the party. If I'd had more time I could've found more holes in Hudson's absences at various times. But I was supposed to keep Burck from getting killed. Time was running out."

"I thought something like that," Applegate said. "But it was more of a suspicion based on where we found the black sedan, and where the sedan had been stolen. Hudson's apartment on Twin Peaks was right between the two points. Not enough to convict, obviously, but enough to bring suspicion until some other evidence came along. Our forensic team would've found hairs and fibers that would match Hudson to the car."

Carver nodded, realizing that Hudson hadn't any chance of getting away with murder. But he might have been able to dance one ballet as the GGBC's leading male dancer. Would that have been enough?

"And we found this," Applegate said, holding a spent cartridge case in his fingers.

Carver looked at it. A bullet casing. A rifle bullet.

"It's a seven point six-two cartridge," Applegate explained. "I know something about ballistics. It's from a semiautomatic weapon. If it had been a bolt-action loader, the sniper could have kept the spent cartridge in the chamber. This one," he looked at it curiously, "was ejected."

Carver remained silent, waiting for the rest.

"In a good light," the homicide detective continued, "you could see the ejection scratches. They're from an operating mechanism not too different from the Kalashnikov. You want my opinion, Bascombe?"

Carver stood there, breathing easily.

"I think it's from a Dragunov," Applegate said, "a Russian sniping rifle. Interesting, don't you think?"

Again Carver heard the applause, faint in the distance.

"I don't suppose you'd know anything about this?" Applegate asked, holding the cartridge to the lights of the ferryboats.

Carver shrugged. Yeah, he thought, a Russian bullet. He didn't doubt Applegate's expertise. But almost anyone could get their hands on a Russian rifle. Even Molerath. Especially Molerath. But did he? Or did it even matter. The Russian certainly had a reason to exact revenge for the death of his partner. Did any of it really matter?

Applegate waited for Carver to say something, then emulated Carver's shrug. He walked back to the prison and the ballet. Carver went aboard the ferry and sat near the stern. He couldn't hear the music but guessed they were dancing *The Thunderer*. He didn't have to hear that, either. The lights of the city across the bay glistened like tears.

He heard steps coming along the deck. He continued to study the city lights. A faint aroma came to him, a subtle mix of floral perfume. Footsteps tapped closer.

Yeah, this was someone who knew a part of him. Someone who knew how to soothe the hurts and pains. Someone who would let him comfort her, be as balm for her wounds.

An arm slid through his, and Carver turned to look at Gloria Loo.

"When we need each other . . ." she said.

Carver Bascombe put a hand over Gloria's and held it tight.

20
Adventures and still counting...

John D.
Mac Donald's
TRAVIS McGEE SERIES

Travis McGee—star of over twenty novels, everyone as good as the last—part rebel, part philosopher, and every inch his own man. He is a rugged, Florida beach bum with a special knack for helping friends in trouble—or avenging their deaths.

"McGee has become part of our national fabric."—Seattle Post Intellegencer